The Rarest Book in the World

This work of fiction is the product of the author's imagination. Any resemblance to persons living or dead is entirely coincidental.

Coypright © 2024 by John W. Conlee

All rights reserved. This book, or parts thereof, may not be reproduced without written permission. Published in the United States by Pale Horse Books.

ISBN: 978-1-939917-28-7

Cover Design: Sally Stiles

www.PaleHorseBooks.com

Also by John Conlee:

    THE DRAGON STONE
    A CUP OF KINDNESS
    THE KING OF MUD & GRASS
    IN THE SUMMER COUNTRY
    THE HEATER
    ROUNDING THIRD
    THE VOYAGE OF MAELDUN
    THE BROTHERS PENDRAGON
    THE LAST PENDRAGON
    CATACLYSM
    THE CHAUCER CODEX
    THE LANCE OF LONGINUS

The Rarest Book in the World

John Conlee

Pale Horse Books

1

The face of the man in the hospital bed looks gray and drawn. One thin wrist protrudes from beneath the bedcovers.

Alwyn Tremayne leans down over him and kisses his brow. "Daddy, we're all here. They're going to give you the best care possible."

The man needs a moment to reply, his lips slowly shaping the words. "I know that, Pet. That's not what worries me."

"No, it shouldn't, Daddy, because you are in the best of hands."

"The book, Pet, it's the book. I don't wish to lose it."

"Daddy, I don't understand."

"Is Charles here? He'll understand."

"Charlie is in the waiting area. Shall I bring him?"

"Yes, Pet, you must bring him."

Allie gives her father's hand a gentle pat, then goes in search of Charles.

Moments later Charles stands at the elderly man's bedside, Allie beside him.

"Ah, Charles, my lad," Rhys Tremayne mutters in a low voice, "so kind of you to come. When did you arrive?"

"Just last evening, sir. Came as soon as I heard. Allie says there's something you'd like me to do for you. Just say the word."

"Charles, I need your help."

"Anything at all, Mr. Tremayne."

"It's a book, Charles, a very special book. I was in the process of purchasing it when my ticker decided to act up. A glorious book, Charles. I mustn't lose out on it. You can understand that, can't you?"

"I can, sir, I certainly can."

"Do you think you might go and fetch it for me?"

"I'll be happy to do that. Sounds intriguing."

"Perhaps Allie could drive you."

"Where is it, Daddy? Who has it?"

"A fellow in Totnes, Pet. His name is Mark Fetherston. He's an antiquarian book dealer I've dealt with a time or two. Not a bad chap, actually." The man's pleasure in talking about books has brought a touch of color to his gray-looking countenance and his voice seems stronger.

Charles gives Allie a quizzical look, then he nods his head with growing comprehension as he recalls the little town on the River Dart. "I know the town you mean, sir."

"I know it too," Allie says, "it's in Devon, about midway between Plymouth and Exeter. Not a terribly long drive from here, maybe an hour and a half. Two at most."

"Pardon my curiosity, sir, but I can't help wondering what this glorious book might be."

"Curiosity is a virtue, Charles, never mind what happened to that poor old inquisitive cat. The book? Why, Charles, given my current preoccupations, it could only be one thing. My boy, it's the Bible."

2

Allie's confident-sounding words to her father about his being in the very best of hands belie her true feelings. It's true that the medical team at the Truro hospital includes some of Britain's finest heart surgeons; and it's also true that Rhys Tremayne's nearest and dearest—his wife, his daughter, his possible future son-in-law—are all there offering their support. But Allie knows she can't rest easy until the by-pass surgery has been completed and the doctors are happy with the results. If she goes off with Charlie running the errand for her father, she won't be there while the actual surgery is occurring; but that's probably a better way to occupy her time than just sitting helplessly at the hospital until it's over.

So, by mid-morning the next day Allie and Charles are well up the A38, nearly out of Cornwall and into south Devon and approaching Plymouth. As Allie maneuvers her little Triumph roadster deftly in and out amidst all the lumbering lorries on the busy artery, Charles can't help smiling at the obvious pleasure her driving gives her. Allie tends to drive faster than she really should, he thinks, not for the first time, but Charles wisely keeps his opinion to himself.

"I called the professor," Charles says to her, after they've traveled for several minutes in silence. She knows he's referring to his Oxford mentor, Professor William

Wentworth of Merton College. "He'd like to come and visit, once your father is back home and has started post-surgery rehab. Do you think that would be okay with Eilish?" Eilish is Ally's stepmother, Rhys Tremayne's second wife.

"It would mean a lot to Daddy to have Professor Wentworth there. And Eilish, I'm sure, would be pleased to have someone else there to deflect or absorb some of Daddy's inevitable crankiness. Daddy being cooped up in bed for several weeks without his daily walk is not a happy prospect."

"How long do they expect the surgery to take today?"

"Five or six hours. They'll have to extract a vein from one of his legs first to use for the bypass arteries. So in a sense it's two surgeries, the leg portion being the minor one."

"Then perhaps we can be back by the time he comes out of the anesthesia."

Twenty minutes later they see the sign for the turnoff to Totnes, and Allie swings the car onto the minor road leading to the small town.

"Did you know," Charles says, "that this little burg we're approaching has long been famous in certain circles?"

"What circles would those be?"

"You should ask Eva Brooksby. She'd be more than happy to tell you."

"In that case, it must have to do with King Arthur." Allie knows that their friend Eva—who has recently finished her D.Phil. at Oxford and now taken a position at Leeds University—is mad-keen about the works of Sir

Thomas Malory.

"Oh, yes," Charles says, "though a good bit earlier than Malory."

"I can just see Professor Wentworth rolling his eyes at the mention of Malory and King Arthur," Allie says.

"But my dear," Charles replies, mimicking the voice of William Wentworth, his beloved mentor, "you would be a making a vast error if you undervalue the importance of Geoffrey of Monmouth and his *Historia*. The work was hugely influential, even if it was one of the greatest literary frauds of all time. All the man did was pen the most important book of twelfth-century England."

"He did? Gosh," Allie says, "guess it slipped my mind."

"Geoffrey not only provided the plots for some of Shakespeare's best plays, including *King Lear*, but he single-handedly created the overarching outline of the entire King Arthur story, an outline that later writers took it upon themselves to fill in. And, of course, he essentially invented the figure of Merlin the Magician. I could go on, if you'd like."

"Please don't, okay? But no offense intended." A moment later she says, "Oh, look there, Charlie, what a cute little castle!"

"Wow, it is. Normally the words 'cute' and 'castle' don't belong together, but . . ."

". . . but this time they do," she says, finishing his sentence.

"Must be Totnes Castle."

"Good guess, my dear Sherlock. Oh, and Charlie, the GPS says we're nearly there. I see a parking spot up ahead right on the street. I'd better nab it." Allie pulls her little car neatly into the spot without even needing to back in.

Out over the sidewalk, half a block away, they can see a sign for the Anne of Cleves Tea Shop, their destination. And as they draw nearer, they see that a tallish man stands out in front looking expectantly in their direction. Probably the book dealer they'd arranged to meet, the man named Mark Fetherston.

"Hello," he calls out as they approach, "and welcome. I'm Mark. And this," and he points to the teashop, "is my office away from the office." He holds the door for them, then follows them inside. He directs them to his table, where various items are already laid out—briefcase, laptop, pens and a pad of paper, half-filled coffee cup. A sport coat is draped over the back of one of the chairs.

"I've gone ahead and placed an order for cream teas for the three of us. There's coffee, if you prefer."

"Lovely," says Allie.

"Coffee for me," Charles says.

"I hope the drive wasn't too bad," Mark says, motioning them to seats on one side of the table. He moves his laptop and briefcase from atop the table to a chair on the other side to make room for the tea trays.

Charles studies the young businessman for a moment, noting that his brown hair has begun to recede and there is the first hint of a double chin. He'd be well advised to go easy on the cream teas, Charles thinks. The man affects a breezy style in both speech and appearance; his pinstriped Oxford shirt is open-necked, the cuffs folded back neatly on his forearms. Charles guesses he's probably in his mid-to-late thirties.

"I'm so terribly sorry about Mr. Tremayne's health," he says to Allie. "I sincerely hope all will be well."

"Thank you," she replies.

"You and Mr. Tremayne have had previous dealings?" Charles asks.

"Three or four times. He's a man who knows his books. And I've sought his advice a time or two also, as a matter of fact, and he's always been most helpful. He's a man who knows a great bargain when he sees one, too.

"Well, Alwyn and Charles, welcome to my office." He spreads his arms wide to encompass the whole tearoom. "My actual office is in my home, only a few steps hence, but I always find it far more pleasant to transact business here. And the kind ladies are most accommodating."

As he says that, two smiling women appear bearing trays. "These charming ladies are Robin and Mavis," he says. "They always brighten my day."

"Let us know if you need anything else," Mavis says.

"Thank you so much," Allie says. "This looks wonderful."

They spend a few minutes enjoying scones with strawberry jam, clotted cream and tea—coffee for Charles—and listen to Mark Fetherston sing the praises of Totnes. "That's a perfectly preserved Norman motte-and-bailey castle just over yonder," he said, "one of Britain's finest. Twelfth century, of course."

"Yes, we were admiring it as we drove past," Allie says.

"So, the book," Charles says, "tell us about the book." He's had enough of the pleasantries and wants to get down to business.

"Yes," Fetherston says, "just as soon as the ladies have removed the trays." When they have, he reaches toward the briefcase on the chair beside him and extracts a sturdy box, which he places on the tabletop. Then, opening his glasses case, he slips on a pair of half-glasses. He hasn't yet opened the box.

"The book that's inside this box," he states proudly, tapping his finger against it, "is the 1572 edition of the Geneva Bible. You may know that this version of the Bible, which was produced shortly after the first great Protestant Bibles of the sixteenth century, was far and away the most popular English Bible throughout the Elizabethan period."

"Printed in Switzerland," Charles says, "in order to circumvent the wrath of Queen Mary."

"Quite right."

"Queen Mary," Allie says, "our beloved Bloody Mary."

"Oh, yes, she certainly was that," Fetherston says.

"1572," Charles says. "So, that would make this a copy of the Bible from the second of the printed editions?"

"That's exactly what it is. The first edition of the Geneva Bible, the 1560 edition, is now virtually unobtainable. Not unless you could nick a copy from the British Library." He pauses a moment to glance at them over the top of his half-glasses, a thin smile on his lips. Allie smiles politely at his weak joke.

"Prior to the publication of the great King James Version in 1611, the Geneva Bible had become the standard English Bible for Protestants. Even after the KJV, it continued to be extremely popular, going through several more editions throughout the seventeenth century. I read somewhere that this was the Bible your Pilgrims carried with them to the New World on the Mayflower," he says, looking at Charles.

"I've heard that too," Charles says. "I've also heard that this Bible is sometimes referred to as Shakespeare's Bible. Isn't that right?"

"Yes, that is also correct. There's a whole sector within the Shakespeare Industry that's entirely devoted to such matters as finding verbal parallels between the text of this Bible and the texts of Shakespeare's plays."

"So I take it that this copy of the Geneva Bible, the one right here, is the one you're offering to Rhys Tremayne."

"That's correct."

"Is it an especially good one?"

"Without a doubt. I have seen several copies of this edition over the years but none as fine as this one. Whoever owned it put it to regular usage, to all appearances, but he also took great care with it. And then after that, apparently, it has had no usage at all. Seems to have sat securely in its covers—for several centuries, in all probability—without anyone even looking at it. Something for which we must be grateful, I warrant."

"How did you come by it, if I may ask?" Charles says.

"Sheer luck. It was a minor item included in a huge estate sale. Lots of very nice things in that sale, which may account for the fact that this little gem was entirely overlooked. Fortunately, I didn't overlook it."

"Would you mind telling us a bit more about the estate sale?" Charles asks.

"Oh, well, just your ordinary sort of thing, actually. It was up in the West Midlands at a tumbledown manor house. The old story of a once-affluent family falling on hard times. At some point in the nineteenth century someone had put together a pretty impressive library, though the members of the succeeding generations largely neglected it. The present owners just wanted to get rid of everything they could make a few pounds on. They didn't bother to itemize the books, let alone have then appraised. I only had a few minutes to look them over, but I could see right off there were some real treasures amongst those books. I made them a flat offer, which they immediately jumped at. Glad to 'get the bloomin' things off our hands,' was what the fellow said to me. It wasn't until later that I discovered the real treasure amongst those books, the Geneva Bible. Practically gave me a heart attack when I saw what was inside this box. Goodness me.

"And as soon as I put it up for sale, the offers came pouring in. Your father, Ms. Tremayne, slipped in just ahead of all the others, and I was happy to promise it to him. Right after his offer there were quite a few more, and I'm afraid I disappointed some folks. One of them was so insistent that I sell it to him that he offered me a thousand quid above the original selling price. But I couldn't possibly go back on my agreement with your father. He's been a loyal customer to me. I've never met him, but I've come to consider your father a friend."

Fetherston finally opens the box and carefully lifts out the book. It has no fancy binding, and the thick dark cover bears no words, though an elliptical shape containing a monogram inside an oval has been impressed into it. All in all, the Bible is rather nondescript in appearance. Charles thinks that may be one of the reasons it has escaped attention for so long.

"Not a lot to meet the eye at first glance, eh?" Fetherston says. "Not imposing at all, a happenstance which surely helped to preserve it."

"Would you mind if we have a peek inside?" Charles asks.

"I wouldn't expect anything else."

Charles opens it to the title page. Allie leans forward over the table to look on. Charles proceeds to turn several pages carefully, pausing from time to time to read an occasional verse from the book of Genesis.

"This was the first Bible to assign numbers to the verses within a chapter," Fetherston says, "hence the expression, 'chapter and verse.' And that was only one of the many innovations the editors of the Geneva Bible made, things that became standard practice in subsequent Bibles."

"I'm no expert, but it does appear to be in very fine condition," Charles says.

"Daddy will be truly delighted," Allie says.

"I'm sure he will be," replies Mark Fetherston. "He will have gotten himself quite a treasure."

Exactly how much of a treasure Rhys Tremayne has gotten is something that neither Rhys Tremayne—nor any of the three of them who are now looking at the Bible—could know.

3

"I realize," Charles says, as they are just a few miles into their return drive, "that the coffee shop is named after one of the wives of Henry VIII, Anne of Cleves, but I can't tell you one more thing about her than that."

"*Divorced, beheaded, died; divorced, beheaded, survived*," Allie says, reciting the little mnemonic school kids learn to remember the fates of the six wives of Henry VIII.

"Which of them was Anne of Cleves?"

"She was number four, the one sometimes called 'The Ugly Wife'."

"Ouch."

"Henry took one look at her and started singing, 'It's All Over Now, Baby Blue.'"

"Henry knew Bob Dylan?"

"Henry didn't actually divorce her, though," Allie goes on. "Since their union had never been consummated, he managed to get an annulment."

"He married her sight-unseen?"

"All he'd seen was Holbein's portrait of her, which apparently had been far too flattering. But since the marriage had been mainly for political purposes anyway—to create an alliance with Germany—Henry didn't kick up too much of a fuss. Didn't give her the chop or anything, just the Sailor's Elbow. I do wonder, though," Allie continues, "why there's a tea shop in Totnes named for her."

"Just to draw upon a famous name?"

"That's probably it. I've never heard of there being any historical connection between the town and Anne of Cleves."

"What did you think of Mark Fetherston?" Charles asks.

"Seemed like a decent enough chap. Had kind words for my father, unlike a lot of people."

"Didn't you think it a bit odd that he didn't see us in his personal office?"

"Charlie, I've seen your 'office' in Oxford. Would you want to conduct serious business there?"

"Disparaging my approach to office tidiness, are you? As professors go, I'm near the top of the class. You should see Professor Wentworth's office at Merton College."

"Perhaps I shouldn't."

"No, perhaps you shouldn't," he says. "Anyway, in regard to Mark Fetherston, I did think he was a bit coy on the subject of the estate sale in which he found the book."

"Perhaps he didn't want to give away trade secrets," Allie suggests.

"He was certainly proud of his coup in finding the Bible."

"Worth a pretty penny. But Charlie, as you were turning the pages, I thought I noticed a few small bits of handwriting scrawled here and there in the margins. Were my eyes deceiving me?"

"No, they weren't. You saw what I saw. Looked like

someone made a few widely scattered annotations."

"Would such things detract from the book's value?" she asks.

"Probably not. In fact. depending on what they are, they might even enhance it. For me, they would certainly pique my curiosity."

"How so?"

"The human element. Somebody—who knows who or when—decided to comment on certain passages in the text. What did they say and what prompted them to do that? Haven't you sometimes, in a used book or a library book, come across places where someone's underlined a passage or jotted a word or two in the margin and you'd really like to know why? What was it about that passage that got to them? Why did they feel the need to pencil an exclamation point in the margin?"

"Sometimes," Allie says, "it's just some know-it-all showing off by explaining an obscure allusion or catching the author in a mistake."

"Yeah, often it is. But a lot of times it seems that something in the text triggered an emotional response in that particular reader. When I encounter that, I really like to know why."

"So, in the case of this Bible, you're suggesting that what's been written in the margins might reveal something important about a sixteenth or seventeeth-century reader."

"That's certainly possible. Figuring out what, that's the hard part."

"But also the fun part."

"Allie, I do believe you're getting into the spirit of the

thing."

"Must be your malign influence on me."

"Malign!"

"I thought that would get a rise out of you, Charlie. Call it the human element."

During much of the drive back to Truro, Allie and Charles are lost in their own thoughts, Allie praying that her father's surgery has been successful and that this book they now have, something he'd desired so very much, will help to lift his spirits.

Weighing heavily on Charles' mind is a matter he knows he needs to discuss with Allie, but not just yet—how her father's heart surgery will affect his and Allie's plans to go to America together. Right now, her father's health is more important to her than anything else. He knows she wouldn't want to think about their plans until Rhys Tremayne is safely and completely out of the woods. But it does leave Charles in a kind of emotional limbo.

In the hospital waiting room they find both Eilish Tremayne and, to their surprise, Allie's mother, Lowenna. The two women are sitting together chatting amiably. They look up as Allie and Charles enter, broad smiles on their faces.

"Your father's awake and comfortable," Lowenna says. "The doctors are pleased with the results."

Allie gives each woman a hug, then turns to Charles and gives him an even bigger one, to his considerable relief.

4

Charles watches as the dozen or so passengers from the London train spill down the steps of the Penzance station. Some are greeted by family members, a few head for the taxi rank, and a couple of them set off on foot. The last one to exit the station is Professor William Wentworth, lugging a small suitcase on wheels. He glances about and then spots Charles' raised arm. The two men exchange waves, and the professor moves toward where Charles is parked on the street.

"On your own, Charlie?"

"I am. Eilish—brave woman—entrusted me with her old car. And I have to say I've just about got the hang of this driving on the wrong side of the road stuff. Allie would have come too, but she wanted to be there when the doctor stopped by to check on her father."

"How's the old curmudgeon doing?"

"Very slow progress, I'm afraid. Seeing you will cheer him up. He's eager to show you his newly purchased book, his pride and joy. Of course, he's also eager to rail against your liberal politics."

"Ah, a book. Rhys does love his old books. What is it this time, Charlie?"

"A very early edition of the Bible. Valuable and interesting in itself, but he seems to think there's some mystery connected to it. I've asked him about it, but all he said was that I should wait until the three of us can chat about it together."

"Oh dear, I hope he's not been up to anything illegal again."

"With these sly old antiquarian book folks, you never can be sure."

Both men laugh. Each of them knows that Rhys Tremayne would never do anything seriously criminal—though he is quite capable of tiptoeing dangerously close to the ethical dividing line.

"You are a cautious driver, Charlie," the professor says five minutes later, as they pass through Marazion and head on toward Helstone. "I'm not being critical, it's a good thing with all the madmen on the roads in this country."

"My aim is to get Mrs. Tremayne's car back to her in one piece and mostly unscathed, if at all possible."

Ten minutes later they pass between a pair of gray stone gateposts and onto the long graveled driveway leading to Rhys Tremayne's huge house that overlooks the sea. Charles sneaks a quick glance up at the large stone birds perched atop each of the plinths, birds that look like crows but are actually choughs, the traditional symbol of Cornwall, a bit of knowledge Charles had garnered a year ago.

As Charles proceeds slowly over the graveled drive, they meet a car coming the opposite way. "Probably the doctor," he says. "Must've just finished his examination of Rhys."

Then they have their first sight of the large house. "Well, my boy," the professor says, "here we are again, back once more at the warm and welcoming edifice you like to call Manderly." It's an allusion to the house in the Hitchcock film *Rebecca*, a small private joke he and Charles had initiated a year ago. "I assume that Maria is still overseeing all the domestics operations at Rhys's demesne?"

"Oh, yes. Rhys has entirely forgiven her for her role last year in the manuscript fiasco. Frankly, I think he'd be lost without her. She's as much a part of Manderly as the sloping terraces, the rose-covered trellises, and the squawking seagulls."

To Charles, the sight of lighted windows and smoke curling skyward from the chimneys are really welcoming. He remembers seeing the house for the first time the previous summer when he and the professor drove down from Oxford to examine a mysterious medieval manuscript that had come into Rhys Tremayne's possession. The anxieties he felt then were quite different than the ones he feels now. The ones he feels now largely involve Allie Tremayne, with whom he is in love and with whom he hopes to share a future. Then, he hadn't yet met her, although unknowingly, he'd only been a day or two away from that life-changing event.

Charles pulls into the open area adjacent to the entranceway and parks beside Allie's small roadster. He snatches up the professor's one bag and they climb the brick steps to the portico. The front door swings open just as they reach it.

"Professor!" Allie cries. "I'm so pleased you could come."

"Hello, Professor," comes Eilish's voice from behind Allie. "Do come in." The two women hug him in turn.

"We saw the doctor's car as we drove in," the professor says. "How's everything looking?"

"No post-surgical complications, thank goodness," Eilish says. "The incision is healing nicely. We just have to make sure he does his breathing exercises and other light exercises. It's going to be a long slow process, but we're encouraged."

"All daddy wants to do right now is study his new Bible," Allie says. "When he's not napping or snapping at us, he's hard at it. And I know he's eager to explore several questions with you."

"I never took Rhys for a Bible scholar," the professor says, smiling.

"I'm afraid he doesn't think of it as a Bible qua Bible. He thinks of it as a book," she says.

"Books are his Bible," the professor says. "They are his church and his religion."

"And he always keeps the faith," Charles says.

"Professor," Allie asks, "fancy a sandwich and something to drink?"

"Both would be most welcome. I just couldn't face the so-called food that was available in the buffet car. And then for me it will be off to bed. Been a long day. I look forward to seeing the old curmudgeon in the morning. And to seeing his Bible as well."

"That's sure to cheer him up," Eilish says.

Allie helps the professor with his bag, then goes to spend a few private minutes with her father. Eilish escapes to her own small study just off the main sitting room, a room which houses her personal library and all the music she is so fond of listening to. Soon Charles hears a violin concerto playing behind the partially closed door.

Just as Eilish steps over to close it, she sees Charles standing alone in the sitting room. "Care for a little nip of Scotch, Charles?" she asks, peeking her head around the door's edge.

"Not tonight, thank you, but I might join you for a few minutes to listen to Mendelssohn's wonderful concerto. You seem to be partial to him. A year ago, the first time I was ever in this room, you were playing his 'Songs Without Words.'"

"What a gift the man had for composing beautiful melodic lines. He's the equal of the best of them," she says.

"The best of them being Schubert?"

"You'll get no argument from me, Charles."

She notices that he's been running his eyes over the titles of the books on the shelf behind him. "Please help yourself to anything that appeals."

"I finished the last one I brought with me this afternoon, so I might just take you up on that. You do have a lot of the classics here. Oh, wow, *The Riddle of the Sands.*"

"All yours, Charles. A marvelous read, as book reviewers are wont to say."

"Mind if I take two or three?"

"Or more, if you like. It sounds like you may share with me what I call the ten-pages rule. If a book hasn't drawn me in by about page ten, I cast it aside and try something else."

"That's a higher bar than mine, but pretty similar to what I do."

Charles also selects a Josephine Tey and a Margery Allingham. "These should keep me going for a few days," he says. "Thanks a lot."

"Charles, I'm so glad you are here. It means a lot to Rhys and of course to Allie. And to me as well, I must say. Feel free to use my little sanctum whenever you like. Help yourself to books and listen to music. And you can even help yourself to some of my Scotch. A *small* amount of my Scotch, anyway," she says with a smile.

"Your Scotch is safe, Eilish."

"Just teasing, Charles. Have all you want—unless it's the Glenfiddich, of course."

"Thanks for the loan of the books. See you in the morning. Oh, and to be on the safe side, you'd best hide the Glenfiddich." Eilish laughs.

Charles ascends the stairs all the way up to the little bedroom on the top floor where he'd stayed the previous summer. He steps over to the window which looks out on the rear gardens and the terraced lawns that slope down toward the sea. He loves this view, with its ever-changing sky above the ever-changing sea. Far off to the southwest, dark clouds billow, and Charles imagines seeing a little bit beyond them to the rugged coast of Brittany and the ancient walled town of Saint-Malo, which he'd once visited.

Allie still occupies her own bedroom on the floor below, and they'd put the professor in the guest bedroom on that floor also. The other little room on Charles' upper floor, separated from his room by a small lavatory, is unoccupied, so Charles has this floor all to himself.

He flops down atop the duvet on the little bed and starts in on the Childers classic. He'd read it once before, back when he'd been a teenager. He'd liked it then, and he suspects he still will.

An hour later Charles hears soft footsteps ascending the stairs followed by a light tap at his door. "It's open," he calls out.

Allie slips inside. "I hope you aren't lonely," she says in a soft voice.

"Not anymore," he replies.

"So you won't mind if I keep you company for a bit?"

"I won't mind at all."

Allie gently removes the book from his hands, marks his place with a slip of paper she finds on the bedside table, and sets the book down atop the table.

"Single beds do sometimes have their advantages," she says.

"I remember an old country song about sleeping single in a double bed," Charles says. "I think that sleeping double in a single bed is much to be preferred."

"Oh, yes," Allie replies, "much."

5

The small police car turns into the drive and passes between the gateposts. The two women inside glance up at the stone birds perched atop them without comment. The young woman doing the driving is Detective Sergeant Valery Wilson. She is twenty-six years old, with four years experience in the Devon and Cornwall Constabulary. Seated in the passenger seat is her superior officer, Detective Inspector Eileen Corrigan, five years Valery's senior. The two women became partners six months earlier, and while initially they seemed a rather mismatched pair, they've quickly discovered that their distinctive personalities actually mesh well and that their skills are complementary.

Each of the women is satisfied with her job in the police, and each of them imagines having a long career in police work—unless or until something more attractive lures her in another direction—and both are open to that possibility. Neither aspires to be like Jane Tennison on the BBC "Pime Suspect" series, though Eileen does bear a slight resemblance to Helen Mirren, as some of her male colleagues are wont to remark amongst themselves.

They are arriving at the home of Rhys Tremayne unannounced, a common strategy when interviewing persons of interest. Not that they really suspect Alwyn Tremayne or the American, Charles Bascombe, of any misdeeds. Indeed, they are doubtful that any misdeeds have even occurred. But the jury is still out on that.

Maria ushers them in and directs them to seats in the sitting room, then goes off to round up Allie and Charles. The policewomen sit side by side on a sofa arranged at a ninety-degree angle to a large fireplace. Another sofa is positioned straight across from them, beyond a glass-topped coffee table. A third sofa faces the fireplace.

When Charles and Allie come into the room, the two women rise to their feet and introduce themselves, then sit back down. Allie and Charles take seats on the sofa across from them.

"Please accept our apologies for barging in like this," DI Corrigan says. "We were in the neighborhood on other business and thought we'd take a chance on your being available." Mendacity, the policewomen know, is just a basic part of their job. Both of them are well practiced in the art.

"How can we help?" Allie asks.

"We wanted to ask you about a book dealer named Mark Fetherston," DS Wilson says. "It turns out you were two of the last people to see him alive."

"Mark Fetherston is *dead?*" Allie exclaims, her face displaying shock and disbelief. "We saw him just the once, what was it Charlie, ten days ago?" Charles nods in agreement. "It was the day of Daddy's surgery. Yes, that would have been exactly ten days ago."

"Can you tell us about that encounter?" Inspector Corrigan asks. Sergeant Wilson, beside her, has taken out a pen and pad, poised to take notes.

"We went to see him in order to pick up a book for

Daddy. Daddy was in the process of buying it from him. We met him in Totnes, in a small teashop there."

"We were probably with him for under an hour," Charles adds. "Chatted with him for a bit, satisfied ourselves that the book looked to be just as advertised, said our farewells and headed back to the hospital in Truro." He notices that the other policewoman is jotting down notes on her pad.

"How did he seem to you?" DS Wilson asks, looking up from her notes.

"Pleasant and cheerful," Allie says. "He seemed quite pleased with the transaction."

"You never went to his home or his office?" Inspector Corrigan asks with lifted eyebrows.

"No, we never did. I believe he said his office was in his home. We did think it a bit odd meeting him in a teashop like that, but he said that was his normal practice. The ladies there appeared to be used to him using their establishment in that way and they seemed quite in tune with it."

"Yes," Valery Wilson says, nodding her head, "that's what they've told us too."

"When did he die?" Allie asks. "And, if I may ask . . . *how*?"

"His body was discovered—in his office—three days after your visit. It appears that you were among the last people to see him alive. When he hadn't come by the teashop for a couple of days, the teashop ladies became worried. They were accustomed to seeing him, alone or with customers, almost daily. It was his cleaning lady who discovered him. Fridays are when she always comes to do her tidying."

"Some sort of accident?" Charles asks with a slight tilt of his head.

"We're still not sure," Inspector Corrigan replies. "Candidly, it appears to have been a drug overdose. Fentanyl."

"It surely couldn't have been suicide!" Allie exclaims. "I know it's never possible to tell what's going on inside another person's head, but he didn't seem at all the type to do that. All the while we were there he seemed quite upbeat."

"As it happens, suicide *is* what some of our colleagues suspect," Eileen remarks. "But no one we've talked to who knew him well sees that as being at all likely. Nor did anyone have any idea he used drugs. We found nothing in his home to suggest it, no pill bottles or drug paraphernalia or the like."

"I suppose by now you've had the coroner's inquest?" Charles gives an apologetic shrug and says, "I read mystery novels. They're big on coroner's inquests."

"They brought in a verdict of death by misadventure, i.e., accidental death," Eileen Corrigan says, "but we are still treating it as a suspicious death."

"The book you bought from him," Valery Wilson asks, "it was exactly what your father wanted and there was nothing untoward about the entire transaction?"

"Entirely straight forward. Daddy is pleased as anything with the book."

"Did any of you, including your father, have any

further contact with him after the transaction?" Inspector Corrigan asks.

"Daddy had made an initial deposit on the book to initiate the process several days earlier. Then, a few days after we'd picked up the book, we transferred the remaining amount. There wasn't any personal contact involved at all."

"Well, that about does it for me," Detective Corrigan says. "Val, can you think of anything else we should ask?"

"Just one or two things. When you were in Totnes, did you see or speak to anyone else, other than Mark Fetherston and the teashop ladies?"

"I don't believe we did," Allie says, turning her head and looking at Charles. "Did we, Charlie?"

"My recollection," he says with another shoulder shrug, "is that we hopped right into the car and headed straight back to Truro. I would have liked to poke around in a couple of the town's used bookstores, but I knew Allie wanted to get back to the hospital as soon as possible, so I didn't say anything." Allie puts her hand on his forearm and gives it a little squeeze.

The two policewomen nod and then get to their feet. "Well, this has been most helpful," DI Corrigan says. "Your comments about Mark Fetherston tend to confirm what we've heard from others."

"I am really sorry to hear about Mr. Fetherston," Allie says. "He seemed quite a decent chap."

"To me, too," Charles adds.

"I doubt that we will need to speak with you again," she says, "but if we do, we'll try to give you more advance notice. Oh, if anything else comes to mind, please give us a call at this number." She hands Allie a card.

They all shake hands, and then Maria, who's been hovering just outside the sitting room the whole time, shows the policewomen out.

Allie and Charles stand there a moment staring at each other in disbelief.

"Mark Fetherston dead?" Allie says. "Oh, Charlie, I can hardly believe it. But let's not tell Daddy just yet. He doesn't need any more shocks to his system."

"Maybe the guy regretted letting your father's book slip out of his hands so much that he went and offed himself. Or maybe he had one really ticked off out-of-luck customer."

"Charlie, don't joke about something so awful," Allie snaps. "It's not a joking matter."

"They said nothing about the possibility of foul play. Do you think you and I could be murder suspects?"

"*You* might well be, Charles Bascombe. But I most certainly am not." Allie is still riled by his unseemly flippancy.

"You mean you aren't willing to be my alibi witness?"

"Always be wary of the suspect with the best alibi, Charlie. Isn't that what your mystery novels tell you? You, Charles Bascombe, are the prime suspect."

6

Rhys Tremayne looks up and smiles as the professor and Charles enter the small study just off the library. He sits in one of three library chairs arranged about a small table. A thick pillow props him forward. He has donned a baggy gray sweatshirt and a loose-fitting pair of drab olive corduroy trousers. His face has a bit of color, Charles thinks, at least more than it had the day before his surgery.

"William," Rhys says, "thank you for coming. You are a friend indeed. And thank you, Charles, for fetching him from the station."

"I can be your friend, Rhys, as long as we keep our attention focused on books. Not a word on bloody politics," the professor says.

"William, this book of mine might involve politics too, though that remains to be determined."

"Charles, my lad," Rhys says, looking at him, "you are a credit to your Celtic heritage. William, Charles has been a brick throughout this whole ordeal. Don't know how Eilish, Allie, or I could have survived without him. We can't allow the lad to go back to America, can we? We need him too much here."

"The book, Rhys," the professor says impatiently, "the book."

"It's in that box on the side table. Charles, would you

do the honors?"

Charles reaches over and retrieves the box, the same one he and Allie brought back from Totnes.

"Thank you, my boy," Rhys says.

Handling the book gently, Charles takes it from the box and places it in Rhys Tremayne's slightly shaking hands. Rhys positions it on the small table in front of them, then slowly opens it.

"The 1572 edition of the Geneva Bible," he says, "as I'm sure you both already know. Not many surviving copies, and none, I think, in as fine a condition as this one."

"Ah," the professor says, "the Breeches Bible."

The professor's comment causes the two older men to burst into laughter. Charles sits there looking nonplused.

"According to this translation," Rhys explains to Charles, "when Adam and Eve saw that they were naked, they sewed fig leaves together and made 'breeches' to cover themselves." Again, the two men laugh. This time Charles cracks a smile.

"I've heard it called Shakespeare's Bible," Charles says, once the two men's bout of humor has subsided.

"Oh yes," Rhys says. "It was the standard Bible of its day, though eventually nudged aside by the King James Version. It was Shakespeare's Bible, John Donne's Bible, Ben Jonson's Bible, you-name-its Bible. All the greats and not-so-greats used it."

"But I believe, Rhys," the professor says, "you've come to think there might be something special about this *particular* copy, aside from its remarkable preservation?"

"Well, yes, I think there may be. So let's talk a little

about that."

Charles and the professor wait for Rhys to continue. Slowly the man begins to turn the first few pages of the book, one by one. Then he stops. "Look there. What do you see?"

The other two lean forward, with the professor adjusting the reading glasses perched on his nose. "Ah," the professor says, "someone has made an annotation in the margin beside that particular verse, written in that dratted Elizabethan secretary hand."

"Yes," Rhys says. "Marginal comments like this one occur sporadically throughout the entire Bible. All of them in that same hand. There are also a few places where words or phrases have been underscored. In a couple of cases an entire verse or short passage has been underscored. There's not a vast number of instances of either practice, and they are widely scattered. I'm sure I haven't found them all, but several of the ones I have found strike me as quite intriguing. For example, I know you're both familiar with that verse from Revelations, 'I am the Alpha and the Omega, saith the Lord,' yes? Beside it in the left-hand margin the annotator has drawn a Chi Rho, and then in the right-hand margin, something I haven't yet deciphered—possibly a Greek letter or monogram also."

"Wondrous strange," the professor says.

"The Chi Rho," Charles suggests, "probably stands for Christ. The Chi Rho monogram was commonly used in medieval texts as an abbreviation for Christ as, for example, in those intricate and beautiful Chi Rho pages in *The Book of Kells* and The *Lindisfarne Gospels*."

"Indeed," says Rhys. Then he turns cautiously to the final pages of the book and finds the spot he's been referring to. The three men examine it intently. "Your explanation, Charles, is probably the right one," Rhys says at last. "God and Christ are all encompassing, from the very beginning of things to the very end. They are the Alpha and the Omega."

"So," Charles says "this Bible you've said is commonly called Shakespeare's Bible. Do you think there's any possibility, remote as that may be, that this particular copy could actually have been owned by Shakespeare, that it could *literally* be Shakespeare's Bible? He certainly must have had one. Is it possible that Shakespeare made all these marginalia?"

"No, I wouldn't think there's much chance of that," Rhys says. "Though few copies of the Geneva Bible exist now, back then they were extremely common. So the odds against that would be extremely high."

"And," the professor adds, "it would be a hard thing to prove, since we have almost no samples of Shakespeare's own handwriting, aside from those few scrawled signatures on legal documents."

"The annotations here," Rhys says, "appear to me to be the work of a somewhat scholarly chap, certainly someone with more than just a grammar school education like Shakespeare had."

"Remember Ben Jonson's snide remark about Shakespeare having only 'small Latin and less Greek,'" the professor says.

"Well, it was just a random thought," Charles says. "I

knew it was a long shot. Anyway, Shakespeare's not my field, I'll be the first to admit it."

"But, Charles,'" Rhys says, "I happen to know that there's one thing that *is* very much your field—paleography. You, Charles, you are a dab hand at reading ancient manuscripts."

"Argh," Charles says, "I can see what's coming. You want to foist off on me the job of deciphering all these Elizabethan scribbles. Correct?"

"Oh, my boy," the professor says, "you're just the man for the job. And you'll have a barrel of fun doing it. You love solving mysteries, so you just turn that fine brain of yours in the direction of solving this one."

"All I need you to do," Rhys says, "is go through the book carefully and transcribe each of the annotations. Copy them out in a modern hand and make a master list of where they occur. As I said before, there isn't a great number of them. Shouldn't take more than a few hours for a talented fellow like you. Then, once we have them in readable form and have a master list, the three of us can go through them together and see if we can make heads or tails of them. A barrel of fun indeed."

"Argh," Charles says again. The professor reaches over and pats Charles on the shoulder.

Rhys Tremayne beams at him joyfully. "'O frabjous day, callooh! callay!'" he sings out.

"I think, Charlie, you are making my old friend a happy man," the professor says to Charles. "Come to my arms, my beamish boy!"

"Argh," Charles says again.

7

DS Valery Wilson carefully negotiates the twisty little road from the village of Widecombe-in-the-Moor to the home of retired rare books librarian, Nigel Cummings. While she is eager to learn what Nigel can tell her about the antiquarian book trade, she finds this drive into the heart of Dartmoor delightful in itself. During her undergraduate years at Exeter University she had often hiked—and a few times camped—in Dartmoor, and the allure of this ancient and mysterious place was a factor in her accepting the job with the Devon constabulary rather than taking the much higher paid position she'd been offered with the Metropolitan Police in London.

She listens as the voice from the GPS device on her mobile phone directs her to a narrow, grassy lane—more a broad pathway than a road—that leads up a steep hill to a stolid-looking, gray stone house. An old estate wagon is parked before a tumbledown shed to one side of the house.

As she steps from her car, the door of the house swings open and a man she recognizes as Nigel Cummings raises a hand in greeting. "Valery," he calls out to her. "My dear, you look just as I remember you, just as you looked, what was it, five or six years ago?"

"Seven, sir. And don't look too closely. Don't want to

spoil your illusions."

She follows him into the house, accepts his offer of a cup of tea, and takes a chair across from one where a book lies open on its seat.

"You were the best student assistant I ever had, Valery," he says, as he carries the tea tray in from the kitchen. "I'd always hoped you would go on and take an advanced degree in Library Sciences. Not you. Too boring for you," he says smiling at her. He likes what he sees, her light-brown suit, white shirt, and tawny eyes. She'd been a stocky young woman as an undergraduate but now, to Nigel Cummings she looks a good bit trimmer. Her tan suit nicely complements her eyes and short brown hair.

"I seriously considered it, sir. And there are moments when I really wish I had. On the whole, though, I've been happy doing what I've been doing. Provides a lot of challenges, not to mention a good many disappointments and frustrations, but also some real satisfactions."

"That's called life, my dear—disappointments, frustrations, and the occasional satisfaction."

"Sir, what a delightful location you have. I envy you. I've always loved Dartmoor."

"Yes, it is delightful—though perhaps not so delightful on cold, winter nights when winds shake the windows in their frames and come whistling down the chimney. Also, it can get a bit lonely at times, living all alone as I do. Of course, I always have my books. Well, here's to you and your visit, Valery." He raises his teacup and reaches it out toward her. She reciprocates, and they touch cups.

"Speaking of books, sir," she says, "'would you happen

to be acquainted with a Cornish bibliophile named Rhys Tremayne?"

"Ah, Rhys. No, not personally, only by reputation. He was a few years ahead of me at Oxford, but we have mutual acquaintances. I've heard him give talks a couple of times at academic conferences, too. To his credit, Rhys is a serious scholar. Rare book librarians tend to view private book collectors as the bane of our existence. But Rhys is a special case—he's a rapacious collector but also an accomplished scholar. Truth be told, it's people like Rhys who are often our salvation. They take such meticulous care of their collections and then, in the end, bequeath them to *us*."

"Do you think he's likely to do that?" Valery asks, with a tilt of her head.

"From what I've heard, it's a near-run thing between us and the University of Edinburgh where he did his graduate studies. The Bodleian has no chance, nor does the British Library, given his antipathy to the English. If you come to know the man and can win his favor, maybe you could tip the scales in the direction of your old university," he says, grinning. Valery smiles and nods.

"It's interesting that he would think of Exeter as not being English."

"That's probably because Rhys thinks of this whole West Country area as being part and parcel of the ancient Celtic kingdom of Dumonnia. British, but not English—rather like Wales and Scotland."

"Ah, I see. Well, sir, one of my purposes in coming here is to learn more about antiquarian book dealers. Do you think you could fill me in a bit about them?'"

The man rubs his chin, tilts his head back, and ponders her question.

"Hmm. Well," he says at last, "those fellows, I have to say, are rather a mixed bag. They range from being serious and responsible business people to being totally unscrupulous, with most of them probably closer to the unscrupulous end of the spectrum than to the other."

"Would you happen to know a bookseller named Fetherston?"

"The chap in Totnes?"

"Yes, that's the one."

"Never dealt with him, Valery, but I heard that quite recently he offered for sale a copy of the Geneva Bible. I'd been wondering how in the world he happened to come by it. Rare as hen's teeth, if you'll pardon the cliché."

"Then I guess, sir, you hadn't heard about his recent death?"

"Oh my, no." His face bears a startled look. "I hadn't heard that. The poor fellow. What happened?"

"An accidental drug overdose is what's generally believed. Or possibly, suicide."

"How awful. I didn't know the chap, but from what I always heard, he was one of the more respectable persons of that ilk."

"It was Rhys Tremayne who ended up purchasing that copy of the Geneva Bible from him."

"Now, *that* doesn't surprise me at all. Just the sort of book Rhys has always had a passion for." Without asking, he tops up her cup with tea, then pours more into his own.

"How valuable would such a Bible be?" she asks.

"Oh, my, hard to say. Of course, its condition would be extremely important. But putting a price on a book that rare is most difficult. It's rather like pricing a work of art. What it's worth is whatever someone is willing to pay for it."

"Could you hazard a guess?"

"Oh, Valery, put me on the spot, why don't you? Well, if it's in good condition, perhaps in the range of fifteen to twenty thousand pounds? My dear, I don't really know. I've been retired for five years, so I'm a bit out of touch. Even back then, I wouldn't really have known."

"You are too modest, sir. I was always impressed by how much you knew."

"And I was always impressed by how quickly you grasped things about our field."

They chat amiably for a few more minutes before Valery says, "It was a pleasure working with you back then, sir, and a real pleasure seeing you again today. Thank you for the tea and for all the information."

"It's been a great pleasure for me, too. If you think of anything else I might be able to help you with, don't hesitate to call. And maybe you'll drop in on me sometime when it's not strictly on business?"

"I'll definitely do that, sir."

As he watches her return to her car and then drive back down the steep lane, he realizes that a strange feeling has crept upon him. "Oh, dear me," he says to himself, realizing that the feeling that has crept upon him is a twinge of desire.

✣ ✣

The local policeman, a round-faced PC with ruddy cheeks who looks like he's eaten more than his fair share of pork pies, ushers DI Eileen Corrigan into the half-timbered house. She glances at the leaded windows and the red geraniums in their neat window boxes. Mark Fetherston had obviously been going for the traditional English cottage look, she thinks. All he needs to complete the picture is a thatched roof and a marmalade cat napping on the inside windowsill.

The few rooms in the house are small but tidy and Fetherston's study is chock-a-block with glass-fronted bookcases. On his neat desk sits a desktop computer, a monthly calendar, notepad and penholder, and a desk lamp.

"You've been able to open his computer and access his email files, correct?" she asks the PC.

"Oh, yes ma'am. One of our young blokes is a wizard with the bloomin' things." Being called "ma'am" always startles Eileen, but she knows she needs to get used to it.

"But no sign of a mobile phone?'"

"No, not just yet. We're still searching."

"Really important to find it, constable. I'm counting on you."

"Yes, ma'am. Well, I'll leave you to it. You have the keys and will lock up when you're finished?"

"Yes, I do and I shall."

"If you need anything, just ring me on my mobile."

"Umm-hum," she says, eager for him to depart.

She begins by examining Fetherston's email files,

starting with his "sent" messages. It is clear right off that he had sent out the same basic message about the Geneva Bible to a good number of possible buyers. Although the messages were basically boilerplate, each one gave the appearance of having been crafted for that recipient. Eileen would need to make a master list of all these people.

Then she turns to examining the received messages. Rhys Tremayne's reply had come in less than half an hour after Fetherston's message had gone out, so he had indeed been the first one to express a desire to purchase the Bible, as Fetherston had told Allie Tremayne and her American friend. Eileen sees that several others had also replied in short order. One of them even told Fetherston to name his price and he would "cut a cheque today."

DI Corrigan then turns her attentions to the man's meticulously kept financial records. He must have made life easy for his tax accountant, she thinks. Finances aren't her strong point, but his records are in such good order that she has no trouble getting a quick grasp on all he'd been doing.

In regard to the books he'd purchased from the estate sale, it appears that he'd paid a flat fee of £1,500 pounds for twenty-one cartons of books. Then, just a week later, he'd sold twenty cartons of books to one of the biggest bookdealers in Hay-on-Wye, the little town in Wales that boasted a plethora of secondhand bookstores. Apparently, he'd rented a van and transported the books there himself.

So, she concludes, he bought twenty-one cartons and turned right around and re-sold the bulk of them, no doubt after having cherry-picked the lot. In fact, she soon finds a sheet which lists the books he'd hung onto from the estate sale. They include, among others, the Geneva Bible and another Bible, not quite so old; first editions of *Vanity Fair* and *Bleak House*; the first British edition of Louisa May Alcott's *Little Women*; hardback editions of several Edgar Rice Burroughs novels; and an early volume of poems by W.H. Auden.

Eileen forwards Fetherston's email files to her office computer, and she takes a photo of the book list with her mobile phone. She will share all of this information with DS Valery Wilson. Valery will have a better idea of the value of the books than she does.

Fetherston, she muses, bought the books for a flat fee of £1,500 and turned around and re-sold them for £3,500. That gave him a tidy profit, even before he sold the ones he'd held back. Those books, she guesses, would bring a pretty penny, too; and all of that was before the *big* score he'd make when he sold the Geneva Bible. The whole business was perfectly legal, perfectly above board. It had surely been Mark Fetherston's lucky day when he found that copy of the Geneva Bible amongst all those other books—if, indeed, luck was what it had been.

To assuage her curiosity about this man, Eileen spends a few minutes exploring all the other rooms in the small house, with particular attention to the kitchen and the man's bedroom. The kitchen is immaculately tidy, but it also appears to have been often used. She'd learned from experience that one could learn a lot about a person from their kitchen. (She just hopes no one ever studies *her* kitchen.) The fellow clearly enjoyed cooking, she thinks, but it appears to have been cooking for one.

There are no surprises in his bedroom. A few pill bottles rest atop the bedside table, including a common sleep aid, a paracetamol bottle, and a vitamin supplement. Nothing unexpected appears in any of his drawers, and the shoes and clothing she finds in his wardrobe are entirely predictable. There is no sign that anyone else has ever been in this room, let alone shared it with him. To all appearances, Mark Fetherston was an old-fashioned bachelor whose only beloved companions were rare books. It appears that he preferred keeping his home his own private sanctuary. Perhaps that explains why he conducted business at the local teashop.

On the walls of his bedroom and sitting room are a few well-chosen prints, but nowhere in the house does Eileen find any photographs—either of family members, friends, or even of himself with the Egyptian pyramids forming a backdrop. She knows that his parents are still alive and living in Shropshire, but there is no sign of them anywhere in Mark Fetherston's home.

She quickly scans his sitting room bookshelves. The books are mostly works of fiction, ranging from popular works by writers such as Dick Francis and Agatha Christy, to more substantial ones by P.D. James and John le Carré, to the serious literary works of John Fowles, Richard Adams, and A.S. Byatt. Clearly, he enjoyed reading both serious fiction and popular entertainment. She sees one shelf entirely devoted to writers of spy thrillers, particularly those by Graham Greene and Ken Follett. There is a le Carré here, too. One shelf holds a curious mélange of international fiction, by the likes of Michael Ondaatje, Vladimir Nabokov, J. M. Coetzee, and John Updike, writers Eileen has never read.

Eileen, despite her training and her nine years of experience, can't help thinking that Mark Fetherston's solitary life was kind of a sad one. But then, who was she to judge, if that was what he'd chosen for himself?

8

Charles Bascombe sits at the table in Rhys Tremayne's library, the same table where a year ago he'd spent several days poring over a curious medieval manuscript. That manuscript, as it turned out, contained a poem that was possibly a lost work of Geoffrey Chaucer. That had been an exhilarating experience. What he is doing now he finds far less exhilarating. Still, he knows that this particular copy of the Geneva Bible could prove to be of real significance to scholars of the Elizabethan period.

Verse by verse, chapter by chapter, book by book, Charles works his way through Rhys Tremayne's copy of the Geneva Bible. In the earlier Old Testament books he finds only the occasional marginal annotation, but when he reaches the "wisdom books"—Ecclesiastes, Job, Proverbs, Psalms, The Song of Solomon—he encounters quite a few. In Isaiah there are even more, though there they tend to be mostly of the underlined-passage variety rather than actual annotations. Could these markings have been made by a different hand? Hard to tell for certain, but he thinks it is a real possibility.

At first it's slow going and Charles finds himself longing for a nice, neat fourteenth-century book hand. But after half an hour of frequent head scratching and close scrutiny, it begins to get easier. He's finally begun to get a handle on the style and eccentricities of the annotator's writing, as he knew he would.

By noon, after three hours of intense concentration, his brain has become muzzy, and he needs a break and a bite of lunch. He decides to look in on Allie and then he will go and see if her father and the professor need anything.

Allie, he knows, has set up a temporary art studio on the small, north-facing screened-in porch at the back of the house. That's where he finds her, standing and staring at the nearly blank canvas on her easel. She is deep in thought. One hand props up her chin, the other rests on her left hip. Charles imagines that she is envisioning a finished painting, despite the canvas being nearly empty. He knows this is not a good moment to interrupt her.

He stands quietly for a long minute, and then says in an apologetic voice, "I'm about to make myself a sandwich. Would you like one too?"

"Oh yes, kind sir, indeed I would." As she speaks, her eyes never leave the canvas. "Could you make it roast beef on rye? Gobs of horseradish but hold the butter?"

"I believe I could. Back in ten minutes."

When he returns, he steps softly into the little studio and sets the plate with the sandwich down on a small table beside a ceramic jar holding paint brushes, pencils, and palette knife. Also on the table are cans containing turpentine and linseed oil and other bits of paraphernalia. Allie doesn't even look in his direction. She is lost in her thoughts.

Charles wanders back into the house and heads toward

the sitting room where he expects to find the two older men. There they are, Rhys stretched out on one of the sofas, his eyes closed, and Professor Wentworth sitting close by reading to him from a novel.

Charles stands and listens. It isn't long before he recognizes what the professor is reading—*Treasure Island*. He smiles at the thought of the two elderly men immersed in the timeless classic by the famous Scottish author. They are like two young lads again, sailing the seas on the *Hispaniola* with Jim Hawkins, Dr. Livesey, and Long John Silver. "Fifteen men on a dead man's chest, yo-ho-ho and a bottle of rum," Charles chants to himself, smiling.

✣ ✣

DI Eileen Corrigan has set one of her underlings to work at sifting through Mark Fetherston's email messages. His task is to extract from them the names of all of those who'd responded to Fetherston's announcement about the copy of the Geneva Bible he was putting on sale. After an hour, the man has compiled two lists, one with the names of the eight people who immediately expressed strong interest, and a second one with the names of people who'd shown *some* interest but who weren't champing at the bit. DI Corrigan tells him to concentrate on the first list for now, working up background information on each of those eight people. Not having Fetherston's mobile phone nags at her. She knows there's likely to be crucial information on the phone the emails wouldn't reveal.

At a nearby desk, DS Valery Wilson studies the list of books Mark Fetherston had kept back from among those he'd purchased at the estate sale. A cursory glance at the list suggests to her that the sale value of those books alone probably surpassed the total amount he'd paid for the entire lot. So, even before selling the Geneva Bible, the deal would have proved quite lucrative. Add in Rhys Tremayne's initial deposit of £2,000, shortly followed by another £15,000, and Mark Fetherston stood to come out around twenty thousand pounds to the good—an amount that was more than half of Valery's annual salary.

After their first several months of working together, Eileen Corrigan and Valery Wilson had come to realize that they often experienced similar intuitions. While they knew that intuition was not supposed to play a big role in serious police work, they knew that it often did. And at the moment, each of them found herself thinking there was something fishy about the estate sale where Mark Fetherston had made his big score. Was it simply a case of blind luck that he'd stumbled upon a very fine copy of the Geneva Bible? Or was there more to it than that? Both women were inclined to suspect the latter.

Over their lunches eaten at their desks, the two women share what they've learned so far.

"I think we need to find out more about this estate sale," Eileen says as she refills her teacup from her flask. "I wonder if Fetherston could have been tipped off in advance and nipped in there and snapped up that Bible before anyone else had a chance to."

"You think he may have had a confederate?" Valery asks. "Someone on hand who was in the know?"

"I don't know, but I think it might be worth finding out."

"I could go up and do some checking," Valery says.

"Yes, I think you should. Maybe nothing in it, but then again, maybe there is. Let's find out. Too late in the day today, but why don't you run up there tomorrow."

"I'll do that happily," Valery says. And it's true. She always prefers it when she isn't stuck behind her desk. She loves being out in the field.

DS Valery Wilson doesn't know the Peak District of Derbyshire well, though she knows the roads are notoriously twisty. After skirting Stoke-on-Trent, she takes the A53 toward Buxton, then pushes on toward Edale. She knows that this village is the most southernly point of the Pennine Way, the popular hiking trail that traverses "the spine of Britain."

It's getting on toward mid-afternoon by the time she finds Wintermoor Manor, a red-brick, Georgian stately home that once must have been quite impressive. Now, it looks somewhat woebegone.

She turns into the entrance drive and pulls to a stop beside a small brick lodge. An old fellow totters out from the lodge and approaches the car. Valery climbs out and holds up her police badge. The geezer nods, then asks if she'd like to come in for a cup of tea and a biscuit. "That would be lovely," Valery says.

The lodgekeeper proves a garrulous old duffer. First he regales her with his version of the history of the manor house before moving to a recitation of its successive owners, sprinkled with anecdotes and digressions. He shows no signs of slowing down, and Valery decides he'd make Coleridge's Ancient Mariner seem downright taciturn. But, she's probably the only person he's spoken to in a good long while and is making up for lost time. Without being rude, Valery finally manages to shift his disquisition in the direction of the recent estate sale and then to the man who'd bought all the books in the library.

"Ah, he were an eager chap, that one," he says. "Rather jumped the gun, he did. Turned up out of the blue on the Friday afternoon before the sale was to begin. Talked his lordship inta selling 'im the whole lot o' them books right off, the whole shootin' match, ya might say. That evening the fella loaded up his van and headed off. His lordship was pleased to have them blamed things out of here. Next day he sold all them empty bookcases ta another fella who'd turned up looking for books."

"Do you think the man had contacted anyone about the books prior to the sale? Or did he just show up hoping for the best?"

"Don't rightly know. Might've been just taking a flyer. It's possible, though, he could've had some dealings with Master Audley."

"And who is he?" Valery asks.

"Thomas Audley, the lord's secretary. Smart young chap, been the lord's secretary for the last several years. He were in charge of the whole thing, and he run it right well, too. By day's end on Saturday, most everything was gone, just as his lordship wanted."

"So now the house is empty?"

"Except for the few bits of furniture the new owners wanted ta buy along with the house."

"So no one is there?"

"I think Master Audley is still around. You could run up and check."

"Yes, I think I shall."

Near the entrance to the great house Valery can see indentations in the gravel that must've been made by the moving vans. The whole edifice gives off an air of dereliction. Kind of sad, really, she thinks, though she herself is no big fan of the old British aristocracy.

A slim, neatly attired young man comes forth to meet her. He looks puzzled by her unexpected arrival, and his face bears a quizzical smile. Valery assumes he must be the person the gatekeeper had mentioned.

"Thomas Audley?" she says, holding up her police credentials. "I'm DS Valery Wilson of the Devon Constabulary."

"Ah, my goodness, a copper. A bit off your patch, wouldn't you be? So, DS Valery Wilson, what brings a copper like you to this remote neck of the woods?"

"Just doing a bit of background checking."

"Seeking corruption in high places? I can assure you that his lordship is pure as the driven snow."

"You're Thomas Audley, the lord's secretary?"

"I'm *Tom* Audley. Thomas Audley, my namesake, was one of Henry VIII's cronies. Talk about corruption in high places. No, I'm just plain Tom."

"You were in charge of the big estate sale they had here not long ago?"

"I was indeed, I'll confess it. It was my last big job for

his lordship."

"I'm interested in the man who bought all the books."

"Oh, yes?"

"Was he someone you knew?"

Audley's hesitation in replying to that simple question tells Valery the answer, and it also tends to confirm her suspicion of chicanery.

"I'm trying to come up with the chap's name," he says, pretending to be lost in thought.

"Fetherston?" Valery suggests.

"Yes, that was it. Did I know him? No, not really. It turned out that we'd been in school together, just a year apart. He said he remembered me, but I didn't remember him, though I said that I did. Didn't want to hurt the chap's feelings, you know."

The man was lying, but Valery is impressed by how quickly he's extemporized.

"Yes, Fetherston," he continues. "Got himself quite a deal on the books because his lordship was so eager to have 'em gone. Made my life easier, too."

"Have you had any contact with him since that time?"

"Not a word."

"So you were in school with him?"

"Yes, at Rugby. Didn't know him, though."

"Now that this place is shutting down, will you be moving on to a new position somewhere?"

"Actually, going back to my old school. They've offered me a nice, cushy job there in the admissions office. Begins in early fall. In the meantime, I'm going to spend the summer in Italy—Ravenna, Siena, Firenza."

"Going to the Palio?"

"Actually, yes. Say, you wouldn't like to come along, would you?" His lopsided grin creates crinkles around his eyes.

"Oh, Mr. Audley, I think you are teasing me."

"No, not a bit of it. Why don't you join me? That's a serious invitation."

"I've one last question," Valery says, moving the conversation away from what she found an awkward and uncomfortable moment. "Did anyone else turn up on the Saturday morning of the sale who was particularly interested in the books?"

"Actually, yes. Two chaps did, as a matter of fact. One of them was rather disappointed that they were already gone, though he ended up buying a couple of the empty bookcases. But it was the other fellow who was quite miffed. Called it an outrage that we would sell any of our items before the sale had officially begun. Said he'd come by earlier and seen several books that he especially wanted to purchase. I didn't recall his earlier visit, but I was away for a few days, so it's possible he'd done that. Anyway, he left in a bit of a huff. At that point, of course, nothing we could do. The books were long gone."

"Do you remember what each of the men looked like?"

"Hmm. Let's see. The grumpy chap was probably late fifties, maybe as old as sixty, with thin, graying hair, though he looked quite fit. Maybe ex-military. Slim face. Wore a light-gray sports coat, I think, and charcoal trousers. Ah yes, purple tie. Over-dressed, I thought, for a weekend estate sale."

"And the other?"

"Much younger. Maybe thirty or so. Dark hair, dark eyes. More casually attired. Navy blue sweater, blue denim trousers, I think. That's about as good as I can do."

"Well, I'm impressed. Did you happen to mention to either of them who it was that bought the books?"

"Oh no, I certainly wouldn't have done *that*. The older chap did ask, actually, but it wouldn't have been fair to Fetherston to have the fellow nagging at him."

"Well, thanks for your time," Valery says. "Very helpful." She hands him her card. "Call, if anything else comes to mind. Oh, could you give me a contact number for you?"

"In case you change your mind about Italy?" he says with a wink. "The offer will remain open right up until the end of June. Think about it, eh?"

"Thanks, but no thanks," she says. "Besides, I've already seen the Palio."

As DS Wilson drives away, she realizes she hadn't thought to ask him if he'd heard about Mark Fetherston's death. If he *did* know of it, she thinks, he would surely have mentioned it—unless there was a reason why he preferred not to.

9

Eilish Tremayne, Allie's stepmother, is away at her job in Truro. And Charles with a few minutes to kill before their evening meal is taking her up on using her little private office just off the main sitting room. He thumbs through her CDs, puts on the Overture to *The Magic Flute*, then begins taking a closer look at the books on her bookshelves. He'd already discovered that he and Eilish had similar tastes in leisure reading.

Charles can smell the enticing aroma of their upcoming dinner that Maria, Rhys' cook and housekeeper, has prepared for the four of them. With Eilish away, they will take their evening meal in the little dining nook off the kitchen rather than in the main dining room. The two older men, Charles knows, have been resting in their rooms but will soon be coming down. Allie is also upstairs tidying up from her day's painting in her little makeshift studio.

Charles runs his eyes over the bookshelf, then pulls down one of H.C. Bailey's Josh Clunk novels, *The Red Castle*. He's read it before but not in a good long time. He considers this series of yarns from the golden age of English mysteries seriously underrated. He thinks he will read this novel over the next day or two and see if he still feels that way. He smiles as he reflects on the central character, Joshua Clunk. The sanctimonious little London lawyer, known as the criminals' lawyer, is a whiz at defending criminals while at the same time lining his own pockets. The lads at Scotland Yard despise him. Josh Clunk, Charles recalls, loved to recite the lyrics to obscure (or maybe invented?) Christian hymns as he goes about his business.

"Well, Charlie, how are things progressing?" the professor asks, as they start in on their salads.

"I've finished recording almost all the annotations. Another hour or two should do it. Then I'll go back and do a thorough double-check."

"I realize that it's way too soon to be drawing any firm conclusions, but any initial impressions?"

Rhys looks on without comment. It seems to Charles that the man's pre-dinner glass of wine has brought a little bloom to his pale cheeks. Rhys has been doing his best to resume a pattern of normality without overdoing it, but he still has a good ways to go. The hardest thing for him, Charles knows, is not being able to take his daily walk, a deeply ingrained habit that may have saved his life by keeping him in good condition. Perhaps in a week or so, he and the professor will be able to do some small-scale roaming about in the Cornish countryside. For now, his fascination with his new copy of the Geneva Bible is the thing keeping him energized. He looks at Charles, waiting to hear his reply to the professor's question.

"Well, actually, I've come to suspect that there may have been *two* annotators," Charles says. The older men glance at each other with raised eyebrows. "One who did the bulk of the annotating, and a second who underlined a handful of passages. That person may have added a few marginal comments as well."

"My word," Rhys murmurs, "two annotators. Who would have thought it?"

"Yes," Charles says. "At this point, I can't say that for certain, but it's definitely a possibility. In a day or so we can all sit down together and go over things carefully."

"Anything else?" the professor asks.

"I think it's likely that there are some discernible patterns in the annotations," Charles says, "patterns reflecting the different interests or temperaments of the two annotators."

"How close did you say you were to being finished with cataloging the annotations?" the professor asks again.

"Pretty close. I've reached the letters of St. Paul in the New Testament. I think I should have it all wrapped up by noon tomorrow. So far what I have is a handwritten list. I'll still need to get it safely into a file in my computer."

Rhys reaches over and pats Charles on the forearm. The man smiles but doesn't speak. Allie takes in the gesture and exchanges glances with Charles. It pleases her that her father so clearly approves of the man she has chosen—he's smart, not English, and he even has a Celtic surname.

"It's grand to be here with the three of you," Professor Wentworth says. "It's too bad, though, it had to take a heart attack for Rhys to reveal that the milk of human kindness really does flow through his veins."

"Professor," Charles says, with a frown of disapproval.

But Rhys just smiles at his old friend's wry remark. He is used to them, and he enjoys them. He also knows there's some truth to that particular one.

10

Charles and Allie, walking hand in hand, move along the grassy pathways that lead down through the terraced gardens behind the house toward the sea cliffs, 200 yards before them. Flowerbeds border the grassy paths. They pass beneath a pair of flower-covered pergolas, one where wisteria vines are in their full glory and another bedecked with clematis. As they near the cliff's edge, sea sounds greet them—the surging of the surf, crashing of the waves and raucous cries of the gulls. Surprisingly, at this pleasant evening hour, no one else is in view on the coastal path. Puffs of clouds ride the gentle breezes and float toward them from the southwest.

They walk just a short distance along the clifftop path until they reach one of the wooden benches placed sporadically along it. "Let's just sit for a while, Charlie," Allie suggests. He nods his agreement, and they plop down on the bench, their hips and thighs pressing together.

"Charlie," Allie says, after a minute of silence. "I guess you know that I'm facing a horrible dilemma."

"Yes," he replies, "I do know that. And before you say anything more, I want to assure you that I will be fine with whatever you decide. The truth is, Allie, I want you with me more than I can say. But if that has to be delayed—no matter for how long—I can live with that. You mean more to me than anyone I have ever known. Nothing is going to change that. If you need to stay here and take care of your father, I completely understand. It won't change a thing about how I feel."

Allie is nibbling on her lips. Finally, she says, "If I do have to stay, maybe it won't be for so *very* long. Maybe just a few months. And Charlie, there's at least some chance that Daddy's recovery will go so well in the weeks ahead that I *can* go with you as planned. It's only early June now, and you won't be going until the middle of August, right? Can we put off making a final decision for a while, maybe till the end of July?"

"Of course we can. Allie, the last thing I want you to feel is that I'm putting pressure on you. When you are ready to decide, just tell me. You know that what you want is what I want."

Allie turns her body toward Charles, then reaches out and places her hands on the sides of his face. She pulls him toward her and presses her cheek against his. Then, lowering her lips, she finds his. "You're my fella, Charlie Bascombe," she says following their kiss. "And don't you ever forget it."

"You're my mysterious Cornish mermaid, Alwyn Tremayne," he replies. "And I want you desperately. So desperately, Ms. Mermaid, that I don't give a fig *how* incredibly dangerous you mermaids are to us mere mortal men—if you lure me to my destruction, well, what a way to go!"

"Oh, Charlie!" she says suddenly pulling back from him. "That reminds me. There's something I've been meaning to tell you. You remember how we went and looked at that bench end carving of a mermaid last year at the church in Zennor? Well, sir, I have another special sight to show you, this one much closer, just a ten-minute drive. You game?"

"Ah ha. Must involve another mermaid, right? Well, if that's the case, I am definitely game."

"I can guarantee you, sir, that what I plan to show you will definitely amuse you."

"You want to know a secret, Ms. Mermaid? You amuse me."

"I suppose that's better than boring you."

"There's no danger of that—though you do pose a real and present danger to a mortal man such as I."

"Of course I do, dear Charles, of course I do. I'm a mermaid. That's my job."

11

When DS Valery Wilson gets to the police station in Plymouth the next morning, DI Corrigan is already at her desk staring into her computer. From the look of things, she's eaten her breakfast at her desk and is probably on her third cup of coffee. Eileen, even when she looks a bit rumpled and weary as she does now, is an attractive woman.

She brushes back a stray lock of silver-blonde hair and looks up. "I hope it was a worthwhile trip, Val."

"I'm pretty sure it was."

Valery needs only a few minutes to report what she'd gleaned about the estate sale—how Mark Fetherston had slipped in early and snapped up all the books; how two other men had turned up the next day and been irked by missing out; and possibly most important of all, how the man named Thomas Audley—who she felt certain had lied to her—surely shared some kind of connection with Mark Fetherston.

"So, Audley and Fetherston were at Rugby College at the same time?"

"Yes, a year apart. Audley claimed he didn't remember him."

"Audley gave you the name of the man who bought the bookcases but didn't know the name of the man who'd been so enraged at losing the books?" Eileen asks.

"Yes. Although he didn't have the fellow's name, he did give me a surprisingly detailed description of him."

"Let me see if the name he gave you matches up with any of those on my list of the people who contacted Fetherston about buying the Bible." It took her only a couple of seconds to determine that it did—the man's name was Michael McMasters and his office was located in Gloucester.

"So your lads have already worked up the background info on the people who responded to Fetherston's announcement? My word, that was quick," Valery says.

"Yes. They're capable chaps, at least when it comes to using the new technology. So here's what I suggest, Val. We divide up these people and each of us tracks down four of them and personally interviews them. Fortunately for us, all eight people live or have offices in southern areas of England: three in London and one in Surrey; the others are all in the West Country—Bath, Gloucester, Cardiff, and Chepstow.

"So, how about you taking Wales and Avon, I'll do the London area. Would that suit you?" Eileen knew that Valery wasn't much of a London person, while she, a graduate of the University of London, always relished a trip back to the great metropolis.

"Those are all places I know and like," Valery replies. "It will be easy for me to nip about to each of them by car. Might be able to do it all in one day."

"First thing tomorrow I'll scoot up to London on the train," Eileen says. "It's likely to take me two days, so don't feel like you have to do it all in one. Now, I'll just print out copies of the list and all background information we have on each of them." Moments later she hands a copy to Valery.

Valery runs her eyes over all eight of the names, then pays closer attention to those of the four people she will be interviewing: Cyril Harrington in Bath; Michael McMasters in Gloucester; Hywel Evans in Cardiff; and James Addison in Chepstow."

"Now," Eileen says, "let's take a few minutes and devise the set of questions we'll want to be asking these folks when we see them."

An hour later they've completed the list. Then each of them spends the remainder of the day writing reports and clearing away other routine matters so their decks will be relatively clear when they head off on the journeys which will occupy them for the next couple of days.

It's a little before eleven on Friday morning when Valery reaches Bath. She parks in a public lot near the center of town, then walks a short distance to George Street where the Jane Austen & Co. Book Store is located. She called earlier to be sure that Cyril Harrington will be in the store, and the woman who answered said he was there.

It's a charming little building perched along with several other shops on a low terrace overlooking the street. Valery climbs a short set of brick steps and enters the bookshop. Glass-topped display cases occupy the center of the room, and tall bookcases crowd three walls. The bookstore obviously specializes in Austen and other nineteenth-century writers, particularly women writers such as the Brontë sisters and George Eliot.

A young shop assistant greets Valery as she enters the store. "Looking for anything in particular?"

"I was hoping to have a word with Mr. Harrington, if he's available. I'm Valery Wilson, I called a bit ago."

"Oh, yes. Let me just see." A moment later she is back and then she leads Valery toward an office just off the main room.

Valery enters and sees a chubby middle-aged man seated behind his desk. He looks up and smiles. "How can I help you, miss? Looking for an Austen first edition?"

Valery shows her police badge. "Looking for information," she says. "After I've retired, maybe then I'll be in the market for first editions."

"Never would have pegged you for a policewoman," he says. Valery takes that as a compliment.

"Mr. Harrington, recently you indicated an interest in buying a copy of the Geneva Bible—is that correct?"

"Yes, I was quite interested in it when I heard of it being for sale, even though it's a bit far afield from our usual. Still, the folks who wander into this shop often have diverse interests, and a book like that is always a fascinating thing to have on display, a real attention getter. And you never know, someone might turn up who actually wants to have it. But someone else beat me to it, alas, and I lost out. Not a big deal, really, though I would have liked to have it."

"How well do you know the man who offered it for sale, Mark Fetherston?"

"Not well at all. I bought quite a nice copy of Austen's *Persuasion* from him a couple of years back. Then I turned right around and a week later sold it for twice what I paid for it. I'd hoped to have it around for longer, it was such a lovely thing, but no such luck. Well, that's business."

"You've never met Fetherston?"

"No, not that I recall. Chatted on the phone is all. Pleasant chap. Enjoyed doing business with him. I was very sorry to hear about his death. Accident, was it?"

"That's the common thinking."

"Shame, really." He shakes his head to underscore his words.

"This is a routine question which I'm afraid I have to ask," Valery says.

Harrington stares at her for a beat then says, "Ask away."

"Would you mind telling me where you were between May 31 and June 3?"

'Ah. Well, I don't mind at all. I was on holiday in the south of France—for the entire last week of May and the first week of June—so that would include the dates you just mentioned. With friends. There's a place there we rent each year."

"That sounds lovely. Oh, and would you happen to know a Cornish bibliophile named Rhys Tremayne?"

"Name rings a faint bell. But no, I don't know him. Can't be an Austen man, or I'm sure I would," he says with a slight tilt of his head.

"No, so far as I know he isn't an Austen man."

"Anything else, then?"

"Not right now. If I think of anything I'll give you a call." She hands him her card. "I'm grateful for your time and cooperation. You've been most helpful."

The shop assistant shows Valerie out. As she descends the few steps to George Street, the bell at Bath Abbey is chiming the hour of noon. Not being pressed for time, Valerie walks a roundabout route back to the car park, being sure it takes her past the weir on the Avon behind Pulteney Bridge. When she crosses the little square between the Abbey and the Roman baths, a couple of buskers are doing their thing for the tourists—a bearded guy is strumming a guitar and singing English folk tunes, and not far away a young woman is playing a creditable rendition of Mendelssohn's "Violin Concerto." The young woman smiles at Valery. Valery gives her a thumbs-up and drops a pound coin in the open violin case.

At this slack time of day, it's no more than a forty-five-minute drive from Bath to Cardiff. Valerie hops onto the M4 and heads west. Soon she is zipping across the broad expanse of the Severn River Bridge. Just on the other side, she comes to the "Croeso y Cymru" sign, welcoming her to Wales. She smiles at the warm Welsh welcome.

When she reaches Cardiff, Valery follows the GPS directions and soon finds the office of Hywel Evans, which is located on the corner of a short street not far from the National Museum and the University. She gets lucky on parking and nabs an open spot only half a block away. As she approaches the shop door, she sees that it is flanked by a stand displaying the Welsh flag, and another flag emblem of the Red Dragon of Wales adhering to the inside of the glass panel of the door. Inscribed on the door just below it are the words "H. Evans, Books."

A sturdy woman with iron-gray hair and wearing a dark blue cardigan sits at a receptionist desk, and Valery shows her badge. "Is Mr. Evans available?" she asks.

"I'm sure he is," she replies, getting to her feet. "Just a moment, please."

Mr. Evans, having heard the voices, comes out himself to greet her, a cheerful smile on his broad, ruddy face. A pair of half-glasses hangs from a chain about his neck. To Valery, the man's physique and body movements convey the image of a Welsh rugby player. "Croeso," he says. "Please come in and sit. Miss Jenkins," he says, addressing the receptionist, "would you mind bringing us a coffee? Or perhaps you'd prefer tea?"

"Coffee would be grand," Valery says.

"So, what kind of books would a member of the Devon constabulary be in the market for on this fine day?" he asks, beaming a broad smile at her.

"Alas, today only in the market for information, not for a single book. But you are speaking to a book lover. If I were to be in the market, what could you offer?'

"In the area of antiquarian books, pretty much anything you might want. My *personal* specialty is sixteenth-century books, primarily poetry—Spenser, Sidney, the other sonneteers, as well as Marlowe's and Shakespeare's long poems. My personal favorite is a lesser-known chap named George Gascoigne. But, detective, all modesty aside, I am the premier antiquarian bookseller in Wales. There's a fellow in Bangor who disputes that claim, but the man doesn't even come close." He gives a hearty chuckle, and Valery can't help joining him.

"By looking at me you might wonder how this burly Welshman ever developed such an interest. Well, blame it on Oxford. You see, I won a scholarship to Jesus College, Oxford's 'Welsh College,' and it was there I caught the scholarship bug. I'd gone there primarily to play rugby—which I did, even becoming a member of the Oxford Blues. But at the same time I got hooked on sixteenth-century poetry, as unlikely as that might seem. I took a lot of ribbing from my rugby teammates, as you can imagine."

"Would you be able to tell me where you were between May 31 and June 3?"

He tilts his head forward and looks at her over his glasses, fixing her with his stare. "Well, that sounds a lot like a serious police question. The answer is that I can remember very well where I was. I was in Scotland during those dates with the rugby team, first in Glasgow, then in a couple of other towns. We had a series of friendlies against several of the better Scottish clubs. We didn't return until the 5th."

"So, you are still playing?"

"Oh no, no, no, but don't I wish. No, blew my knee out ten years ago at the age of thirty-three. Been hobbling about ever since. No, I'm on the coaching staff of the National team. After ancient books, it's my greatest passion. Do you care for rugby?"

"I follow it some," she replies, "though I follow football more closely."

"You and almost everyone else."

"Mr. Evans, have you ever had any dealings with a fellow named Mark Fetherston?"

"Oh, yes, Mark. So *that's* why you're here. I was very sorry to hear of Mark's death. As a matter of fact, I had just contacted him about a book he'd put up for sale, a very early Bible."

"He sold it to a fellow in Cornwall, a collector named Rhys Tremayne. Do you know him?"

"Know the name, but that's all." He held out his arms apologetically, palms turned upward.

"To be honest, we're looking into the death of Mark Fetherston, talking to everyone who had any contact with him in the days preceding his death."

"Yes, Miss Wilson, I had already cottoned onto the real purpose of your visit."

"Anyway, sir, here is my contact information. If anything comes to mind you think I should know, please do call." She hands him her card.

"And, DS Wilson, I do hope you will come back and visit us again one day when you aren't on such a grim errand, maybe sometime when you are in a book-buying mood," he says, grinning. "You know, I could make you an incredible deal today on an early copy of *The Faerie Queen*. You look like a woman whose credit is good. What do you say? Only set you back a couple of thousand."

"Good-bye, Mr. Evans," she says, smiling. "I've enjoyed meeting you."

As she walks to her car Valery thinks, "That big, bluff Welshman is nobody's fool. But it doesn't seem at all likely he's a killer. At least, when he's not on the rugby pitch."

Valerie knows that the drive from Cardiff to Chepstow should take her less than an hour, but as the afternoon is drawing on, she decides she will wait until first thing in the morning before trying to see the book collector there. She wants to be fresh. After that, it's not far to Gloucester and her final interview. She hasn't contacted either of these men in advance, but she is willing to take her chances. Besides, she prefers to catch people when they are off guard.

When she stops at a petrol station, she phones ahead to the Two Rivers Hotel in Chepstow. The rivers, she concludes, are surely the Severn and the Wye. She remembers from her school-trip visit to Chepstow Castle fifteen years ago that the Wye flows right through the middle of Chepstow before merging with the Severn. Her call succeeds and she books a room.

As Valery pulls into the little town half an hour later, a gentle rain has begun falling. It should be a perfect night for sleeping.

In London, Eileen Corrigan is wrapping up her Friday activities also. She has successfully interviewed three of the four people she hoped to see—her day being successful in the sense that she'd been able to find the people quite easily, and successful in that she could scratch all three off the list of possible suspects, since each had a rock-solid alibi for the days in question. Eileen tried to reach the fourth chap, the one in Surrey, to set up a Saturday interview but without any luck. She plans to try again in the morning. Then, interview or no interview, she will head back to Plymouth tomorrow afternoon.

Eileen wonders how Valerie has done with her interviews but decides not to call her. They can compare notes soon enough. She takes a room for the night in a small boutique hotel near Paddington Station. Tomorrow, she will walk to the station to catch the train back to Devon.

12

On the same Friday morning in which the policewomen are conducting their interviews, it's quiet at the Tremayne home in Cornwall. Professor William Wentworth, whose stomach is just a pinch upset—the consequence of unwisely eating a few bites of railroad food?—has chosen to remain in bed. Eilish Tremayne, Rhys's wife, is still in Truro, dealing with a minor crisis at BBC Cornwall. She isn't expected to get back before late in the evening. Allie had set off early for her three-day weekend stint at the art gallery in St. Ives, and Friday is Maria's day off. She's gone to visit Allie's mother, Loweena, as she commonly does on her off days. And Rhys's physical therapist wouldn't be coming until Monday. So, it's up to Charles to hold down the fort, looking after Rhys, the professor, and a nearly empty house.

Since the two older men have kept to their rooms, Charles spends the whole morning without interruption entering his transcription of Bible annotations into a file on his laptop. By late afternoon, he finally has a chance to settle down on the sofa in the sitting room with a novel from Eilish's shelves. Allie's father, who had come down and joined Charles for lunch, is now snoozing on a sofa just across from him. The professor has remained abed all day;

and when Charles looked in on him, he said he was feeling somewhat better and expected to be fine by tomorrow.

About 4:30, Rhys rouses himself, sits up, and looks about.

"Ah, Charles, my boy, there you are. Had myself a most refreshing nap. So, it's just the two of us, eh? What would you say to taking a little stroll? Oh my, how I've been missing my daily constitutionals."

"Have something in mind, sir?"

"I do, I do. Maybe if we were to head out onto the moor, I could introduce you to my girls. You'd like that, I should think."

"Your *girls?* Sir, what girls would those be?"

"Ah, so Allie hasn't taken you there as yet. Shame on her. Tends to confirm what I've always suspected—she's a bit jealous of them. She needn't be. I don't love them any more than I love her."

"Mr. Tremayne, I think you're being coy."

The older man smiles and says, "Grab a sweater, my boy—might get a bit blustery—and then let's set off, eh?"

"Sir, you really aren't supposed to do anything strenuous this soon after your surgery."

"Oh, Charles, now don't be such an old woman. It's not much of a trek, just half a mile, a very easy stroll out onto the moor. I'll take my waking stick and I'll have your arm to lean on if need be.

"Your girls, sir?" Charles asked again.

"Nine of them, Charles. Some folks refer to them as sisters. That might even be true."

"Sheep?" Charles asks "Ewes?"

"Oh, no. They certainly aren't sheep."

Five minutes later the two men exit the house and move off slowly, Charles making sure the older man isn't pushing himself too hard. The direction in which they proceed is away from the sea. Since Allie prefers hiking along the coastal path, Charles hasn't had much chance to see the inland countryside. Viewing it from the car, the landscape had struck him as unexceptional, but as they advance slowly along the trodden pathway, he sees that the surrounding grasslands are punctuated with colorful wildflowers and a variety of berry bushes.

"Pick me a few of those raspberries, if you would be so kind," Rhys says. Charles picks a handful, giving most of them to the older man but saving a few for himself. Tart but tasty, he thinks.

Charles assists Rhys over an old wooden stile. Then the grassy path before them narrows and is bordered by taller bushes that almost form a lush green tunnel. When they are through it, they come out into a cow pasture where they need to step carefully to avoid cowpats. They climb another stile before reaching an open upland lea that extends before them. There, fifty yards away, are Rhys's "girls."

Rhys pauses and stands in silence, giving Charles a chance to take in the sight of a low circle of stones. Their rough and rugged appearance reflects the many centuries during which they've had to endure the winds and rains of Cornwall. In height they appear to range from about three and a half feet to five feet. Charles knows that each of them also extends at least a couple of feet down into the earth. Most of them are slender in shape, with only a couple of them being more rounded. Two of the taller ones have a slightly northward tilt, probably the result of the Cornish winter winds.

"They look grand, sir," Charles says. "No wonder you're so fond of them. How many are there?" He begins counting the megalithic stones for himself.

"Nine upright stones at present."

"Your own miniature Stonehenge," Charles says.

"Oh, no, Charlie, not mine, and not even a poor man's Stonehenge. Locals call them The Nine Sisters."

As Charles studies the ancient Neolithic grouping, he sees that there appears to be two gaps in the circle. "Are there two missing stones? Or were those openings to allow an avenue to pass through the circle?" he asks.

"Quite perceptive, my boy. But I can't answer your question. What I can tell you is that there is at least one missing stone, though it's not from either of the openings. It's quite certain there was once a center stone, presumably one that was a good bit taller than these. On close inspection, the indentation made by its insertion hole is still visible. And its shattered remains, they say, were discovered a good time back. The betting is that the Puritans—perhaps in the seventeenth century—made quick work of it. The other stones they just knocked flat, where the grass could grow over them. Those old Puritans had no love for anything that smacked of being an ancient pagan monument or sanctuary, oh no they didn't."

"Then along came the Victorians with their love of

antiquity," Charles says. "They tidied the place up and re-erected the stones."

"Quite right, quite right. According to folklore, these surviving stones, were nine young maidens who came here and foolishly frolicked about on the Sabbath. As a result of their impiety, they were turned to stone."

"I've heard similar tales," Charles says, and then after a pause adds, "I would say that Lot's wife's crime was worse than that. And she was only turned into a pillar of salt."

"Indeed," Rhys says with a chuckle. "Why, Charles, I'm getting the impression that you've been reading the Bible lately, drawing a comparison to Lot's wife like that."

"You might say that I have. Reading around the edges of it, in any case. Entirely finished with it, too."

"Oh, that's wonderful news. As soon as William feels up to it, we must all sit down and pore over everything you've found. I'm terribly eager to see your results."

"Maybe we'll be able to do that tomorrow."

"Charles, my lad, I have to say that it's grand to be out here with you. It brings great joy to my poor old heart."

"This is a truly delightful spot, sir, magical and mysterious, as all the megalithic remains are. And I find myself drawn to these girls of yours quite a lot—though not as much as I find myself drawn to your real-life daughter."

"Charles, you may not realize it, but you have been a wonderful influence on Allie. Until she met you, she was pursuing a rather rackety lifestyle, as artists often tend to do. After meeting you, not so much of that anymore, thank goodness. I'm most grateful to you, dear boy."

"Oh, golly, sir. I've always thought my own lifestyle

could stand to be a little bit *more* rackety. Most folks find me rather boring."

"Now, Charles, that can't be true. And besides, one should never care too much about what most folks think."

"Sir, that is an attitude with which I definitely concur."

Rhys rests his bottom atop one of the smaller stones for several minutes while Charles wanders about the stone circle, making a close examination of each individual stone. None of them is more than five feet high, and a couple of them seem to have crude, weathered carvings on them. Charles doubts that they are ancient carvings; more likely graffiti added by visitors in more recent centuries.

Rhys is happy to wait while Charles satisfies himself. It pleases him that the young man shares his enthusiasm for this ancient monument.

After the two men progress about a hundred yards into their short return journey and reach the first stile, Charles realizes that Rhys has begun to breathe heavily.

"Why don't we pause here and take a short rest," Charles suggests.

"Yes. Just let me catch my breath a bit and then we can go on."

Charles takes out his plastic water bottle and holds it out to Rhys. The man takes it and sips gratefully. "Ah," he says. "Just a moment more and I'll be ready to continue."

The house is in sight when Rhys halts and presses his hand firmly against his chest. "Ah, dear me," he utters with a gasp. He loosens his grip on his walking stick and it topples in front of him. As the man slumps forward,

Charles catches him before he collapses to the ground.

"I've got you, sir. Let's just stand here. Then I'll get you inside."

After a minute Rhys begins to breathe more normally. "I'm okay to go on now, Charles. Do keep ahold of my arm if you would."

Together they inch forward, the older man shuffling his feet slowly. At last, they reach the back door of the house.

When they get there, Charles notices that the door is unlatched and slightly ajar. He's certain that he'd shut it firmly and locked it. Maybe Eilish has returned early and entered through the back entrance.

But the house lies in silence as Charles helps Rhys to his bedroom. Charles gets him settled on his bed, pulls the duvet over him, and places a glass of water on his bedside stand. "I'll be fine now, my boy," the elderly man mutters softly. "Just need to shut my eyes a few minutes."

Charles tiptoes out, then slips upstairs to the professor's bedroom and peeks in. The man is still asleep so Charles doesn't disturb him.

Maria has left them a casserole for their evening meal, so Charles goes to the kitchen. As he is retrieving it from the fridge, he thinks he hears a small sound from the front part of the house. Maybe it's Eilish.

Charles creeps softly down the hallway and into the sitting room. Nothing. Then he notices that the door to Eilish's little office is partially open and the overhead light is on. Yes, she must have returned earlier than expected—though he doesn't remember her ever using that light.

Charles steps quietly to the open door and looks in. A woman is leaning over Eilish's sideboard. It isn't Eilish—this woman is taller, slimmer, and darker-haired.

Charles pushes the door all the way open and says, "What's going on?" The woman starts and turns halfway towards him, her eyes wide, her mouth open.

Behind him, Charles hears the hardwood floorboards creak. Just as he begins to pirouette about, something smashes against the side of his head. For a split second he feels excruciating pain. And then Charles Bascombe finds himself plunging into a deep, dark tunnel where everything is . . . *black*.

13

It is just after nine on Saturday morning when Detective Sergeant Valery Wilson raps on the door of the man's residence, only a few steps down the High Street from Chepstow Castle. She raps a second time before the door finally opens.

The man standing there couldn't be more different from the burly Welshman she'd seen the day before in Cardiff. The face and body of this short, slim bespectacled man look like they've been sucked dry. The man is probably just reaching middle age, but he could easily pass for a senior citizen.

"Hello," she says, "Mr. Addison?"

He nods nervously.

"Would you mind if I come in for a minute? I'm DS Wilson of the Devon Police." Valery holds up her police badge.

"Yes, of course you may. Step into the sitting room if you would. Maybe we could keep our voices low? Mother is still asleep, don't you know."

"You are Mr. James Addison?"

"Yes, yes, that's who I am." The man seems to have a nervous tremor, which Valerie suspects might be his normal condition. Her immediate impression is of a shy, reclusive fellow who is very uncomfortable in the presence of others.

"You collect books, Mr. Addison?"

"Bibles. I collect Bibles. *Only* Bibles."

"Recently you contacted a man in Totnes about buying a sixteenth-century Bible. Is that correct?'

"Oh yes, I did. That's correct. I did do that. Mark Fetherston. It didn't work out." Now he is blinking his bespectacled eyes like a nervous owl and twisting his hands together just above his waist.

"How is it that you know Mark Fetherston?"

"I don't actually know him. I bought a Bible from him a couple of years back, a choice early edition of the Douay-Rheims. This time he announced that he had a fine copy of a very early edition of the Geneva Bible. *That* I would have greatly liked to have. I already have one Geneva Bible, but it's not such an early edition or in such fine condition. If I was able to get this one, then I would have tried to sell the one I have back to Fetherston. Anyway, it didn't work out."

"Do you mind telling me where you were between May 31st and June 3rd?"

He looks at her in astonishment. "Where I *was*? Where could I be but here? I would never go away and leave mother on her own. That would be unthinkable."

"You don't sometimes go off by yourself for a few hours at a time?"

"Why would I do that? No, ma'am, I never do that. I leave the house once a week to do the shopping at

Tesco. Maybe a time or two I nip into the Tesco Express down the way for the odd item or two. But I'm never gone for more than an hour at most."

"Well, Mr. Addison, I think that's all I wanted to ask you. Thank you for your time. You've been most helpful."

"Umm, do you think you could tell me what this is all about?"

Valery hesitates a moment before saying, "Mr. Addison, I'm sorry to tell you that Mark Fetherston died a week ago. So we've been checking out a few things about his death."

"Oh, my word!" The man's pale face turns even paler. "Oh, dear, I hadn't heard that. The poor fellow."

"James!" comes a querulous voice from upstairs.

"Your tea's on the way, mummy," he calls up. "It will be just another minute."

"Thanks again," Valery says softly, handing him her card. "If you think of anything we should know, please give us a ring." Mr. Addison nods.

14

It requires an effort for Charles to open his eyes, but he manages it.

"He's awake!" It takes Charles a second to realize the voice is Allie's. He feels her reach out and touch his cheek delicately with her fingertips.

"Hey, you," she says. "Decided to return to the land of the living, have you?"

"I'm still considering it," he croaks. "I'll let you know in a week or two."

"Here comes the doc now," the professor says.

"I hope you were having sweet dreams, Charles, but I'm delighted you are back with us," says Rhys Tremayne.

"Don't remember any dreams, sir. Nothing but a deep, black hole."

Maria ushers a tall, dark-haired man into the sitting room where Charles is propped up by pillows on one of the sofas, an icepack against his head.

"Allie!" the man says. "I *wondered* if I might see you here."

"Hello, Ian," she says, with what seems to Charles, still in a muzzy state, a lack of enthusiasm.

"So you know my daughter?" Rhys asks.

"Oh, Allie and I go way back," he says. "We were several years in school together."

Charles feels a quick spasm of jealousy, an experience he hasn't had since college.

"Who is this Ian fellow?" he thinks. "And what gives him the right to greet *my* girl so gleefully?"

"I didn't know you'd gone to med school, Ian," Allie says.

"Still in my future, I'm afraid. Right now, I'm still a Physician's Associate, but I'm qualified to do most things—short of performing heart surgery," he adds, smiling at Allie's father, who doesn't smile back.

"Well, let's just have a look at the first of these many patients, shall we? Smart that you put an icepack on it." He removes the icepack and gently feels the side of Charles' head. "That's quite a bump," he says. "No bleeding. That's fortunate. Scalp wounds are notorious bleeders. This time you were in luck."

"Easy for you to say," Charles thinks.

"Don't think there's any need for x-rays. Do you have any history of concussion?"

"No," Charles says grumpily, "never had one."

"That's good. Well, it looks like you'll be having a sore head for a few days, but that's about it. I'll prescribe a painkiller for you, but simple aspirin might do you as well as anything. Any questions for me?"

"Should I continue to ice it?"

"Oh, yes, sorry. Thought that was obvious. Yes, do keep ice on it for another day or so."

"Maybe it was obvious to you, asshole," Charles thinks

but doesn't say.

"We'll take good care of him," Allie says.

"And what about you?" he says addressing the professor.

"Oh, I've had a touch of stomach flu. All cleared up now."

"For good measure, let me check your vital signs, since I'm here."

"Ian, it's my *father* you should be checking on," Allie says.

"All in good time, Allie." After he checks the professor's pulse and blood pressure, he nods his approval. "Pulse 74, blood pressure 130 over 80. So all of that looks pretty good," he says.

But that wasn't the case with Allie's father.

"Hmm," he says. "I think Dr. Brannigan should have a look at you tomorrow. Your heart and lungs seem to be doing fine, but since you had that fainting experience yesterday afternoon it would be safer to have an expert opinion."

"Well, if there's nothing else, I'd best be off. Wonderful to see you again, Allie. Maybe we can get together sometime soon, eh?"

"No way on God's green earth that's happening, asshole," Charles thinks.

"Thank you for coming," Allie says. "Good luck with getting into med school." Charles thinks he detects a slight note of sarcasm in Allie's words. He hopes so.

When Ian is gone, the sense of relief in the room is palpable.

Finally Charles says, "Would someone mind telling me

what the heck happened last night?"

"As best we can figure," the professor says, "while you and Rhys were on your walk, the house was broken into. Eilish returned about eight and found you sprawled out unconscious on the floor just outside her study. I was upstairs in my room and unaware of any untoward events. Rhys was dozing. Eilish came and got me and with maximum effort we lifted you onto the sofa. Your breathing and pulse seemed fine, so we put an icepack on your head and kept watch over you. Allie came back from St. Ives straight away when Eilish phoned her. Allie insisted on calling the doctor. That's why that chap was just here."

"What about the police?" Charles asks. "Have they been called?"

"Yes," Eilish says, "they should be turning up any moment now."

"Besides bashing me, what else did they do? Is anything missing?"

"We haven't done a thorough job of checking just yet."

"The Bible," Charles asks. "Is it safe?"

"First thing I checked," Rhys says. "If they tried to take it, they failed. Couldn't breach *my* secret treasure trove, oh no they couldn't."

"Charlie," Allie asks, "what about your laptop? I didn't see it on the table in the library where you usually leave it."

"If it isn't there, they must've snatched it. Were my notes and transcriptions still there?"

"I didn't see them. They must have taken them, too.

And didn't you have a flash drive with the computer?"

"Yes, I did."

"It wasn't there, so they must've pinched it as well."

"Well," the professor says, "if they walked away with all of Charles' excellent handiwork, we still have the Bible, that's the important thing. They were thwarted in getting it."

"It may look like they nabbed all of my handiwork, but there's a good chance we're still okay on that," Charles says. "At least I think I can still access it."

"And how would you do that, dear boy?" Rhys asks.

"After putting all the annotations into the computer, I saved the file, then attached it to an email message I sent to myself. If I didn't mess up, the file should be safe and sound in my email."

"Clever lad, Charlie," the professor says. "Your mother didn't raise any fool."

"One learns from harsh experience," Charles says. "When you've lost as much work as I have the last few years, experience teaches you to back things up like a maniac."

"Looks like the police are just pulling up," Allie says. "Took 'em long enough."

The local police lads have come and gone, but they haven't impressed anyone with their intelligence or diligence. "Typical plods," the professor says. "File a report, no doubt, and that will be that. Good-bye Charlie's laptop."

"Listen," Charles says, "it seems almost certain to me that the break-in and theft of my things has to be related to the Bible. It's even possible that it could be connected to Mark Fetherston's death. I think we ought to contact those policewomen in Plymouth and let them know about all of this. Those two seemed pretty sharp, far more competent than the local lot. In the meantime, I suggest we steer clear of any of the places where we know the thieves had been to avoid contaminating any traces of evidence they may have left."

"Charles is talking sense," Eilish agrees. "I'll keep out of my study, and everyone must stay away from the library."

"And from where my treasures are stashed," Rhys adds. "Even though they didn't get in, it's quite likely they gave it a try."

"In the meantime, why don't we try to have a quiet day," Allie suggests.

15

Later on Saturday morning after leaving Chepstow, DS Valerie Wilson sets off to track down Michael McMasters, the book-selling chap in Gloucester, but she has no success. First she tries his office in town, then his home in a Cotswold village a few miles away—no one answers at either place. It seems likely he is away for the weekend. She leaves her card and a written message for him to call her, and voice messages, too. Then she heads for the M5 and the drive south to Plymouth.

Just after she passes Bristol her mobile buzzes. The caller is Eileen so she answers.

"Hey," Valery says, "how's it going?"

"Okay, I guess. I missed out on one of the four. How about you?"

"Exactly the same. I missed out on one of them as well. The three I saw seem almost certainly to be in the clear as regard to their whereabouts. No obvious motives and pretty definitely no opportunity."

"Listen, Valery, I just received a call from one of the chaps in the office. You remember that couple in Cornwall, the ones who went to Totnes and picked up the Bible from Fetherston?"

"Yes, I do."

"They had a break-in last night. The American was attacked and received a good knock on the head. Sounds like he's going to be okay, but his laptop was taken, along with all his notes and the work he'd been doing on the Bible."

"Oh, my."

"Just before he was knocked silly, he caught a glimpse of a woman. Then he was attacked from behind. So we know that at least two people were involved."

"Were they after the Bible?"

"That's their guess. But if so, they didn't get it. The father, the old book collector, has a security setup to rival Fort Knox. I've sent the tech team down to process the scene. They're on their way now."

"Sounds like we need to talk to the American and the others straight away."

"We absolutely do. I'll take the train to Penzance. Think you could meet me there this evening?"

"Not a problem. I'm well on my way now. I'll probably beat you, so just give me a call and let me know when you'll arrive. I'll give those folks a heads-up to let them know we'll be coming. Guess they'll have to clear their Saturday evening for a visit from the police."

"There goes *our* weekend, too."

"Weekend? I didn't know we had weekends."

16

Maria, the Tremaynes' housekeeper, ushers DI Corrigan and DS Wilson into the sitting room where a small group awaits them. "Good morning," Allie says.

"First," Eileen begins, "we'd like a quick word with Mrs. Tremayne and then we'll want a few minutes with Mr. Bascombe. After that, we'd like to have all of you here together. Okay? Mr. Bascombe, why don't you stay here while we talk to Mrs. Tremayne." The others, politely dismissed, drift away.

"Mrs. Tremayne," DI Corrigan begins, "tell us what happened when you returned home last night?"

Eilish describes her experiences succinctly for the third time, having already told them to the others in the house and then to the local police.

"You saw no sign of intruders at that point?"

"No. The house was dark and quiet and everything seemed normal—until I discovered Charles lying on the floor just outside my study. It wasn't until later that Allie discovered things were missing."

"What time did you return?" Valery asks, her note pad at the ready.

"Half past eight. It was still light outside, though my

husband and the professor were in their rooms."

"And what about your study?"

"The door was open, the lights off. I didn't go in because I was attending to Charles.

"What did you do for him?"

"Tried to rouse him but he remained unresponsive. I got the professor to come and help me move him, and together we were just able to get him up onto the sofa. By then my husband was aware of our activities, and he brought a wet washcloth for Charles' head. Then I called Allie in St. Ives. She said she would call the doctor and the police and be on her way. She got here about forty minutes later, and then the young doctor—physician's assistant, actually—arrived about fifteen minutes after her. The local police got here maybe an hour later.

"So Allie was the one who noticed things were missing?"

"Charles regained consciousness just after Allie arrived. Right away she went to the library and discovered that his laptop and all of his notes were missing."

"That would have been about ten o'clock?"

"Yes. Or just after."

"Well, all of that is very helpful. Any questions for us?"

"None that spring to mind. Oh, is it okay now for me to use my study?"

"Yes, that's quite okay. Our technical people have fully processed the room. Sorry if it still requires a little tidying up."

Maria comes in carrying a tray with a teapot, a small pitcher of lemonade, cups, and a variety of biscuits. She sets it down on the small coffee table before them. "Thought you might be in need of a snack," she says.

The women smile and nod.

"That's great, Maria. Thank you," Charles says.

Valery pours tea for Eileen and lemonade for herself. When she looks toward Charles, he indicates he'd like lemonade as well.

"How's your head feeling now?" Valery asks him.

"A steady ache. But it's still intact, so far as I know."

Eileen sips from her cup, then sets it down. "Just before you were attacked," she says, "you caught a brief glimpse of a woman inside Mrs. Tremayne's study, is that correct?"

"Yes. She seemed to be rummaging through Eilish's papers. I only saw her for a few seconds."

"Could you describe her?"

"Umm . . . I'll try. Above middle height but slim-ish. Dark-haired. When I spoke to her, asking her what she was doing, it startled her and her mouth fell open. I was surprised by the contrast between her white teeth and her very red lips."

"Eye color?" Valery asks.

"That I don't recall. I guess I should since she opened them wide with surprise."

"Did she say anything?" Eileen asks.

"No, nothing at all, except maybe a small gasp."

"That's when you heard a noise behind you?"

"A creak in the wooden flooring. As I was swinging about, that's when I got bashed."

"Did you see anything of your attacker?" Valery asks.

"Nothing at all."

"And you blacked out immediately?"

"Oh, yes. There was a split second of intense pain, then . . . nothing."

The two women sit silently for a moment, looks of sympathy on their faces.

"I'm glad the pain is more bearable now," Valery finally says.

"It's still there, but I'll live."

"The items that were taken," Eileen says, "could you tell us about them?"

"Allie went to the library and took a good look. She saw immediately that my laptop wasn't on the desk where I'd left it, then noticed that all my notes were gone, too. I'd backed up my work on a thumb drive, but it was missing as well. Allie's father went to check on his rare books collection. Everything was safe and sound. Our biggest concern was the Geneva Bible, and we were relieved to know it hadn't been taken. As far as we can tell, nothing else is missing in the entire house."

"The Geneva Bible is the Bible that you picked up from Mark Fetherston in Totnes," Eileen says. "Yes?"

"That's the one."

"How valuable is it, would you say?" Valery asks.

"Quite valuable. I believe Rhys paid about £20,000 for it."

"What makes it so valuable?" Eileen asks.

"Its early date and its excellent condition. The earlier editions of the Geneva Bible are quite rare, and this is an especially fine one."

"Could there be anything else about it that makes it

especially valuable or that sets it apart from other extant copies?" Valery asks.

Charles purses his lips and seems to be pondering her question. He wonders if he should say anything about the annotations. In the end he decides not to.

"We'd just begun our study of it," he says. "I'd made some preliminary notes but hadn't had a chance to share them yet with the professor and Mr. Tremayne. There's no question, though, that it's a remarkable book."

"The question that's been in our minds," Valery says, "is whether the sale of this Bible to Mr. Tremayne could have some bearing on Mark Fetherston's death."

"You think someone might have killed him because he sold a book?"

"A very *valuable* book," Eileen says.

"Still . . . ," Charles says.

"People have killed for far less," Eileen remarks.

"And maybe, if he *was* killed by someone, whoever did it hadn't realized he'd sold it and thought he still possessed it," Valery suggests.

"You seem to be discounting the possibility that his death was some kind of accident," Charles says.

"No, not entirely," Eileen replies. "We're keeping an open mind about it."

Charles looks skeptical.

"The items that were taken," Valery says, returning to her earlier question. "Your laptop, your notes, your thumb drive. That's the whole list?"

"As far as we've been able to determine. There are quite a few valuable things in this house, but none of them seem to have been touched."

"Could you tell me about your notes?" Valery asks. "What did they contain?"

"Oh, just basic information about the book. It's the second edition of the Bible, and I was describing some of its unique features, things that set it apart from the first edition. The editors made quite a few additions and improvements to that edition. I don't think my notes say anything especially monumental, just basic information of possible interest to scholars."

Now it's Valery's turn to look at Charles with slightly skeptical eyes. She senses that he is holding something back, that there is something there more important than he is willing to admit.

Eileen, though, seems perfectly accepting of his explanation. "Well," she says, "you've been most helpful. Now, let's bring everyone back in, shall we?" She raises her tea cup to her lips and empties it.

When everyone has reassembled in the sitting room, DI Corrigan tells them they'd learned pretty much all they needed to know from Mrs. Tremayne and Mr. Bascombe. "But if any of you have anything you want to tell us—or ask us—now's your chance."

"Yes," Professor Wentworth says, "I was wondering if you've identified other potential buyers for the Bible. And if so, have you managed to track them down?"

"An astute question, sir," she says with a smile. "Maybe we should add you to our team. The answer is yes, we've been doing precisely that. Mr. Tremayne, it turned out, was quicker to respond to the offer than any of the others, but there were indeed several others who were keenly interested. So, yes, we are taking a good look at them."

"Can you say whether or not your technical team found any useful evidence?" Allie asks.

"Too soon to be sure about that," says DI Corrigan, "but they are quite good at what they do, so it is certainly a possibility."

"One last thing before we leave," DI Corrigan says, looking at Rhys Tremayne, "would you mind, sir, if we could have a quick look at this Bible of yours?"

Rhys pauses for a brief moment before saying, "Yes, I believe that would be all right. I'll just fetch it for you. It will take me a moment."

It's nearly five minutes before he returns carrying the box containing the Bible. He opens it, extracts the book and hands it to Eileen.

"You hold it Val, you're more the book person than I am."

Valery opens it slowly then, after perusing the title page, carefully turns a few pages. "Remarkable condition," she says. "I assisted the rare book librarian at Exeter when I was an undergraduate, but I don't think I ever saw a sixteenth-century volume in this condition. Quite extraordinary, really."

Her words bring a wide smile to Rhys's face; they are music to his ears.

Valery turns a few more pages, and when she's reached the Cain and Abel story, she notices a faint underlining of one of the verses. As she looks more closely, she also sees a few faintly scrawled marginal annotations in among the printed annotations the editors had provided. Her initial inclination is to ask about them, but on second thought she decides not to. She wants to see if they will comment on them, but they don't.

"Would you mind if I were to take a quick photo with my mobile phone?" she asks.

Rhys considers her request a moment before saying, "Yes, miss, I would mind. I don't mind showing you the Bible, but I do mind your taking it with you, so to speak. You see, I can't help feeling quite proprietorial about the book. I hope you understand."

"Quite all right, sir, I do understand."

"Well, thank you all so very much," DI Corrigan says. "Is there anything more you think we should know? If not, please resume your normal activities. We have interrupted your lives enough."

"And I'm sure you will take good care of Mr. Bascombe," Valery says, giving Charles a smile.

"You needn't have any fears about that," Allie replies.

"Well, if there's nothing else, we'll leave you to yourselves, and we'll be off," Eileen says.

On the drive back to Plymouth, the two policewomen go back over their conversations at the home of the Tremaynes. They are both convinced that the break-in concerned just the Bible and that the attack on Mr. Bascombe had been inadvertent, caused by his unexpected return. It also seems probable to them that the death of Mark Fetherston, the sale of the Bible, and the break-in are all connected.

"I don't think the perpetrators were experienced housebreakers," Eileen says. "If they'd been pros, they would surely have snatched up a few other items to make it look like a normal robbery. Concentrating on the Bible and related materials is a dead giveaway."

"And the attack on the American," Valery says, "that was rather strictly amateurish also. Lucky for everyone it didn't have more serious consequences."

Valery keeps to herself her feeling—since it's *only* a feeling—that Charles Bascombe had been holding something back about the Bible. His slight hesitation in answering her question caused her to think he'd discovered something significant about those additional markings she'd noticed in the margins of the Bible. She hasn't mentioned the markings to Eileen, but she can't help wondering about their possible importance. Perhaps she should have another conversation with the retired rare books librarian from Exeter.

17

"DS Wilson," says the reception desk staff member who enters Valery's office, "There's a visitor out at the front desk asking to see you."

"Oh yes? Who is it?"

"Some fella who says he knows you, says it's important he speak with you."

"Well, okay then, you can send him back."

Standing before Valery's desk a minute later is Thomas Audley, the man she'd interviewed a few days earlier in the Peak District about the estate sale. Now he's attired in a tan sweater vest over a pale blue golf shirt and wearing off-white flannel trousers. To Valery he looks like a character out of an Oscar Wilde play.

"Well, hello again," he says cheerily. He beams her his toothy grin.

"Mr. Audley," she says, "come to confess your high crimes and misdemeanors?"

He holds out his hands for the cuffs, still grinning. "Tie me up, tie me down," he says. "No, actually, DS Wilson, I just happened to be in the neighborhood, so I thought I'd stop by and see if you've had any second thoughts about taking a little summer trip to Italy. I've had my hopes up."

Valery isn't sure how best to respond. She doesn't have to, because after a moment's pause, he continues.

"I'm just kidding, DS Wilson. You made yourself perfectly clear last week. To my great regret, I must say. But, I am a fellow who can definitely take a hint."

"What can we do for you, Mr. Audley?" Valery asks, not charmed by his folderol, which she finds tiresome. "I suspect there's some real purpose for your visit?"

"Yes, in fact, there is. I'm in need of information and perhaps some advice, and I thought you were the ideal person to turn to."

"Advice? Pertaining to what, exactly?"

"Detective, I must chide you for not being entirely forthcoming with me last week. When you were asking about the books from the estate sale, somehow you neglected to say anything about Mark Fetherston's untimely demise. Now, I've been wondering why you didn't mention that rather significant fact."

"Mr. Audley, you told me you hardly knew the man. I saw no need to burden you with sad news about someone with whom you were barely acquainted."

Audley tilts his head slightly and squints his eyes, giving her a dubious look. "Well, if you say so," he replies. "Anyway, I was sorry to learn of the fellow's death. And my real purpose for being here does concern him. Well, not him exactly but rather his books. I've been wondering what will happen to them now. In addition to the fine ones he bought in the sale, I assume he must have quite a stock of other valuable books in his inventory that were for sale.

His web site, which is still up, certainly indicates that."

"Yes," Valery says, "that's an interesting question. We should take a look at that."

"Now here's the thing, DS Wilson. I have a dear friend who has just decided to take a whirl at the antiquarian book trade herself. If she could manage to obtain Fetherston's books, it would give her a leg up. She'd be quite interested in accruing everything Fetherston may have had—in the event, of course, that his executor would be interested in unloading them for a substantial amount of cash."

"Mr. Audley, I think you would need to contact his executor or his surviving family members about that."

"Yes, that's what I think as well. I was hoping you could provide me with that information."

"We can probably do that, yes. Would you mind telling me a bit more about your friend who's interested in the books?"

"Oh, well yes, I can. She's a brilliant young woman, Cambridge educated, who's now been working for a few years in a London publishing house. But she's become tired of that and wants to make a career adjustment. She knows a boatload about books, so she's decided she'd like to take a shot at the antiquarian-books side of things. I'm sure she will be good at it, and I am personally willing to contribute some startup money to support her endeavor. Fortunately, she has a good bit of family money too, so it seems financially feasible."

Valery nods. "Can we contact her directly with this information?"

"Probably best if you were to give it to me, and I can

pass it on."

"Okay. But could you at least give us some contact information on her?"

Tom Audley ran two fingers across his chin. "Yes, sure. Can I phone you later and provide it? That be okay?"

✢ ✢

"Those bloody Tudors," Professor Wentworth says, "all that bedding and beheading!"

"I suspect Henry VIII took the prize for bedding," Charles says. "Did he do more beheading than Mary or Elizabeth?"

"All three of them did their fair share," Rhys says. "Maybe Bloody Mary did more *burning* of the Protestant martyrs than beheading, but she was plenty 'bloody,' too. Lopped off the head of poor Jane Seymour, 'the nine days queen', amongst others.'"

"When it came to dispatching enemies, Elizabeth was no saint either," the professor says. "Mary Queen of Scots is probably her most famous victim, but there was no shortage of others."

"Henry's most famous victim," Charles avers, "was probably Sir Thomas Moore, with Anne Boleyn and his fifth wife, Katherine Howard not far behind. In the end he even disposed of his long-time henchman, Thomas Cromwell. Some scholars even suggest that Thomas Wyatt's poem with the line, 'these bloody days have broken my heart,' was composed after he'd witnessed the beheading of Anne Boleyn from his prison cell in the Bell Tower."

"Quite plausible," the professor says. "That poor fellow, like so many others, was besotted with the woman. But sadly for Wyatt, it was a case of *'Noli me tangere'*—'touch me not, for I belong to Caesar.' Anne was certainly Henry's private property."

"Ah, yes," Rhys says, "*Noli me tangere*, the famous phrase from Wyatt's 'Whoso list to hunt'— a wonderful Petrarchan sonnet."

"Do you know the other important context for that phrase?" Charles asks.

"I'm afraid you must remind me, dear boy," Rhys replies.

"It's what Christ said to Mary Magdalene in the Gospel of John, on Easter Sunday morning just after the Resurrection. He was no longer human flesh and physical contact with the Divine was forbidden."

"Ah, Charles, you've been dipping into the Scriptures again."

"Just working about the edges, sir, so to speak."

"On that note," the professor said, "I think it's time we had a good look at what Charles has learned about these annotations in that Bible of yours, don't you think?"

"I've printed out copies of my notes," Charles says, "so whenever you are ready, we can go over them." He places one in front of each of the older men.

"I need just another little splash of coffee to fortify myself," the professor says, "then I'll be all set to go."

✧ ✧

"I've tracked down the chap in Surrey," Eileen says to Valery. It's Monday morning, and the two policewomen sit at their desks across from each other in the Plymouth police station. "He's planning to call back at 10:30. I'd like you to listen in, Val."

"Of course, I'm happy to. Still no word on my missing guy in Gloucester, the fellow who bought all the bookcases at the estate sale. It's beginning to look like that chap is ducking me. If so, it might place him high on our list of suspicious persons."

"Audley said he didn't know the fellow?"

"That's what he claimed. I've begun to have my doubts about Tom Audley's ability to speak truthfully. I'm quite sure he was lying when he said he hardly knew Mark Fetherston, and lying again when he pretended he hadn't known of Fetherston's death until after I interviewed him. Thomas Audley, like his sixteenth-century namesake, appears to have a veracity problem."

When the call comes from the book dealer in Surrey, both women pick up their desk phones.

"Inspector Corrigan?" says the gruff, nasally voice of the man on the other end of the line.

"Yes, sir, I'm here. My colleague DS Wilson is on the line as well."

"Splendid. Two for the price of one, eh?" And the man gives a little cackle. "Well, yes, then, this is Robin Estabroke. Detective, I believe you've been trying to find me. So, madam, here I am. And how can I help you?"

"You attended an estate sale in Derbyshire about ten days ago, is that correct, sir?"

"Oh, yes, and what a colossal disappointment! Their pre-sale information ballyhooed all the wondrous books they were offering, yet when I got there—precisely at the time the sale was scheduled to begin—the books were already *gone*. Believe me, I was beside myself! A long trip into that god forsaken country for nothing, an entire day wasted."

"Were there particular titles or works you were hoping to buy?"

"Well . . . their announcement had listed several first editions of some famous authors and quite a large collection of nineteenth-century fiction, all of which interested me."

"But you weren't in the market for anything specific?"

"I deal in a wide variety of old books in almost all genres."

"History, biography, and religious works?"

"All of the above. Fiction is my biggest seller, then biography, then history, then poetry."

"What about Bibles?"

"Well, yes, Bibles too, especially early Bibles. They can bring a pretty penny. There are collectors who specialize in them, don't you know. I have a couple of choice Bibles on hand, if you might be interested." He gives another hoarse cackle.

"Hello, sir, this is DS Wilson joining the conversation," Valery says. "I was wondering, sir, if you recently tried to buy an early Bible from a man named Mark Fetherston, a book dealer in Totnes?"

"Ah, Fetherston, yes, indeed I did. He was offering an early edition of the Geneva Bible that I very much wanted. I made Mark an outrageously generous offer—and to my chagrin, the blighter turned me down! Said I was too late. Mark owed me one, and still he turned me down!"

"He owed you one?" Valery asks. "Why did he 'owe

you one'?"

"Oh, well, I suppose I can say. A few months back I put him on to a great deal, and he snatched it right up. He turned that great deal into a stupendous one. He's a cagey old bird is Mark Fetherston."

"You aren't aware then, sir," Eileen says, "that Mark Fetherston died over a week ago?"

"Oh my . . . I'd heard a rumor along those lines. Had no confirmation of it as yet."

"Sadly, it's true."

"Oh, my word. The chap was a credit to our profession. I shall miss him."

"Sir, could you tell us more about his stupendous deal?" Valery asks.

For a moment the man is uncharacteristically silent. "Umm . . ." he finally says, "I think I'd rather not. I'm not certain it has been fully consummated yet. Would hate to say anything that might queer the deal."

"But if Fetherston is dead, how could you queer the deal?"

"Yes, good point. His death creates a complication, doesn't it? I'd best think about it a bit more before saying anything further."

"Fair enough," says Eileen after a pause.

"Getting back to the Geneva Bible," Valery says, "do you know to whom it was sold?"

"No, Mark didn't tell me that, and my usually reliable grapevine hasn't coughed up that information either."

"Well, sir," Eileen says, "if you are able to tell us more about this big deal Mr. Fetherston had in the works, that would be much appreciated."

"And if you learn to whom he sold the Bible, could you pass that information along as well," Valery says, even though she already knew the answer to her own question.

"I certainly will. Well, it truly saddens me to have Mark's death confirmed. I was hoping there was nothing to the rumor. Like I said, he was a real credit to our profession—unlike some I could name."

They say their goodbyes and ring off.

Valery and Eileen sit quietly for a moment looking at each other.

"What did we just learn?" Eileen says aloud, her words more her own musing rather than a question for Valery.

"We may have just learned," Valery says, after a moment's reflection, "that there was a reason to kill Mark Fetherston that is totally unrelated to his sale of that Bible."

"You mean that someone wanted to prevent him from making his 'stupendous' deal?"

"Yes. And that that someone might be the man we were just talking to."

"Okay, I'll buy that. So we keep an eye on him and his dealings. And at the same time we track down the missing bookcase buyer who's been ducking you."

"Yes. And we don't forget Thomas Audley and the woman he says wants to buy Fetherston's books," Valery adds. "In the meantime, though, I want to learn more about the Geneva Bible, and if possible, the particular copy of it that Rhys Tremayne possesses."

"How do you plan to do that?"

"I think I'll start by picking the brain of the rare books

librarian I once worked for at Exeter. He should at least be able to point me in the right direction."

"Good plan. I'll set the boys to digging up all the information they can find on Mr. Robin Estabroke in Surrey and see if they can't trace the whereabouts of your chap from Gloucester."

Valery nods and picks up the phone.

When Valery calls Nigel Cummings, the retired rare-books librarian she'd once assisted at Exeter University, the man sounds genuinely delighted to hear from her.

"Why don't you come to Widecombe and have lunch with me, Valery? There's a couple of quite decent places on the town square."

"I would really enjoy doing that, sir," Valery says, "Actually, I could come tomorrow, if that's not too inconvenient."

"Oh, splendid," he replies. "And the weather is expected to be good, too. We could sit outside at the Café on the Green. What time suits you, Valery?"

"Would an early lunch be okay? Say, eleven-thirty?"

"Works perfectly for me. It will be like having our elevenses together in times past."

"I'll see you then, sir."

"It will be my pleasure."

18

"As you both already know," Charles says to his older compatriots, "I believe there are two kinds of annotations appearing in this Bible. They were made by two different hands and for differing purposes—though discerning what those purposes were might require the brain of a Merlin or a Sherlock."

"Fortunately," Rhys says with a grin, "we have the learned professor with us." He smiles at his dear friend, Professor William Wentworth.

"Too bad you don't have him as he was forty years ago," the professor replies. "Back then he might have given Sherlock a good run for his money. Fortunately for us, though, we have Charles' fresh, young brain."

"Ah, shucks," Charles says with a grimace.

Just then Allie pokes her head around the door and says, "Excuse me for interrupting the scholars at work, but I wanted to remind Charlie we have an outing planned for about five. Right?"

"Yes, indeed," Charles says. "I have not forgotten. I'm eager to go and be edified."

"Edified you shall be, sir," she replies before departing.

"What, pray tell, is *that* all about, Charlie?" the professor asks.

"There's a church fairly nearby with some medieval wall paintings Allie wants me to see. She says I'll be thrilled by them. She's probably right."

"I think I know the church she has in mind," Rhys says. "Oh yes, Charles, those wall paintings are right up your street."

"How come *I'm* not invited?" the professor exclaims, in a pretended huff.

"Let the youngsters have a bit of time to themselves," Rhys says. "They don't need any old duffers like us tagging along. Besides, I thought you and I were going to have a game of chess. You're not trying to wriggle your way out of it, are you?"

"Against *you?* Hah. I've no fear of your devious and unorthodox strategies."

Allie stands before her easel in her temporary studio on the screened-in porch. But her mind is elsewhere. It's on her father and on Charlie Bascombe. Her father's recent setback concerns her deeply. How serious is it? So serious it might scuttle the plans she and Charlie had been making?

Allie also feels concerned for Charlie and the bang he'd taken on the head. She is fairly certain, though, he will be back to his normal self in another a day or two. Charlie, she knows, is a hard-headed fella—in more ways than one.

Allie stares at the canvas and tries to re-focus her attention on the partially completed painting. It just isn't happening. Too many other things crowd her mind. Uppermost amongst them—Charlie Bascombe, this shy, quiet, thoughtful young American academic who'd somehow insinuated himself smack-dab into her life. It still perplexes her how what on her part had begun as a mild flirtation—more a lark than anything serious—had gradually modulated into something quite different and unexpected. On the face of it, the two of them were completely incompatible beings. She was fully aware of her tendencies to be flighty, unpredictable, and susceptible to sudden impulses and the pursuit of immediate gratification. She's always been fiercely loyal to both of her parents, but *never* to anyone else other than herself. For her, Charlie was an entirely new and unexpected experience. He was unlike any man she'd previously known—kind, gentle, and considerate, with a few mild eccentricities she finds both amusing and endearing. Charlie is old-fashioned to a fault, but he was open-minded and certainly no prude. He possesses a tender side she's never seen in a man, and she admires his great passion for his scholarly pursuits. But what she likes most of all is his great passion for her.

Allie so wants to be able to go with Charlie at summer's end. But what about her father? As things stand right now, she can't conceive of abandoning him. She knows that Eilish, her stepmother, cares deeply about her father and would look after him well. But despite that, Allie's and her father's relationship is of a different, deeper sort. Maybe, she thinks, there is one other person who understood the magic in the father-daughter relationship as well as she did—a fellow named William Shakespeare.

✣ ✣

When DS Valery Wilson is only a few miles from Widecombe-in-the-Moor, she spots the tall tower of St. Pancras Church rising up amidst the surrounding hills and tors. She loves this little gem-like village tucked so neatly into the heart of Dartmoor.

With schools still in session, it's a quiet Monday morning in Widecombe, the summer invasion of family groups still a month away. Valery sees several open parking places near the Café on the Green and pulls into one of them.

Nigel Cummings is already there seated at an outdoor table, and as she approaches, he stands up to greet her.

"I am so delighted you could come, Valery," he says, ignoring the fact that it was she who'd asked to see him. She smiles, says "Hello, sir," and takes the seat across from him.

"They have quite a nice selection of soups, sandwiches, meat pies and pasties," he says, handing her the menu. "For me, though, it's just going to be a boring old ploughman's lunch."

"And for me maybe a boring old Cornish pasty and an order of chips," she says. "But I'm wondering if I should be adventurous and indulge in a half pint of Devon cider?"

"A good pint of best bitter for me," he says. "Nothing adventurous about that—or about a half of cider, either—I would aver."

"Not really supposed to drink on the job," she says, with a small shrug of her shoulders.

"I wouldn't call a half of cider really drinking," he says, "not unless it's scrumpy jack. And besides, this is just a social call on an old friend from times passed. You're hardly on the job."

"Not on the job? You'd best wait until I've plied you with all my questions, sir, then tell me I'm not on the job."

"Questions about old books? That will be pure pleasure, my dear."

When the young woman waiting on them has gone off with their orders, they sit for a moment in companionable silence. Valery stretches out her arms and tilts her face backward to allow the warm June sun to fall directly on it. "Oh, what a perfect day," she says.

Nigel Cummings says nothing. He can't help looking at his attractive young companion admiringly. He imagines what the few others nearby might be thinking about this elderly gentleman and his much younger female companion—a woman probably too young to be his daughter, yet too old to be his granddaughter. He doesn't mind being the subject of their curious glances. Maybe they see me as a sly old dog, he thinks, smiling to himself.

"Sir, when last we spoke, you gave me a good bit of helpful information about antiquarian book dealers. I would like to continue that discussion if you don't mind, only this time a bit more specifically?"

"Ah ha! So this really *is* a professional visit more than a personal one."

"It is both, sir. Seeing you is always a treat. Having a chance to talk with you about books makes it doubly so."

"It's a double pleasure for me, too, Valery. So . . . books. Fire away."

"When last we spoke, you mentioned that you were

aware of the fact that Mark Fetherston, before he'd died, had offered for sale a copy of the Geneva Bible."

"Yes, I remember that I did."

"Would you mind telling me more about the Geneva Bible?"

"I can do that, of course. And I'll try not to make it too boring."

"It won't bore me, sir. I love old books almost as much as you do."

"Don't say you weren't warned." He proceeds to give her all the background information on the Geneva Bible, much of which she already knows.

"So, it was the most popular Bible of its day, up until the King James Bible began to dominate?"

"Quite right. There was another Bible called the Bishop's Bible which competed with it for a few years but never really displaced it from its preeminent position as the people's choice."

"You may recall, sir, that Mark Fetherston sold an especially fine copy of it to the Cornish bibliophile Rhys Tremayne?"

"Oh yes, I do recall that. In fact, I believe I learned that from you."

"There may be something about that particular copy that makes it especially valuable. Do you have any idea what might make one copy far more valuable than all the others?"

Nigel tilts his head to one side and runs a hand across his chin. "Hmm. No, I really don't, not beyond the fact that it's quite a scarce early edition and apparently is in truly fine condition."

"If a book like that contained marginal notations in a contemporaneous hand, how might that affect the value?"

Nigel raises his eyebrows and pursues his lips. "Well, I suppose if the notations are at all interesting, it might increase the value a bit. If they are dull and intrusive, they might actually decrease it a bit. However, marginal notations in old books always create a curiosity factor, so it would likely depend on how intriguing they proved to be."

"What if they lent a clue to the identity of the person who wrote them?"

"If they did that, and if the person was someone of historical importance, that could enhance the value of the book a very great deal."

"For example?"

"Well, for example, if this particular Geneva Bible had been owned by Queen Elizabeth herself and had marginal notes that were written in her hand, that would be of monumental significance. The value would shoot through the roof. That would be true to a lesser degree for well-known historical figures such as Sir Francis Drake, Sir Walter Raleigh, or perhaps John Dee."

"John Dee?"

"Not familiar with Dee?"

"I'm afraid not."

"Well, John Dee was a fascinating fellow at the court of Elizabeth, a brilliant eccentric who dabbled in a variety of things. He was kind of a sixteenth-century Welsh Merlin, as a matter of fact. His grandfather had come along with the first of the Tudors, Henry VII, when the Tudors arrived from Wales. Later, Dee's own father was a minor figure at the court of Henry VIII. As a young man Dee himself was something of a prodigy, and he served Queen Elizabeth in various capacities. He was also one of the ones who pushed her to the making of explorations in the New World. I believe he is credited with coining the phrase 'the British Empire.' He was especially keen on scientific pursuits, particularly those relating to astronomy, and he amassed an impressive array of early scientific instruments. Later in life, sadly, he became fixated on the realm of the occult. That probably contributed to his undoing."

"Goodness. He sounds kind of like a Faustian figure."

"Not a bad comparison. And it's not inconceivable that Christopher Marlowe had met the man. In any case, he must surely have been aware of him."

"So, annotations by a famous historical figure could increase the Bible's value considerably?"

"Yes, I should think so. Valery, your questions suggest to me that this book does possess marginal notations. Is that the case?"

"Yes, sir, it is."

"Then, it would behoove the owners to try to ascertain the identity of whoever is responsible for them—not necessarily an easy task, of course. I take it you have seen this Bible?"

"Yes, but only for a brief moment. I have no idea how extensive the marginal notations are or if they might reveal anything about the identity of the writer."

"Valery, this is all quite intriguing. You've piqued my

curiosity. I find myself wishing there was some way I could take a look. Unfortunately, I don't know Mr. Tremayne personally, only by reputation."

"I wish you could as well. But in his own words, he 'feels very proprietorial' about it, so I have no idea how I could make that happen. I will certainly bear it in mind."

When they've finished their meals and the trays taken away, they sit sipping cups of coffee. Nigel Cummings looks appraisingly at this young woman across from him. There are so many things about her that he admires—her intelligence, her confidence in herself as a professional woman, and not least, her lovely amber eyes. Today for the first time, it dawns on him that she has a truly delightful voice, mellow and just a little deeper pitched than that of most women—"her voice was ever soft, gentle, and low, an excellent thing in woman"—he thinks, though he hopes this able policewoman will never experience a fate like Cordelia's.

"When we spoke before," Valery says, "I asked you if you knew Mark Fetherston. I'd like to ask the same question about a few others, if that's okay."

"Of course. Ask away."

"Do you know Cyril Harrington, bookseller in Bath?"

"The Jane Austen man? By reputation but not personally. His reputation is good."

"Hywel Evans?"

"Ha, ha, the jolly Welsh rugby fellow. I do know him a bit, and I have to say, he's a delightful chap. A colorful bundle of contradictions—rugby, Oxford, and sixteenth-century poetry."

"What about a fellow named James Addison?"

"Hmm, no, I don't think so. Who is he?'

"Lives in Chepstow, collects Bibles."

"Doesn't ring a bell with me."

"Michael McMaster, Gloucester book dealer?"

"Again, I can't say that I do.'

"And lastly, Robin Estabroke," Valery says, remembering that Estabroke is the man in Surrey that Eileen has so far failed to track down.

"Ah, yes, Robin I do know."

"Tell me about him?"

Cummings grits his teeth, wondering how openly he should speak.

"Give me all the dirt, sir, if you would," Valery says.

"Well...okay, then. You may recall that when we talked before I said there was a broad spectrum of antiquarian book dealers, from entirely scrupulous ones like Mark Fetherston to the opposite extreme? Robin I would place amongst the latter group. He's a former intelligence officer in the military. Bright and knowledgeable, and he's as slippery as a slithy tove. Robin can be charming—when he's trying to manipulate you, but if he has a grievance with you, he can be a right bastard. I believe at one point he got into some trouble with young women."

"Young women?"

"*Very* young women. But I'd best say no more."

"Ah, I see. Well, you've been most helpful, sir. And I appreciate your candor about Mr. Estabroke."

They sit in silence for a few more moments before Nigel Cummings says, "If you still have a few minutes,

Valery, maybe we could walk over and take a peek at the church? It has some quite remarkable features, including a fascinating array of roof bosses."

"I would love to do that, sir, but I see it's nearly gone one. So, I had better decline the offer and head straight on back to the 'cop shop,' as the fellows refer to it. People will think I've been dilatory if I'm away for much longer. But next time we will do the church, for sure."

"It's a deal," he says, smiling.

As she drives away, Valery sticks her arm out the window and gives him a farewell wave. Nigel Cummings can't help feeling a sense of joyousness, knowing that there will be a "next time" with this bright and appealing young woman.

19

Rhys, William, and Charles huddle closely together staring down at the Bible that lies open before them on the library table. At his elbow Charles has placed the notes from his computer, printed copies of which also lie before the other two.

"There's nothing at all in the first few chapters of Genesis, not until we get to the Cain and Abel story."

"Nothing on the 'breeches'?" Rhys says, trying to suppress a chortle.

"Maybe you could scribble in an annotation of your own," the professor says.

Charles ignores them. "Now, with Cain and Abel, the first of the annotations, we also get the first instance—and one of the few—when both kinds occur."

"How can you be sure the marginal scribbles and the underscoring weren't made by the same hand?" Rhys asks.

"Initially, you can't. But as you become more accustomed to each of them, you begin to recognize subtle differences—in the thickness of the ink on the page, for example, and in the relative steadiness of the hands (one's a bit shaky, one quite steady and firm); and in most instances the ink of the underscorings tends to be slightly darker. I think you will agree after you've seen a fair number of each kind."

"So the Cain and Abel story?" Rhys says. "Why the shared interest in that one?"

"You tell me," Charles says, looking at the two older men and shrugging his shoulders.

"Uh, Charlie, you tell *us*," the professor says. "Yours is the fresh young brain."

"Maybe we should ask John Steinbeck," Charles replies.

"Ah, *East of Eden*," the professor says.

"Yes," Charles replies, "for a lot of readers down through the ages it's a morally perplexing episode. Why was Abel's sacrifice wholly acceptable to God and Cain's not? Cain was a vegetable farmer and he offered some of his finest produce. What was wrong with that?"

"I always assumed," Rhys says, "it was because meat was far more valuable—and thus it represented a far more significant sacrifice on the part of the giver—far more than a mere basketful of vegetables. One was a rather paltry sacrifice, the other constituted a genuine hardship on the giver."

"But Cain gave what he had to give; vegetables were what he had," Charles says. "Why should one kind of farming be preferable to another?"

"I guess it proves that God is not a vegan," the professor says.

"Anyway," Charles says, "you can see the moral quandaries this story creates. Of course, the story goes on to reveal Cain's serious character flaws when he flies into a jealous rage and murders his brother."

"The primordial act of kin-slaying," Rhys says.

"Charlie, what did the marginal comment have to say?" the professor asks.

"Like us, he wondered why one sacrifice was acceptable and one wasn't. He says, 'Is the Deity really so capricious as this makes it seem?' " Rhys says, reading the words from Charles' printed notes.

"He clearly found the situation morally questionable as well," Charles says.

"Apparently he did," Rhys agrees.

"Well, let's move on," the professor says. "What's the next one, Charlie?"

"A marginal comment on Lot, his wife and daughters, and the cities of the plain."

"More moral complexity," Rhys says. "Seems to draw attention, doesn't it?"

"Yes," Charles says, "especially for the writer of the marginalia. He finds Lot's negotiations with God upsetting."

"No underscorings this time? Er, no, I don't see any," Rhys says.

"No, no more of them until we get into Exodus," Charles says.

"Those infamous Ten Commandments, I suppose," Professor Wentworth says.

"Yes, but before that we have one on Joseph's brothers selling him into slavery and then another one dealing with the Plagues of Egypt," Charles replies.

"Ah, those beastly things," Rhys says.

"They do seem to focus their interest on some of the bleaker bits, don't they?" the professor says.

✣ ✣

When Valery answers her mobile phone, the now-familiar voice of Thomas Audley says. "Detective Wilson, I want to thank you for the contact information you provided for Mark Fetherston's family. Most helpful. A transaction is now proceeding with dispatch."

"Glad to have been of assistance. So, Mr. Audley, how soon do you depart for Italy?"

"Having second thoughts about coming along?" Valery hears him give a small chuckle. "Actually, there's been a last-minute change in plans. Looks like I will be having no Italy escape this summer after all. I've decided to stay here and help Diana get all set up. Thanks to you, she's off and running. Remarkably, she's been able to buy up Mark Fetherston's whole enterprise, lock, stock, and barrel—not only his books but his house and office as well. It looks as though she will soon be doing everything he'd been doing and from the exact same place. It's working out grand for her."

"But not so grand for Mark Featherston."

"Er, no, not for Mark. Most unfortunate business, that."

"Oh, Mr. Audley, I was wondering if you've heard anything from Michael McMasters."

"From whom?"

"Michael McMasters, the antiquarian bookseller in Gloucester. He's the chap who bought up all the bookcases at your estate sale."

"Oh, yes, I do remember him. No, I know nothing of the chap. I'd never spoken with him before that day and haven't since. I do remember how disappointed he was that all the books were gone. Happily, he was pleased with the bookcases, which I have to say he snapped up for a song. Worked out well for all parties—great buy for him, great for us to have them off our hands."

"So, you've had no subsequent contact with him?"

"No, none. As I say, I don't know the fellow. I just met him the one time when he showed up at the estate sale."

Valery has long suspected that Tom Audley is a consummate liar. Is he lying now? "If you should hear from him, could you let us know?"

"Yes, of course. Though I don't know why I would."

"Oh, your friend who you say is in the process of buying all of Mark Fetherston's possessions. Her name is Diana?"

"Diana Southgate. Comes from a prominent family in Essex. We overlapped at Cambridge. Named after Princess Diana, of course."

"A lot of girls born during the '80s were."

"Well, I just wanted to thank you. So nice to hear your voice again, Detective Wilson."

"Sorry about the abortive trip to Italy, Mr. Audley."

"Next summer for sure. Do keep it in mind, DS Wilson. It would be wonderful if you were game." Then he rings off.

DC Corrigan looks up from her desk when she sees that Valery is off the phone and asks, "Want to see the file the lads have worked up on Mr. Robin Estabroke?"

"Yes, but for now just give me the gist?"

"He attended Rugby School, just like Audley and Fetherston, but almost two decades earlier than them. Then he went on to Oxford for his B.A. and after that, he did graduate studies at Sandhurst. Then he had a thirty-year career in military intelligence, with postings all over the world including Hong Kong, Shanghai, Budapest, Vienna, and London. When he was in the Far East, he seems to have developed a taste for acquiring quite old items, antiquities and antiquarian books, as well as a taste for quite young women. Both pursuits came to involve him in some legal hot water. Military intelligence had had enough of him, and he of them. So he retired to his family home in Surry and then began his book business."

"Quite a biography. Any legal issues since his retirement?"

"No, apparently none at all. He seems to have been on his best behavior."

20

It takes only ten minutes for Charles and Allie to reach the small Cornish village of Breage and the church with a medieval wall painting that includes a mermaid.

"It's pronounced Breage," Allie says, "rhymes with 'vague'."

The square church tower, with its four corner pinnacles, rises impressively above the otherwise unexceptional-looking church. As they walk from the car to the west porch and the main entrance, they pass through an atmospheric graveyard filled with ancient, weathered tombstones and Celtic crosses.

"The present church is mostly fifteenth-century," Allie says. "It replaced a much older one that stood on this spot for several centuries."

Inside, the church offers several features that would normally absorb Charles' interest if his eyes weren't immediately drawn to the north wall and the late medieval paintings that adorn it. Ignoring for once the impressively carved bench-ends and the medieval floor tiles, he and Allie make a beeline for the wall paintings.

The right-hand painting displays a large figure of Christ wearing only a loin cloth. Blood springs forth from all of His wounds. Arranged about Him is an extensive display of medieval tools and implements—shears, saws, hammers, a scythe, a wheelbarrow, even a few musical instruments.

"That's really something," Charles says. "Do you suppose it celebrates or alludes to the fact that Jesus had been a carpenter? A kind of tribute to blue-collar workers?"

"That's one interpretation," Allie says. "The prevailing view, though, is that it's an admonition not to work on the Sabbath. Doing that re-opens Christ's bloody wounds, as you can see."

"*That* again, hmm?" Charles says. He remembers Rhys' stone circle and the young women who were punished for frolicking on a holy day.

"It's a violation of one of the Commandments, you know," Allie says.

"The Fourth, if I remember correctly."

"But this isn't the painting I lured you here to see, Charlie. It's the other one." Allie takes a few steps to the left and Charles follows her.

"My word," Charles says, "it's St. Christopher, larger than life. You know, some of the St. Christopher legends say the man was seven and a half feet tall. Here he's even taller than that."

They stand silently studying the striking depiction of the Patron Saint of Travelers. On the huge man's shoulder sits a small child who, unbeknownst to the man carrying him, is the Christ Child. In one hand St. Christopher holds a huge staff, and water swirls about his thighs as he strides through a river. Fish lurk in the waters about him. But the most remarkable creature—and the one Allie has brought Charles to see—is a mermaid. She possesses a mermaid's traditional accouterments, a comb and a mirror. Remarkably, on the front of the mirror the artist has painted her reflected face.

"A fresh-water mermaid," Charles exclaims. "Didn't know there were such things."

He and Allie stand there studying the painting. "When I was a kid," Charles says, "some of my pals wore St. Christopher medals. Actually, so did Chaucer's Yeoman in the *Canterbury Tales*, as the professor would be quick to remind us."

"This artist had a real flair for the original," Allie says. "And very likely, a sense of humor, like your Chaucer."

"Putting in that little mermaid is truly a wonderful addition," Charles says. "I'm sure there's no mention of any mermaids in any of the written accounts of St. Christopher. She's a real treat."

"Control yourself, young man. She's not all that enticing, is she?"

"Sorry Allie, but she is."

"Give a man a pornographic image, and that's all he needs."

"Pornographic? Not even close. You, as an art expert, should know that."

"The entire painting is a bit primitive," Allie says, "one has to admit it. But the artist does have a certain unexpected sophistication."

"The mirror she's holding is a stroke of genius," Charles says. "Look at her face!"

"Her face in the mirror is a brilliant touch."

"I loved that bench-end mermaid you showed me a

year ago, and I love this one, too."

"And what about *this* one?" Allie asks, pointing a finger at herself.

"That one?" Charles says. "I have to confess, that one's the best of the lot. And, alas, she's the one who's likely to lure me to my destruction."

"Let's hope so," Allie says. "We do aim to please, you know."

Charles grins, then he reaches out and pulls this lovely, enticing mermaid into his warm embrace.

As they drive back to Manderley a few minutes later, Allie says, "Tell me a little more about the legends surrounding St. Christopher, Mr. College Professor."

"If you insist. First of all, I believe his name derives from Greek words meaning 'bearer of Christ.' He took that name after carrying the Christ Child across the raging river. In the story he's been helping pilgrims and other travelers cross this dangerous stretch of river, and then one evening a tiny little boy turns up and asks for his help. He manages to carry the little tike across, but just barely because as he moves deeper into the water, the weight on his shoulder grows greater and greater and before he can reach the farther shore it's almost unbearable. After he's reached the shore he asks the child how it was that he'd become so heavy. The child says, 'You merely bear the weight of people on your shoulders. I bear the weight of the whole world on mine'—or something to that effect."

"What happened to Christopher later on?"

"Oh, just the usual. When he was ordered by a pagan

tyrant to bow down to his pagan gods, he refused, so the tyrant ordered his head to be chopped off. That wasn't easy to do, but after several attempts they managed to complete the execution."

"Never easy being a martyred saint."

Rhys Tremayne has won the chess game, and he's feeling chuffed. When Charles and Allie walk into the sitting room, the two elderly men are well into a bottle of Johnny Walker Black.

"Daddy," Allie says, "I don't think you should be drinking. Didn't the doctor tell you not to?"

At that moment. Eilish swoops in and snatches up the bottle of whiskey. "William," she snaps at the professor, "what were you thinking, allowing Rhys to indulge like that?" The professor looks suitably chastened.

"I'm sorry, my dear," Rhys says. "I so rarely defeat my learned friend that I couldn't help feeling jubilant. Just a little nip has surely done me no harm."

Eilish steps over to her husband and embraces him. "Oh, my dear, you mean too much to us for us to allow you to take any chances. Winning a game of chess is no reason to get all worked up."

"But, Eilish, it's merely the innocent celebration of a happy man. Here I am in my own home surrounded by the best people I will ever know. I have survived a terrible hospital ordeal, I am the owner of a truly remarkable book—perhaps the rarest book in the world—and I have just won a game of chess off one of Oxford's finest players." After Eilish releases her hold on him it's Allie's turn to come and hug her father.

"Rhys," the professor says, "I hope you aren't going to break with tradition. Since you won, it's your turn to declaim. To the victor goes that honor."

"Oh, dear, I didn't expect to win. I have nothing prepared."

"Just give us something off the top of your head, then."

"Ah, okay I think I can come up with something. But perhaps the women should step from the room. Just a bit off-color, this one."

Neither woman moves a single step.

"It's a little ditty I heard many years ago concerning our beloved Oxford:

> *There was a young man from St. John's*
> *Who wanted to roger the swans.*
> *No, no said the porter,*
> *Make free with my daughter.*
> *The swans are reserved for the dons.*

"Very droll," William says.

"Makes me think of that story in Genesis when Lot offers the men of Sodom and Gomorrah his daughters," Charles says. "Didn't want them to have at the angelic creatures who'd come to visit him."

"Charlie, my boy," Rhys says, "your mind seems much preoccupied by the scriptures these days. My fault, I suppose."

"Sir," Charles asks him, "were your undergraduate days at Oxford really such an unpleasant experience for you?"

"They *weren't*," the professor chimes in. "Rhys just

likes to play the business up."

Rhys shrugs. "In some respects, Charles, I have to admit that being at Oxford was a grand experience. It was there I was able to form my lifelong friendships with people like William and my old friend Neville Smallwood, the fellow who became a clergyman up in North Cornwall. They don't come any better than those two. In other respects, though, it was quite repugnant. Too many toffs, too many frauds, too many people looking down their noses at you. And indeed for my taste, too many chaps who preferred the swans to the porter's buxom daughter. I suppose that marks me as being a bit narrow-minded. Well, my boy, I am what I am."

21

DS Valery Wilson sits at her desk ruminating. Finally, she says aloud, "What if Tom Audley and the late Mark Fetherston were in cahoots?'

DI Eileen Corrigan, sitting across from her at her own desk, looks up. "Go on," she says to Valery, "you've got my attention."

"What if Audley knew before the estate sale that he had a valuable Bible on his hands, one he could sell to Mark Fetherston for a relative pittance, and then later on receive a substantial kickback from him when Fetherston sold it for a bundle?"

"Why wouldn't Audley just sell it himself and keep all the profits?"

"Maybe because it's a business for specialists. He needed Fetherston's contacts, his knowhow, and his standing in the profession to optimize the deal."

Eileen considers Valery's remarks and nods her understanding. "Okay," she says, "go on."

"Suppose that after Fetherston had put the Bible up for sale, someone else somehow came to realize that the Bible's true value far exceeds what Audley and Fetherston had assumed. But unfortunately for them, Fetherston immediately sold the Bible to Rhys Tremayne without anyone else being the wiser."

"So your hypothetical 'someone' whacks Fetherston, thinking he still has the Bible?"

"Yes, that seems within the realm of possibility to me. I am, I realize, serving up a lot of hypotheticals here; but they are the things that have been nagging at me."

"Well, Valery, fair enough. No harm in considering such things, of course. But it seems to me that the real key is the break-in down in Cornwall. Once we've tracked down the perpetrators of that, then things may begin to sort themselves out."

At that moment one of the younger members of their team approaches and places a folder on DI Corrigan's desk.

"This just came in, ma'am," he says. "Thought you would want to see it." He glances over at Valery and gives her a wink. Valery rolls her eyes.

"Thank you, Matthew," Eileen says, and opens the folder. "Ah, good. Here's some more detailed information on this Ms. Diana Southgate, including some photos."

"Excellent," Valery says. "So far Diana Southgate is the only female in our rogues gallery. And if we accept the American's account, we know that a female was involved in the break-in."

"Maybe I can get the lads in Helston to run a photo lineup past him. See if he picks out our Ms. Southgate."

"Yes...," Valery says. "Or better yet, maybe I should run down there and do it in person. It's often more productive to view at firsthand the expressions on a witness's face."

"I don't see the need for you to do that, Valery, but if you really want to, I've no objections," Eileen says, giving a little shrug.

"I really would like to. Those Helston lads are probably okay, but I have to say they haven't hugely impressed me."

"Nor me, to be honest."

"I'll give the young American a call straightaway and try to arrange it."

When Valery reaches Charles by phone, he suggests that she come around mid-afternoon on Friday, a time that works for him and won't inconvenience anyone else, since the women will be away at their jobs and the two older men will probably be napping.

Valery likes Charles' suggestion for an additional reason to those he gave. Lurking in the back of her mind is the possibility that she might be able to persuade him to let her have another look at the Geneva Bible. And if she can, maybe he will also allow her to take a quick photo of an annotated page. That's a long shot, but he seems a good bit more tractable to her than Rhys Tremayne. And if Charles flatly refuses, she certainly won't push the matter—though it might be worth a try. She smiles to herself, thinking that if worse comes to worst, she can always exert her feminine charms on the young man. She has known that to work in the past—even though it caused her some slight twinges of conscience when it had.

✣ ✣

"'*Vanitas Vanitatum et omnia vanitas*,'" the professor intones.

"Yes," Rhys says, "all is vanity indeed and a striving after the wind. A very sobering book is Ecclesiastes."

"But one that seems to hold special interest for our

annotators," Charles says.

"Which suggests that the both of them—assuming there *are* two—had a philosophical bent," Rhys says.

"I've never found Ecclesiastes to be as dreary a thing as a lot of folks do," the professor says. "To me, the writer touches upon many positive aspects of human existence too, suggests that our lives are not *entirely* pointless, not entirely a worthless striving after the wind."

" 'A time to dance, a time to laugh, a time to love,' " says Charles.

"You chaps are cherry-picking the text," Rhys says.

"'A man should rejoice and do good in his life,'" the professor observes, "'and he should eat and drink and enjoy the fruits of his labor for they are the gifts of God. Those are the writer's very words.'"

"That's pure sophistry," Rhys says. "You Oxford intellectuals are trying to turn a darkly pessimistic treatise into a spiritually uplifting one. Pure sophistry, I say."

"I've always liked the verse about casting your bread upon the waters," Charles says.

"A rather soggy metaphor, if ever I heard one," Rhys replies. "And if one were in Oxford, those dratted swans would cobble up the bread before it had a chance to get soggy."

"Still fixated on swans, eh, Rhys?" The professor says, with a chuckle.

"I think the verse has to do with believing in yourself," Charles says.

"I agree with you, Charlie," the professor says.

"Perhaps so," Rhys admits, "but that verse isn't one of

the ones our annotators were concerned with, now, is it? No, I think not. Their attention is far more focused on the 'all is vanity' bits. I think they had a much clearer notion of what the writer of Ecclesiastes was getting at than you two rose-colored glasses chaps do."

"Charlie?" the professor asks, pointing to something scrawled in the margin next to verses 26-28 of Chapter 7, "what do you make of this little squiggle here? It looks like a single word."

"With the help of my trusty magnifying glass," Charles replies, "I read it as a name. I think it says 'Helen'."

"A woman more bitter than death? One whose heart is snares and nets?" says the professor, reading phrases in the biblical text adjacent to the word in the margin.

"Sounds to me like this Helen woman, whoever she is, may have seduced and then dumped the poor lad," Rhys observes.

"Maybe so, maybe so," Charles says softly, gently rubbing the furrows of his forehead. "Or, maybe it was even worse than that." For a long moment the three men sit there silently, reflecting on the annotation and the words presumably associated with it.

"Goodness," Rhys finally says. "Well, I don't know about you chaps, but I can't help feeling a bit low. All this vanity of vanities business always does that to me. It's just too damned depressing. Charles, I thank you for all your fine work, my boy," he says, patting Charles on the shoulder, "but I believe I shall be taking to my bed for the remainder of the day."

"That does it for Ecclesiastes, sir," Charles says. "Psalms

is up next, and there you will probably find the annotated passages quite a bit more uplifting."

Rhys just nods wordlessly. His hands hang slackly at his sides, his eyes seem to gaze into the distance. To Charles, the man doesn't look at all well. And when Charles assists him to his bedroom, Rhys shuffles his feet slowly and leans heavily on Charles' arm.

"Professor," Charles says upon returning to the library where Professor Wentworth still sits staring down at the words of Ecclesiastes, "we need to call Doctor Brannigan *now*. We can't wait until his next scheduled visit."

"Right as usual, Charlie," he replies, nodding. "And I've been wondering if maybe I shouldn't call my wife, see if I can't persuade Janet to come down and help. Take some of the load off Eilish and Allie's shoulders."

Charles doesn't know Janet Wentworth, the Professor's wife, at all well. But he knows she can be a formidable force and that the professor tends to stay out of her way whenever the woman takes the bit between her teeth—which, apparently, she often does.

"No," the professor says, "on second thought, maybe not such a good idea. Might be a case of too many cooks." Charles nods his mute agreement. Three strong-willed women in the house at one time is plenty. They don't need a fourth.

Charles doen't think Allie or Eilish would mind having someone else come in and start managing things in her own fashion, though Maria, the Tremaynes' housekeeper, certainly would. Maria considers Manderley her personal bailiwick. Charles is relieved that the professor has had second thoughts.

"Maybe you should run up to Oxford for a few days, sir. Let your wife know that you haven't totally abandoned her."

"Oh, I'm sure she knows that. Besides, I'm going nowhere until we finish up our work on the Bible. You dig?" he says, using a phrase he'd picked up in America in the late '60s.

"I dig," Charles replies.

22

Diana Southgate couldn't be more pleased about how things are working out. Last night she'd arrived in Totnes to familiarize herself thoroughly with the property she is in the process of acquiring. Members of Mark Fetherston's family had already come and removed the few personal things of his they wanted to keep. They'd left her a set of keys, and when she entered the small house, she saw that most of its furnishings were still in place. She liked the look of these things that would soon belong to her. Mark Fetherston, she thought, had had good taste. She wouldn't need to make a lot of changes, at least not right off.

Of greatest interest to her, of course, are Fetherston's books. A quick examination of his many and assorted bookcases in his sitting room and in his office reveal that he possessed more books than she would have guessed. Some of them, her practiced eye told her, were truly rare and valuable. Yes, getting in before the vultures had circled had been a major stroke of good luck. For that, she was much indebted to Tom Audley. His help in bringing it about had been essential. Tom's a slippery operator, she thinks, smiling to herself; but then, so am I. We deserve each other.

Diana spends the night sleeping in Mark Fetherston's

guest bedroom. She can't quite bring herself to sleep in a recently deceased man's bedroom. Not yet, but it wouldn't be long before she will make that bedroom her own.

Now, on her first morning in her new abode, Diana brews a morning cup of tea in his kitchen and toasts an English muffin, which she spreads generously with the butter and marmalade she's found in Mark's refrigerator. By nine-thirty she's seated at Fetherston's desk—soon-to-be *her* desk. Right off she transfers his contact files from his computer (the password to which she's been given) to a flash drive. Diana is adept with computers and accessing the files in Mark's computer has been easy for her to do. But there was one exception, one file which refused to open when she applied the usual tricks of the trade. Most strange, she thinks. She herself has had a lot of experience with encrypted files—she's encrypted a fair number herself—and she believes herself to be highly skilled at unencrypting them. Diana Southgate, a woman who likes a challenge, grits her teeth and sets about it. It is a tough nut to crack. But after the better part of an hour, she succeeds in besting the blessed thing.

But what is this? Yes, she's opened it, but at first glance she can't make heads or tails of it. It seems to be written in some sort of cipher or code. One thing is certain. Mark Fetherston went to great lengths to keep this file away from prying eyes. The man must not have been the open book most people took him for. Oh no, there was a dimension to the man that he'd kept hidden from the world. Diana wonders if the police have been able to access this file. If so, it might provide them with some important avenues of inquiry. But they probably haven't. Considering how much of a challenge it posed for her, she thinks it was probably well beyond their feeble talents. It remains for her to crack the cipher and figure out what the dickens this secret file might actually contain. Once she has, she certainly won't be sharing it with the authorities or with anyone else. Maybe not even with her friend and fellow conspirator, Thomas Audley.

✣ ✣

Rhys Tremayne's medical setback has brought a halt to the three men's analysis of the annotations in the Geneva Bible. The doctor immediately imposes a regimen of bed rest for Rhys. For the next few days, physical and mental exertion of any kind is strictly forbidden.

"Don't you two chaps be going on without me," Rhys orders sternly.

"My friend, we wouldn't think of it," the professor replies.

"Those annotations in the Bible have waited four hundred years for someone to come along and take a look at them," Charles says. "I think they can hang on for a few more days."

"But I don't think *I* can, Charles," Rhys says. "The thought of them just sitting there has infiltrated my poor beleaguered brain. We are *so close* to unlocking this mystery, having to pause our efforts now is galling."

"Perhaps we can resume those efforts in a few days, Rhys," the professor says. "In the meantime, I shall sit with you and together we shall get ourselves back to Robert Louis Stevenson and the adventures of Jim Hawkins and that peg-legged bloke Long John. That's how we shall occupy that infiltrated brain of yours."

"It will have to suffice, one supposes—since the doctor and you two vile brutes insist upon chaining me to my bed. I was so looking forward to what Charles had found in the Book of Psalms, too."

"Sir," Charles says, "here's my best advice. Never trust that one-legged man, he's a tricky bugger. No, the one you can trust is that strange little chap named Ben Gunn."

"Charles, I shall follow your sage advice implicitly."

Over the next two days, Rhys does as the doctor orders, and by Thursday morning, he appears considerably improved.

"You look like more your old self today, sir," Charles says, as he brings the man his breakfast tray. "There's some pink in your cheeks."

"I feel more myself as well, my boy. I also feel up to doing a bit of Bible study today, if my cruel gaolers might permit such a thing."

"Perhaps they will. I shall run the idea by Allie and Eilish. They're the ones whose opinions matter."

After the two women have come to see Rhys, they are both persuaded to allow such a thing. But Eilish imposes a strict limit of two hours.

"Do me a power of good, honey-love," Rhys says to her.

"I think so too," she replies. "But Charles, you must promise to call a halt at eleven o'clock? Fair enough?"

"Fair enough. That might just be enough time to get us through Psalms and Proverbs; not many annotations there. Maybe even Isaiah."

In fact, it did. And when the library clock chimes eleven, Rhys is eager to continue.

"Sorry, sir, no chance of that," Charles declares firmly. "But there's time enough for you and the professor to dip back into the adventures of those bold chaps on the *Hispaniola* before we have our noon repast."

"How about you taking a turn at the reading, Charles?" Rhys says. "Give William's creaky old voice a bit of a breather, eh?"

"I'm happy to. To tell you the truth, I'm rather eager to see what's been happening with those folks out there on that island myself," Charles says. So as Charles reads softly, the two older men lay sprawled on the sitting room sofas, drinking in Stevenson's glorious adventure along with imaginary bottles of rum.

"My appetite is back," Rhys declares, as the men cluster about the table for lunch in the dining nook. "Load me up, pet," he says to Allie.

"A small salad and half a cheese sandwich is all you are allowed," Allie replies, "doctor's orders."

"But you can slide a pickle or two on the half sandwich," he says.

"Only half a pickle."

"You can be a cruel wench,"

"Too right," she replies.

"I have an idea," Rhys says as Eilish and Allie are tidying up the kitchen. "If I feel as chipper after my nap as I've felt all this morning, what say we have a little outing this evening. Just a little one, mind you. A very little one."

The faces of both women bear frowns.

"What do you have in mind, sir?" Charles asks. "I will tell you right off that a walk out to visit your dancing maidens is out of the question."

"Oh, no, nothing so strenuous, just a simple evening meal at the Sickle. You've had me under house arrest for so long that a little change of scenery would do wonders for my spirits. You do want to keep my spirits up, do you not?"

The two women exchange glances and then shrugs. Since this is a Thursday night, Maria will be departing before dinner in advance of her day off, and responsibility for the evening meal will fall upon them. A night of pub grub would simplify things and might prove a welcome diversion for all of them.

"Why don't we wait and see how you are doing by late afternoon," Eilish says, not immediately scotching the suggestion.

The Scythe & Sickle, a country pub just a few miles inland on the Lizard, is located near the little hamlet of Gweek. "Serves the best fish & chips in southeastern Cornwall," Rhys declares, "as well as some potent, locally brewed ales."

"Which you won't be having," Eilish says.

"I shall drink one for you," the professor says. "You can enjoy it vicariously."

"Some friend," Rhys says, glumly.

It's a cool and pleasant evening, and they pass through

the rooms inside the pub to the beer garden out back where they seat themselves on benches around a large wooden table. They are on the early side and the server takes their orders immediately.

"It's fish and chips all around," Charles tells her.

"Five fish and chips," she says. "And to drink?"

"We'd like to try some of the locally brewed ales," Charles says.

"You want the Shipwreck Bitter, or maybe the Frenchman's Creek Pale Ale?"

"How about two of each of those to begin with. That be okay?" he asks, looking at the others.

"Sounds right to me, Charlie," the professor replies. "We can try them both and then make our second round to our individual liking."

"And a bottle of fizzy water," Eilish says.

"Two Shipwrecks and two Frenchman's. And a fizzy water," she repeats as she scrawls their orders on her pad.

"Fizzy water," Rhys grumps. "So it's come to that, has it?"

A few other folks have begun to drift into the beer garden, taking seats at the empty tables. Charles eyes a couple who have come in and sat down at a table not far from them. He wonders if he's seen them before, though he can't imagine where that would have been. The woman is tall and dark-haired, her companion slope-shouldered and balding. Early middle-aged, he guesses. It seems to Charles that the woman is paying his group a good bit of interest. No reason why she shouldn't. Charles, the professor, and the Tremayne group probably aren't the kind of customers that typically frequent this off-the-beaten track establishment.

Five minutes later their food arrives, and they begin tucking in. "Would you be so kind as to hand me the malt vinegar, William," Rhys asks the professor. "At least *that's* not off-limits, is it?"

"You know," Rhys says a few moments later, "this place used to have a different name. I suppose they scrounged up the 'Scythe and Sickle' to make it sound more like Ye Olde Country Pub."

"What was it called before?" Charles asks.

"When I was a lad it was 'The Griffin'. I loved looking at the griffin painting on their pub sign. Fierce-looking bugger. With one taloned foreleg he was cradling a hoard of gold coins, and the other he'd raised as a warning to keep away."

"Maybe they changed the name because that fearsome Griffin was frightening away their clientele," Allie says.

"Perhaps, though griffins are rather commonplace mythological creatures."

"Remind me what a griffin is," Eilish says.

"Head, chest, forelegs and wings of an eagle; hind quarters, back legs, and tail of a lion," Charles says.

"One of a great number of composite beasts found in many of the ancient mythologies," the professor says. "Has a long and complex history. Evil, greedy, and ferocious in the older mythologies, but by the Middle Ages somewhat ameliorated. Some commentators even turned the griffin into an allegory of Christ, saying his dual nature reflected the fact that Christ was both God and man."

"There are some really bizarre hybrid creatures in early legends," Charles says, "sometimes conjoining multiple beasts into one, like the chimera. My favorite, I have to confess, is the Questing Beast in Arthurian tradition."

"Oh, Charles, why don't we leave Malory out of it for once in our lives," the professor says with a groan.

"Describe it, Charlie," Allie says.

"Head and tail of a serpent, legs and feet of a deer, body of a leopard, haunches of a lion."

"Goodness," Eilish says. "Hard to picture such a creature."

"It was the hybrid creatures that conjoined human beings with animals that I always found the most fascinating," Rhys says.

"Satyrs and centaurs and fauns, oh my," Allie says, parodying Dorothy in *The Wizard of Oz*.

"Among many others," Rhys replies.

"And there are some," Charles says, giving Allie a knowing smile, "that involve women and other creatures—sometimes, even, women and fish." Allie returns his smile.

"Well, excuse me for asking about griffins," Eilish says. "I'm sorry I started that hare. Got more than I bargained for. Pick another topic, Charles, would you?"

"You have to be careful what you say around scholars," Charles says. "It's too easy to get them started. Another topic. Hmm. Not politics, not football, not antiquarian books."

"How about Cornwall's hidden glories?" Allie says. "What are your favorites, professor?"

"My favorites aren't so hidden. I love that stretch of

the coastal path between Tintagel and Boscastle. Also, that delightful church at Altarnun, the 'Cathedral of the Moors,'—that's the church where Doc Martin got married in the TV show. And of course my all-time favorite, Brown Willy."

"Brown Willy?" Charles scoffs. "Sir, no disrespect, but you've never climbed Brown Willy. You've never even set foot on its lowest slopes."

"No, but I've seen it from the road. Doesn't that count? I also know the etymology, and I even know that it's the highest spot in Cornwall."

Rhys smiles at his old friend. "Let's let William have Brown Willy, if he insists. As for me, what I love most of all is my little circle of stones."

"As well you should," Charles said. "That truly *is* a hidden gem, unlike the items on the professor's list."

"What about you, Charles?" Eilish asks.

"Hmm. Well, for one, I love Sullen Syd's CD Emporium, or whatever it's called, that place in St. Ives where a year ago we took a stab at recreating the professor's stolen CD collection."

"It's CD *City*, not emporium," Allie says, correcting him. "Emporium violates the alliteration."

"And much appreciated your efforts were, even though I did eventually get most of the lost CDs back," the professor says.

"I hope to have a look around in there this weekend when I'm in St. Ives again," says Charles, who planned to take a little break from the others and spend a good part of the weekend there with Allie.

"Bring me back a surprise, Charlie," the professor says. "For old times sake."

Fifteen minutes later, they get up to leave. Charles notices that the couple he'd wondered about earlier had departed before them. He wonders if the whack on the head he'd had a few days earlier had served to make him a bit paranoid. His concern about the man and woman is surely misplaced.

A few minutes into the return drive, Rhys suddenly bursts into song: *"I'll sing you one-o, green grow the rushes-o."*

The professor, in his gravelly voice, quickly gives answer: *"What is your one-o?"*

"One is one and all alone and evermore shall be so," sings Rhys.

As the two older men work their way through all twelve verses of the old British folk song, the other three can't help but join in, Allie in her light-soprano, Charles in his mid-range baritone, and Eilish in her mezzo. As Eilish turns the car into the graveled drive, passing between the two tall gray plinths topped by gray stone birds, they've reached the song's conclusion: *"Two, two the lily-white boys, clothed all in green-o, but one is one and all alone and evermore shall be so."*

23

The lads had prepared three sets of photo strips for Valery to take with her to show to the American who'd been attacked in Cornwall. Each of the nine frames contained a headshot of a dark-haired woman. The photo of Diana Southgate had been placed in the middle of the second strip. Valery knows it's a long shot that the American will be able to pick out any of them as the woman he'd momentarily seen in the study just before receiving that nasty knock on the head, but it's worth a try. Anyway, that is her ostensible purpose for the visit. But motivating her just as much is her hope that she might be able to get another peek at the Geneva Bible. And if so, then maybe she will get a chance to see—and maybe even photograph?—a sample of the annotations she'd noticed before.

Valery wears the same outfit she wore on her first visit to the retired rare books librarian, Nigel Cummings, a tan suit over a white shirt, an outfit that goes well with her tawny eyes and short brown hair. This morning she's taken more care than usual with her makeup. Since she normally tends to be rather casual about her appearance, it dawns on her that she must want to make a favorable impression on the young American.

When Valery pulls up to the house, Charles Bascombe

steps out onto the portico to welcome her. "Hello again," he says, with a smile. "Why don't we go to the library? Mr. Tremayne and the professor are in their rooms resting, but if they wake up before we're finished, they might appear in the sitting room. Would you care for coffee, tea, lemonade, or a soft drink?"

"I'm fine, thanks," Valery says. She follows him to the library where she sees that the Bible and his notes rest on a small table. They sit down on chairs at another small table close by.

For a brief moment they sit there awkwardly looking at one another. Valery is struck by his light blue eyes and their contrast with his tanned cheeks. Finally she says, "How is your head feeling? There's no obvious swelling or discoloration."

"No, all of that is gone now. There's still the occasional ache, but nothing a couple aspirin can't handle."

"Wonderful," she says. "That was quite a nasty knock."

Charles nods his agreement.

"Well," Valery says, "I've brought along some photos for you to have a look at, Mr. Bascombe, if you'd be so kind." She takes a folder from her bag and extracts an envelope containing the photo strips. "Take your time looking them over. We'd be interested in knowing if you think you've seen any of these women before."

Valery places the first of the three strips down on the table, and Charles examines each of the faces in the frames slowly and carefully. All three women have a generally similar look, each with a narrow face and dark, shoulder-length hair. One has light eyes, two have darker eyes;

two have fuller lips, one hardly any lips at all. All three are moderately attractive though none, Charles thinks, is what you'd call a beauty.

"No," Charles says slowly, "I don't think I've ever seen any of them before. Sorry."

"Nothing to be sorry about," Valery says. "All right, here are three more." She removes the first strip and replaces it with another.

Charles repeats the process of looking at each photo closely. These three women are fairly similar in looks to the first three, but two of them, he feels, he might have seen before.

"Hmm," he says. "Maybe we can come back to these after I've seen the final three."

Valery nods and exchanges photo strips.

"No," he says, after he's had a good look at the final strip, "none of these women look at all familiar to me. Let me take another look at the middle group." Valery removes the last strip and places the second one back on the table.

Charles bends down over it and scrutinizes the photos carefully. "Definitely no to the one on the right," he says. "Attractive woman but I've never had the pleasure," he says, his words drawing a smile from Valery.

"What about the other two?" she asks.

"Both look a little familiar to me, but I can't say why. No, wait a minute, the one on the left, yes, now I know why she looks familiar. That woman was at the country pub we all went to last night. At least, I'm *pretty* sure it was her. She and a man sat at another table in the beer garden not far from us while we had our meal. Yes, I really do think it was her."

Valery, looking downward, jots something on her note pad. Then she looks up again.

Charles rubs a hand along his chin. "The middle one rings a very faint bell with me also—though I can't say why."

"Any chance she might have been the woman you saw in the study just before you were knocked out?"

"Hmm. Well, I suppose that's a possibility, but I couldn't say that with any certainty."

"Well, Mr. Bascombe," DS Wilson says, "I must say, you've done wonderfully." She returns the photos to the folder and the folder to her bag.

"If you don't mind my asking," Charles says, "can you tell me who the two women are who look familiar to me? That is, if you know."

"Oh, we know who all of these women are," she replies. "We have files on each of them."

"But you can't, or rather won't, tell me about the two I picked out?"

"No, I'm afraid I can't do that, at least not at this time. Maybe at some later time."

The two of them sit there looking at each other, each comfortable with the other. The house is quiet, the elderly gents still in their rooms.

Finally Valery says, "So how is your study of the Geneva Bible coming along? It might interest you to know that I once had a good bit of experience with rare books myself."

"Oh yes? How did that come about?"

"Back when I was an undergraduate at Exeter, I worked fifteen hours a week as a student assistant to the Rare Books Librarian. The man took me under his wing and taught me a great deal. I loved the work. It nearly persuaded me to do graduate studies in Library Science and Information Technology."

"He *nearly* persuaded you, but then you joined the police force instead?"

"A much more practical occupation. Given the way things are going, the future for librarians is looking rather bleak."

"As it is for philologists and paleographers," Charles says, pointing a finger at himself.

Valery glances over at the nearby table. "That's the Geneva Bible right there, is it?" she asks, pointing at the book atop the small library table.

"It is. I've just been looking at the . . ." and then Charles puts the brakes on what he was about to say.

"The annotations?" she says. "Is that what you were going to say? I noticed them myself last week when Mr. Tremayne allowed DI Corrigan and me to have a look at the Bible. Actually, I was wondering if you think it might be all right for me to have just another quick peek at it?"

Charles hesitates, considering her request. Then he motions for her to join him at the other table. What harm would there be in doing that?

"I was in the process of looking at the Gospels when you arrived," he says, 'Not a great many annotations in them, but a couple of them could be of real importance."

"Importance in determining who the annotator might

actually be?"

Charles nods. "But mum's the word, right?"

"Right," she says. "Oh, I see that you have a hand-held ultraviolet lamp. I've worked with them before. Really can bring up the fainter bits of writing for you, I imagine."

"Yes, though I can read most of them perfectly fine with just my trusty magnifying glass."

Valery stares down at the biblical text of the opened book. A few words are scrawled beside a passage in the Gospel of John. She can't make them out.

"You can read that?" she asks.

"I can. I'll admit that it took me a while to get the hang of it. But once you've become familiar with the guy's eccentricities, it's no big problem to decipher his scrawls and weird scriggles."

"Well, I'm impressed," she says.

They sit without speaking for another long moment before Valery says, "A bit ago I declined your offer of coffee. Could I change my mind?"

"Yes, you may. Cream and sugar?"

"Yes, please."

"Back in just a couple minutes," he says, getting up and heading for the kitchen.

When Charles is safely out of view, Valery closes the Bible and then opens it to the title page. She takes out her phone and photographs it. There are no annotations on it, so surely she isn't doing anything unethical. At least, that's what she tells herself.

She sees that the Bible has a flyleaf, so she turns back a page just to take a quick look. She knows that people often made the odd doodle on a flyleaf, and she's curious to see if there might be anything on this one.

Valery scans the page quickly and doesn't see anything. No, wait. Is there possibly some very faint writing near the top of the page? Even with Charles' magnifying glass she can't be sure, but she thinks there is. Valery reaches for the ultraviolet lamp, flicks the on switch, and holds it over the top potion of the flyleaf. Yes, there is some writing. It's an inscription: "To Kit, on his First Communion. With much love, your godmother, Margaret."

Holding the ultraviolet lamp with one hand and her phone with the other, Valery takes a photo of the flyleaf inscription. She knows that if she hadn't overstepped an ethical boundary before in photographing the title page, now she really has.

Charles returns with the coffee tray just a minute later. He places the tray—which holds two coffee cups, a French press coffee urn, a small plate of Maria's shortbread biscuits, a sugar bowl and small pitcher of cream—down on the other library table, not wanting to take a chance on any spills near the Bible or his notes.

"Sorry to put you to such trouble," Valery says. "But this will help to keep me alert on the drive back to Plymouth."

"Not much trouble," Charles says. "Besides, my two dear friends will be up any time now, and they'll be wanting half a cup apiece when they re-appear."

Valery's conscience gnaws at her. Finally she says, "While you were gone I took another peek at the Bible. I couldn't help myself." She offers a little shrug of apology. "And I noticed something on the flyleaf. I'm sure it's something you're well aware of, but I thought I should let you know that I'd done that."

"Something on the flyleaf? Show me." Charles opens the Bible to the flyleaf.

Valery picks up the ultraviolet lamp, turns it on, and holds it over the top portion of the page. There, faint but readable, is the inscription about Kit's First Communion.

Charles tilts his head sideways and opens his eyes wide. "Wow," he finally says. "Detective Wilson, that isn't something we'd noticed. And I have to say, it may just provide the confirmation I've been hoping for." Charles continues to stare down at the inscription. "No," he says, "there's no indication of a date. That's a shame."

"Is the absence of a date very important?"

"No, but having one would have been a splendid thing. Well, you can't have everything. But this is a brilliant discovery, DS Wilson. I think you went into the wrong business."

"So the inscription was what you needed to tell you who the annotator was?" Valery asks.

"Well, no, it doesn't tell us *conclusively* who he was. But it provides a really important piece of circumstantial evidence. As they say on all those TV shows, you can make a pretty strong case if you have a tall enough stack of circumstantial evidence."

"And you think your stack may now be tall enough?"

"We are definitely getting there. I have yet to put before my colleagues all the bits and pieces I've been accruing. And my colleagues are bigger skeptics than I am, so, it certainly remains to be seen. But in my opinion, we can now make a pretty powerful case."

"And I suppose you are not about to share with me just what conclusion you are coming to."

"No, not just yet. No more than you are about to tell me who the women are I picked out from your photo lineup a bit ago," Charles says.

"Sounds like we understand each other," DS Valery Wilson replies, smiling at Charles.

24

A gray drizzle has begun to fall as DS Valery Wilson heads north toward Plymouth. But it doesn't dampen her spirits. Her trip to Cornwall, she believes, has been well worth the trouble. The young American scholar *had* seen two of the women in the photos she'd shown him, and one of the ones he'd picked out was Diana Southgate. Although he couldn't be certain it was her whom he'd seen during the break-in, there was a good possibility it had been. Where else would he have seen her?

The fact that he also remembered a second woman was slightly disconcerting, though. For DI Corrigan and DS Wilson were responsible for his having seen that second woman, since they were the ones who'd decided to place the surveillance team there to keep tabs on the male members of the Rhys Tremayne household. The fact that Mr. Bascombe had both seen and remembered the woman spoke well of his powers of observation, but it also meant that their surveillance team was now compromised and would have to be switched out. Before she hits the main road to Plymouth, she stops and calls Eileen on her mobile phone to explain the situation with their surveillance team. "Let's give them a night off," Eileen says. "Then we can get a set of fresh eyes out there in the morning."

Valery feels pleased with herself most of all because she was one the one who'd made a break-through contribution to the scholars' investigation of the Geneva Bible. The men who'd been examining the Bible hadn't spotted the inscription on the flyleaf, but *she* had, and the young American was of the opinion that that inscription was extremely important. She couldn't wait to share that information with Nigel Cummings, her friend, the retired rare books librarian. She would share with him the photos she'd taken both of the title page and the inscription on the flyleaf.

Try as she could, Diana Southgate is stumped by Mark Fetherston's encoded file. She spent most of the night working at it, trying every trick she knew. In the end, she concluded that not even MI6's finest cryptographers could have done it. Maybe it was something so old-fashioned that all the modern programs hadn't ever dealt with it.

And then it struck her. She remembers seeing the row of spy novels in Fetherston's sitting room bookcase, novels by Ken Follett, John le Carré, and Graham Greene—all of them spy novels having one important thing in common—they all involved a book code. Mark Fetherston's secret file, she surmises, could involve some sort of book code. Judging from those specific spy novels, the man obviously had a fascination with them. If so, then she is certainly out of luck. Without knowing the book and without having two identical copies of it, she has no possibility of breaking into his code. These days cryptanalysts, with their sophisticated software programs, would be able to break a book code, given enough time, though that would not have been true fifty years ago. But, alas, Diana lacks such software. Still, out of curiosity she plans to thumb through the pages of Greene's *Our Man in Havana*, le Carré's *A Perfect Spy*, and Ken Follett's *The Key to Rebecca* just on the off chance that he'd left some telltale markings in one of them. If he had, she still might be able to do it.

✣ ✣

Charles Bascombe is in an extremely good mood as he pulls Eilish's old Jaguar onto the main road. He's on his way to St. Ives and in a good mood for several reasons. For one, he's having a two-day break from Rhys and the professor, men he admires and loves, but men best taken in moderation, not in sustained day-in-day-out doses as in the last few weeks. For another, he feels fairly certain he has now identified one of the annotators of the Geneva Bible; and if he is correct, it is *quite* a big deal. But he's happy most of all because he can spend a good part of the weekend in St. Ives with Allie. Of course, she'll be working at the art gallery during the daytime on Saturday and Sunday, but he can visit her there and watch her ply her trade, and they can walk on the beach together during her lunch breaks. He's also looking forward to having a little alone time to haunt the local used bookstores and maybe visit a few of the small town's excellent museums. He knows that St. Ives will be teeming with tourists, but if he were to drive just a few miles out of town, he can visit little country churches where he's likely to be the sole person there. That appeals as well.

It should take him less than an hour to reach Allie's

small flat in St. Ives, and by the time he gets there, she should be back from the gallery. He has no qualms about having abandoned Rhys Tremayne and William Wentworth, since Eilish had arrived home by the time he'd left and since Maria will be back from her day off first thing in the morning. He's left the two elderly gents in capable hands.

As he drives, Charles' thoughts turn to the afternoon's interview with the policewoman from Plymouth. She's an intelligent woman, no doubt about it, not to mention quite attractive as well. Charles, while not oblivious to that latter fact, tells himself he wasn't influenced by that in forming his positive opinion of her. The woman's discovery of the inscription on the flyleaf was remarkable; how could she have found it when three experienced scholars had overlooked it? Well, it *was* written in small and very faint letters, and it did require the ultraviolet lamp to make it out. It was a shame, though, that the inscription hadn't been dated. Still, since the publication date of the second edition of the Geneva Bible was 1572, and since it was likely that the age of the child to whom it was given was probably about ten or eleven, the date was almost certainly sometime in the late 1570s or early 1580s.

With his thoughts thusly occupied, Charles doesn't notice that a small cream-colored car has pulled onto the main road behind him and stays close behind him all the way to St. Ives. When at last he turns onto the little street where Ally has her flat, he doesn't notice the car pause a moment at the street intersection, before slowly proceeding straight on.

25

"Your missing man," DI Eileen Corrigan says, when Valery reaches the office at six on Friday evening after the drive back from Cornwall, "we can now account for him."

"You mean Michael McMasters, the bookseller in Gloucester I couldn't locate?"

"Yes," Eileen says, "your bookseller in Gloucester, a man who is now a *former* bookseller in Gloucester. His body turned up in the Severn this afternoon, found by a pair of fishermen."

"Christ," Valery whispers softly.

"No obvious indications of foul play, so presumably some kind of unfortunate accident. Anyway, helps to explain why you weren't able to track him down."

"Postmortem?"

"Going on now. The Gloucester police are aware of the fact that we were looking for him and will let us know if anything turns up. But they say it's obvious he's been in the water for several days."

"Our persons-of-interest list grows smaller," Valery mutters to herself.

✣ ✣

At nine-thirty on Saturday morning, Thomas Audley watches from his vantage point near the corner fifty yards from Alwyn Tremayne's flat, as Allie sets off on foot for the art gallery where she works. For the last two weeks Tom has been monitoring the lives of the Tremaynes, and he knows that the gallery opens at ten and that it's Allie's responsibility from Friday to Sunday to do the honors. He knows a lot about the Tremaynes but not much about the American, the man he's followed here, beyond the fact that he is tight with the Tremaynes and that he's come to assist Rhys Tremayne with his prized acquisition, the Geneva Bible.

After Allie leaves for work, Charles Bascombe spends the morning marshaling all the evidence he's accumulated to support his belief that he's succeeded in identifying the chief annotator of the Geneva Bible. In his written document, he lists each item in building his case, relating each piece of internal evidence to what he considers significant pieces of external support. Then he drafts his conclusion. He notes that each individual piece of evidence suggests a particular possibility; and then, when all the pieces of evidence are taken collectively, that possibility seems inescapable. Charles believes that Rhys Tremayne and William Wentworth, after careful consideration, will concur.

Charles glances at the clock. It's going on twelve. He quickly assembles a picnic lunch for two—turkey sandwiches, Granny Smith apples, small bags of crisps, and a pair of Snickers bars. He and Allie can pick up water or soft drinks on their way to the beach.

On this busy Saturday morning, the little town is filled with pedestrians, and Charles doesn't pay any particular attention to the fellow lurking behind the tree down near the corner, a fellow who, unbeknownst to Charles spent the whole morning keeping his eyes on Allie's flat. With long, quick strides Charles sets off for the gallery, a five-minute walk away.

Throughout the morning Tom Audley has continued his surveillance of the flat. Finally, at twelve-thirty, the American comes out. He pulls the door shut firmly behind him and sets out on foot also. He carries a small bag, and from the look of it, Audley guesses it contains a picnic lunch. If so, the fellow is probably meeting the young woman and he will likely be away for an hour or more. Tom decides that that should give him plenty of time to slip into the flat and have a look around. He knows there's a workable key under one of the pots outside the front door, something he discovered two days earlier when he'd nosed about her flat. Tom assumes the American didn't bring the actual Geneva Bible, but he wonders if he might have brought his research notes pertaining to it. He hopes so. If he encounters them, he will photograph whatever he finds, leaving the man's notes as undisturbed as possible.

Tom Audley doesn't really know why Robin Estabroke is so keen on acquiring *this* Bible. If only the man had let him know earlier, he could have held it out of the estate sale and they would have been sitting pretty, no muss, no fuss. And he doesn't understand why Robin is so bitter toward Mark Fetherston. The fact that Fetherston sold the Bible to someone else was surely a part of it. But Tom has a strong feeling there's more to Robin's animosity toward Mark than that. Enough to have had him killed? Tom doesn't know for a fact that Fetherston was murdered; and if he was, Tom doesn't know for sure that Robin Estabroke was the responsible party. But, it wouldn't shock him to learn that he was.

Tom Audley is happy to accept the substantial remuneration Estabroke has offered without asking too many questions. What strange bedfellows he makes with Robin Estabroke and Diana Southgate. He's aware of the fact that both of them are using him. But even so, what each of them offers in return for his services makes it all worthwhile. He smiles to himself, knowing that he is indeed a man who can be bought—just like his notorious sixteenth-century ancestor—but only if the price is right.

As it turns out, Charles and Allie decide not to picnic on the beach but rather to walk out on Smeaton's Pier, the quay which partially encircles the small harbor, and eat their lunches there. Charles thinks back to a year earlier when the two of them had eaten fish and chips here and Allie had pointed out the Godrevy Lighthouse, the one that inspired Virginia Woolf's famous novel. Today many others are meandering about on the narrow quay, some of them eating their lunches as well. Several small fishing boats are snugged up beside the quay and firmly secured by cables to bollards.

Allie and Charles sit close together on the low

concrete wall, their thighs touching, while they eat their sandwiches. It's a warm day but a light breeze wafts against them and creates a pleasant, almost musical, sound as the ropes on the boats flap and flutter against masts.

"It's almost like a painting," Charles says.

"One that all the local shops and lesser galleries are filled with," Allie says, sounding bemused. "If you buy one of them, Charlie Bascombe, I shall renounce you."

"Even if painted by a chap named Rousseau or maybe Seurat?"

"*They* didn't paint such clichéd crap."

"The last thing I ever want you to do is renounce me," Charles says. "But this scene is pretty as a picture, if you won't renounce me for mouthing a cliché. And by the way, so are you." He leans over and plants a kiss on her neck just below her ear.

"A public display of affection? What is the world coming to, Charlie Bascombe?"

"You, uh, inspire me," he says.

"I corrupt you, you mean."

"Well, that too. Do you want to know what your father said to me a week or so back? He said he credited me with being a good influence on you."

"There's some truth to that, Charlie, though I've never been quite the wild child he's always feared I might be."

"He said you had a rackety lifestyle."

"Ha, ha."

"I told him I could do with being a little bit *more* rackety."

"Perhaps there's some truth to that, too, Charlie. But

I'll take you as you are, rackety or not."

This time Charles leans down and kisses her on the lips.

"Don't you ever call me rackety," he says.

A young lad who is passing by mutters under his breath, "Get a room, why don't you?"

"Now, *there's* an idea!" Allie says, and they burst into laughter.

Their joyous lunchtime visit is a delightful interlude for both of them. Still, hovering over them all the while is the uncertainty of what lies ahead for them at summer's end. June is now moving toward its conclusion, which means that only the month of July remains before it will be decision time. Allie's father's condition has been roaming all over the map. Right now it is looking pretty good, but he's already taken a couple of bad turns. Was that how things were going to be? Good, bad, good, bad. Who could say?

Inside Allie's flat Tom Audley has struck paydirt. There on the kitchen table, just as if it had been left there intentionally for him to see, lies a copy of the document Charles prepared that morning, the document in which he carefully and fully spells out the case for the identity of the Bible's primary annotator. Tom Audley does not know, however, that Charles purposely left out any references to the possibility of there being a second annotator. That was a separate matter, one which Charles, the professor, and Rhys Tremayne would have to give serious consideration to later on.

Audley photographs the five sheets one by one, then puts them back exactly as he found them. He takes another few minutes to wander about the little flat just on the chance he might see something else pertinent to his endeavor. He doesn't. A plate of Jaffa cakes and digestive biscuits sit on a kitchen counter, and as he'd had nothing to eat since breakfast, he's sorely tempted. But he refrains. He double-checks to be sure his photographs are all there and in good order. Then he stands for a moment peering out the front door to make sure the street is quiet. He has to wait a couple of minutes for a woman walking her chocolate Lab to pass from sight; then Tom slips out through the door and strides nonchalantly away.

Audley heads for a café he knows and likes only a couple of streets away. After lunching there he plans to forward his photos to Robin Estabroke. The fellow should be ecstatic. If they aren't worth the amount to Robin that Tom believes they should be worth, then maybe he and Diana should cut Estabroke out of the picture and set up business on their own. After all, they're the ones doing most of the heavy lifting. For Tom Audley, there has been little joy in working with Robin Estabroke. Tom Audley is no choirboy himself, but he is certain that Robin Estabroke is an out and out villain.

26

At one-thirty, Tom Audley stands in front of a tourist shop across the street from the art gallery, slowly turning the rack of postcards he isn't really looking at; he hasn't a shred of interest in buying a postcard. Out of the corner of his eye he sees Charles and Allie just now returning to the gallery. He watches as Charles gives her a little farewell kiss. She's an attractive woman, Audley thinks, breathing a sigh. But oh how he wishes that right at this moment he were in Italy in the company of that intelligent and luscious policewoman he quite fancies.

As the young American fellow strides off down the street threading his way through the throng of tourists, Tom Audley once more dogs his footsteps. The man pauses for a moment before a used record shop called Sullen Syd's CD City and studies the CDs and records displayed in the window. Audley thinks he intends to go in, but he doesn't. Instead, he walks on down the narrow lane until he comes to Carbis Bay Books. This shop he does enter.

Tom waits outside for a moment, then enters the crowded bookshop. Bookshops are on hard times these days, but this one doesn't seem to be.

Several buyers have queued up at the counter clutching their purchases, and elsewhere people jostle for position in the aisles before crowded bookshelves. St. Ives, Tom knows, is a sophisticated little town, one where people still care about the arts.

Small signs are posted here and there to help customers find their desired sections. The man Tom has followed is evidently heading for the Crime Fiction section. The man waits patiently for a few other browsers to clear a space, and when they finally do, he begins perusing the titles on the shelf before him.

Tom slides up and takes a position behind him. And as he stands there, he has a vivid recollection of coming up behind this very same man once before. A thrill of excitement shoots through him as he recalls the strange and pleasurable sensation he experienced when he landed a hard blow with his electric torch to the side of the man's head. He finds himself greatly desiring to do it again, but of course at this moment, that's out of the question.

Realizing that someone is standing close behind him, the man half turns and then smiles at Tom. There is no hint of recognition on his face. "I'll be out of your way in just a moment," he says.

"No rush," Tom replies.

"Do you like spy novels?" the man asks Tom.

"Yes, just a bit," Tom replies. "Any special recommendations?"

"If you haven't read the novels of le Carré, you have a treat ahead of you. *The Spy Who Came in From the Cold*?"

"Thanks for the tip. I appreciate it. I'll give him a try. Oh, and by the way, would you happen to know what this lovely music they've got on at the moment is?"

"You should be ashamed of yourself," Charles says with a smile. "That's Fairport Convention's 'Who Knows Where the Time Goes.' The singer is the incomparable Sandy Denny."

"She does have an ethereal voice," Tom says. "Well, thanks again. You are a fount of information."

Charles returns to his perusal of the book titles, and Tom Audley drifts away, not wanting to call too much attention to himself. It had been a foolish piece of audaciousness to actually engage the fellow in conversation. Now, Audley knows, the man will remember him for sure. But Tom has never been a fellow known for following the path of cautiousness.

From across the shop Tom continues to watch Charles. After Charles pays for a couple of books at the counter, Tom follows him out onto the street. Tom watches as the fellow retraces his steps to the music shop. This time he does go in. It's a few minutes later when he re-emerges, holding a Sullen Syd's carrier bag.

Tom follows the man back to Allie Tremayne's flat, at which point he decides to break off his surveillance. He feels sure the man will be there for a good while.

Tom Audley makes his way back to the music shop. There he purchses several CDs by the group called Fairport Convention. The truth is that he *has* heard of them; but they'd been a couple of decades before his time.

✣ ✣

It's ten o'clock on Sunday morning and the service of Song and Prayers at St. Pancras Church in Widecombe-in-the-Moor has just begun. Standing beneath a large umbrella and beside the lychgate Nigel Cummings, retired rare books librarian, awaits Valery Wilson's arrival. It's a gray, drizzly morning and the forecast for later isn't any more promising. Today there will be no lunch outside in the town square after the church service for the two of them.

"Sorry," Valery says as she hurries up. "Needed to drive cautiously on the slick roadway."

Nigel smiles at her and holds the open umbrella over both of them as they step toward the south porch entrance. Then he closes it and sets it down and leans it against the wall amongst all the other damp umbrellas already there. As they enter the nave, the congregation is standing and singing "Now Thank We All Our God." The usher nods at them as they slide into a pew near the back. Nigel, knowing the words, joins in the singing, and Valery, who doesn't, sort of hums along anyway. She'd been raised in the Church of England and enjoys attending services, but in recent years the exigencies of her work have prevented her from being a regular churchgoer.

When the congregation is seated again, Valery runs her eyes slowly over the crowded pews. Two-thirds regular congregants, she guesses, one-third visitors. She belongs to the latter group, and Nigel is probably somewhere inbetween. It's a lovely church. As Nigel had told her before, the roof bosses above their heads are striking and unusual. She would like to take some photos, but of course not during the service.

This mid-morning service of Song and Prayer, a service for many centuries known as Matins, is quite short. It consists of scriptural readings from the Old and New

Testaments, the singing of hymns, and prayers offered by the presiding priest as well as communal prayers. There is no Eucharist or sermon, and attendees are in and out in forty minutes, creating a twenty-minute interval between this service and the fuller one at eleven.

As she listens to the reading of the passages of scripture, Valery's thoughts are on the Geneva Bible and the photos she has in her shoulder bag. She hasn't told Nigel what she's brought, but she knows they will interest him greatly.

The service goes by in what seems mere moments, and then the two of them find themselves standing again for the singing of the final hymn. The priest, with upraised arms, intones a final benediction: "Let us go forth in peace; support the needy, help the weak, and honor all people. Let us love and serve the Lord. May His blessings be upon us and remain with us always."

"Amen," the congregants say in unison, then rise to their feet and prepare to depart. As they exit the organist plays a soft piece, a Bach prelude, Valery guesses.

They are among the last ones out, and when Nigel retrieves his umbrella, it's one of the few that remain. When they step from the covered entryway, he doesn't bother to open it, for the rain has stopped falling. For the moment, at any rate.

"Would you mind if we walk for a few minutes in the churchyard?" Valery asks. "It's so lovely and peaceful."

"Let's do," he replies. "We have plenty of time before our lunch reservations. But you'd best keep to the flagstone path. The grass is very wet."

Valery loves old churchyards, and this one is exactly

her cup of tea. She stops before many of the upraised headstones and crosses, reading the names and dates. Some of the earliest stones are so weathered she can't decipher them, but most of the eighteenth and nineteenth-century ones are still readable. The gravestones of young children always cause her pangs of sorrow, as do the ones which might well be those of young mothers who died in childbirth. Now and then, but not often, she sees the dates for someone who enjoyed a remarkable longevity.

"Micha Hankins, 1809-1907," she reads out to Nigel. "He must've been a hardy old fellow. Lived for nearly a century."

"1809. Born the same year as Charles Darwin," Nigel says, with a smile. "I guess he offers support for Darwin's theory that it's the fittest who survive."

"He outlived two wives and seven children," Valery says, after glancing at some of the adjacent stones. "That must have been hard." Then she can't help a sympathetic glance at Nigel, knowing that he, too, is a widower.

From the church come sounds indicating that the eleven o'clock service is just now beginning. They see a few stragglers making their way hurriedly toward the church entrance.

"I've booked a table for half-past eleven," Nigel said.

"Wonderful," she says. "And I've brought a couple of things about which I'd value your opinion."

"Wonderful," he says, echoing her remark. "You have piqued my curiosity."

As the waitress clears away the remains of their steak

and kidney pie, Nigel Cummings looks over the dessert menu.

"Valery?" he asks.

"Just coffee for me. Black, please," Valery tells the waitress.

"I'd like coffee and the raspberry sorbet," Nigel says.

While they await their after-dinner coffee, Nigel Cummings sits and looks across the table at his youthful companion. He has very mixed emotions. He's proud of this young woman whom he considers something of a protégé, and sitting here with her is an absolute delight. At the same time, he recognizes that there must be strict boundaries on their relationship. A close and warm friendship is surely possible and surely not inappropriate, but anything beyond that is out of the question.

"Sir," Valery says, noticing the pensive, wistful look on his face, "a penny for your thoughts?"

For a moment Nigel doesn't reply. Then, dodging her question, he says, "So you've brought some items for me to have a look at, have you?"

"I have," she says, and extracts a folder from her bag. She opens it and places two photos on the table, then slides one of them across to Nigel.

He needs a moment to put on his reading glasses. When he's all set, he peers down at the photo. It's the one Valery has taken of the title page of the Geneva Bible.

"Clear and crisp," he says, "very likely from early in the print run. Rhys Tremayne's copy must be a truly fine one. I am envious. Knowing how much Rhys loves his books, the fellow must be over the moon. I see that this is the 1572 edition, the second edition and by far the best of all. This copy appears to be quite a gem."

"And here's another photo I want to show you," she says. She places it down and pushes it toward him.

As Nigel reaches for it, his fingers nearly touch hers. Then he rotates the photo to face him. "Ah, so you took one of the Bible's flyleaf?"

"Yes. It wasn't until after I'd illuminated it with an ultraviolet lamp that I became aware of this inscription. The inscription is so faded that without the ultraviolet light it's unnoticeable."

"To Kit," Nigel says out loud.

"From his—or maybe *her*?—god-mother, Margaret," Valery says.

"His, I should think. Well, Valery, this is quite remarkable. And most intriguing."

"Any notion, sir, who Kit might be?"

"Hmm. A common enough nickname during the Elizabethan period, so probably no shortage of Kits to choose from. Offhand, though, only one very famous person comes to mind."

"The same one who comes to my mind?"

"Indeed."

"I wonder if it would be possible to discover who Margaret might have been?" Valery asks.

"Another very common name during that time. Would require some serious detective work to do that, and even then, rather a long shot, I should think. Good thing I'm speaking to a very bright young detective right at this moment."

"It's you I was counting on, sir, my favorite book sleuth."

"Oh, you were, were you? Well, Valery, since I am retired and have a fair amount of free time on my hands, and since you are one of my very favorite people, I shall see what I can do. But don't get your hopes too high. Discovering the identity of Kit and Margaret will be no easy matter. Might not even be possible."

"But you are willing to try?"

Nigel chuckles softly. "Oh, yes. For you, Detective Wilson, this old lover-of-books—book sleuth, as you put it—is willing to try."

Valery reaches across the table and touches the back of Nigel's hand.

27

Ally and Charles, each in their own car, drive back to Manderley on Sunday evening. Allie's little red Triumph arrives ten minutes ahead of Charles in Eilish's maroon Jaguar salon car.

When Charles enters the sitting room Allie is nowhere to be seen, and the two older men, engrossed in their chess match, hardly bother to look up, though the professor waves a hand in his direction and Rhys Tremayne utters a low growl which might be "'Ullo, lad."

Charles climbs the two steep sets of staircases to his room and drops off his bag, then takes a quick shower. When he comes back down ten minutes later, Allie is still nowhere to be seen and the two men are still bent over their chessboard. A quick glance at the board and the intense concentration on the men's faces tells Charles they have now entered the endgame. Few pieces remain, and Charles doesn't know which one of them holds the stronger position.

Charles notices that the door to Eilish's study is partially open, which means she's amenable to visitors. Since he's brought her a present, he taps softly on the door, then pokes his head in. He sees her sitting at her desk doing paperwork. She looks up and says, "Charles, do come in."

"I don't wish to interrupt you," he says.

"Oh, you aren't at all. Just catching up on a few bills. Never one of Rhys's strong points. I'm nearly finished anyway."

"Eilish, I've come bearing gifts. Well, one gift." He steps over to the desk and hands her a CD that he'd picked up at Sullen Syd's.

"How did you know?" she says, looking at the front of the plastic case.

"I didn't, but I couldn't imagine that Vaughn Williams and Thomas Tallis wouldn't be right up your street, as they say."

"You're getting to know me too well, Charles," she says with a smile. "Shall we give it a listen?"

For the next few minutes they sit quietly listening to Ralph Vaughn Williams' "Fantasia on a theme of Thomas Tallis," followed by the one on "Greensleeves." As they do, Charles' thoughts wander for a bit before settling on this woman who sits ten feet away. Eilish is an eminent professional woman, the chief executive for BBC Cornwall. She's also a woman who chose to become Rhys Tremayne's second wife and Allie's stepmother. He suspects that she has the potential to go much further in her career with the BBC if she were so inclined, though she seems quite content doing what she is doing now. To all appearances, she loves living in this semi-remote corner of Britain with her eccentric bookworm husband who is fifteen years her senior. She obviously sees things in Rhys Tremayne, Charles thinks, that many people don't, things that he's begun to see as well. He can't help admiring her for choosing happiness and contentment over professional ambition. Then he thinks of the words of Ecclesiastes: "Vanity of vanities, all is vanity." Eilish Tremayne, he thinks, is a woman who has chosen not to "strive after the wind."

"Do you know much about Tallis?" she asks Charles when the pieces have ended.

"I don't think anyone knows a great deal about him, aside from the fact that he somehow managed to negotiate all the dangers that surely swirled about him throughout the sixteenth century. The man was attached to the court of every Tutor monarch from Henry VIII to Elizabeth, all the while remaining a devout Roman Catholic, a perilous thing to do. But he seems to have enjoyed the favor of the Protestants just as much as that of the Catholics. Maybe being a great musician and composer gave him a special status."

"And maybe everyone simply recognized that he was an exemplary human being."

Charles nods his agreement.

Suddenly from the sitting room comes a loud cry: "You insidious old rascal! William, I never would have thought you were capable of such a devious maneuver."

"Sounds like the professor has won the chess match," Charles says to Eilish.

"I'd better go out and calm Rhys down," she says. "Can't be good for his heart."

"Daddy," they hear Allie say, "for heaven's sake, it's only a game."

"Only a *game*? Pah! Well, William, you won, so declaim away . . . my perfidious friend."

The professor begins quoting, in Chaucerian Middle English, some famous lines that are dear to his heart:

> *"A knight ther was, and that a worthy man,*
> *That fro the tyme he first began*
> *To riden out, he loved chivalrye,*
> *Trouthe and honour, fredom and curteisye."*

"I think the professor intends those lines to be about you, Rhys," Eilish said.

"Would that he did and would that they were," he replies.

And then Charles quotes the final verse from the Knight's portrait: "*He was a verry, parfit, gentil knight.*"

✣ ✣

At nine-thirty on Monday morning, Charles, Rhys, and William are huddled about the small library table.

"Today we wrap it up, eh Charles?" Rhys says.

"I think so. Not many annotations left to go. Some pretty important ones, though." The two older men nod and wait for Charles to proceed.

"First off, Matthew 7:1-2. No annotation here but several underlined verses."

"'Judge not lest ye be judged'," the professor says, "from the Sermon on the Mount, one of my favorite biblical admonitions. For me, right up there with 'he who is without sin, cast the first stone.'"

"Hmm," Rhys says, pondering the underlined passage

the professor just read. "I'm wonder if . . . "

"Yes," Charles says, with a tilt of his head, "me, too." Rhys raises his eyebrows.

"What's next, Charlie?" the professor asks.

"Matthew 27. He turns to where he's marked a page with a slip of paper. "You can see that in the margin beside the word 'Barabbas' the annotator has written just one word, 'name.'"

"Hmm," Rhys says again. "Curious. Any comment, William?"

"I have a thought. But why don't we keep on going. What's next, Charlie?"

"Romans 6:23." He turns the pages in the Bible to where he's marked a passage with another slip of paper: "'The wages of sin is death'."

Rhys peers down at it, then reaches for the magnifying glass. "What's he written in the margin? Looks like it says, 'That's hard.'"

"Yes," Charles agrees, "that's what I see, as well."

"Sounds like St. Paul's words make the annotator uncomfortable," the professor says.

"You can't deny it's a rather bleak sentiment," Rhys opines. "All of us are sinners." Charles and William nod in agreement. "But," Rhys continues, "there's no forgiveness if there isn't any sin."

"Take that, St. Paul," Charles says.

"I believe, Rhys, it's, there's no forgiveness if there isn't any repentance," the professor says.

"And there's no need for repentance if there isn't any sin," Rhys shoots back.

"Uh, gents, why don't we push on with the Bible," Charles says.

He proceeds to show them two more passages of minor interest in Paul's epistles, then flips over the pages to the Book of Revelations. He opens it to nearly the final page of the Biblical text where he's inserted another slip of paper. The annotation is next to the famous "I am the Alpha and Omega" passage. Rhys picks up the magnifying glass once more and holds it over the annotations, first the one on the left, then the one on the right.

"Definitely a Chi Rho on the left," he says. "Not sure what it is on the right. Looks like the second letter is Omega, which matches the biblical context."

"That's how I see it," the professor says.

"Me as well," Charles says.

"But the squiggle in front of the Omega, Charles?" Rhys asks. "What do you make of that?"

"I've puzzled over that a good bit. My conclusion is that it's the Greek letter Mu."

"Mu followed by Omega? Hmm. And what do you suppose that could mean?" Rhys asks.

Charles doesn't respond right away. He looks slowly at each of the older men in turn. Neither of them speaks.

"Charlie?" the professor finally says, a question in his voice.

"Okay, here's what I think. The pair of anagrams, the one on the left and the one on the right, taken together amount to the annotator signing his work."

The two older men still looked nonplussed. "Enlighten us, Charlie," the professor says.

"If you put all the Greek letters together, he provides a clear hint. The Chi Rho, I'm guessing, is an anagram for his first name, the other Greek letters an anagram for his surname."

The two older men sit there for a long moment pondering what Charles has just said.

It's Rhys who finally speaks. "The fellow's first name is *Christ*?" he says, sounding dubious, if not actually shocked.

After a brief pause, Professor William Wentworth says, "No, Rhys, his first name isn't Christ. It's Christopher."

"Oh, my," Rhys says, as the man's identity dawns on him.

"And the fellow's surname is Marlowe," the professor says, "with the Mu and Omega being the first and last letters or at least sounds of it."

"So what you are suggesting, Charles," Rhys says, "is that our morbid annotator is in fact the mysterious and controversial Elizabethan dramatist Christopher Marlowe?"

"Yes," says the professor. "Who, by the way, was also commonly known by his friends and associates as *Kit* Marlowe."

The three men just sit there without speaking as the implications of such a possibility slowly sink in.

Finally, Rhys asks, "And what about Barabbas?"

"The name of the villainous central character in Marlowe's *The Jew of Malta*," the professor says.

"And what about Helen, the name he'd written in the margin in Ecclesiastes?" Rhys asks.

The professor doesn't reply but looks toward Charles,

inviting him to do the honors.

Charles draws the moment out before he says softly, "'Was this the face that launched a thousand ships, and burnt the topless towers of Illium?'"

Once more the three men sit without speaking.

It's Rhys who finally breaks the silence. "Ah yes, 'Marlowe's mighty line,'" he whispers.

28

Robin Estabroke is ecstatic. He's carefully gone over the photos Tom Audley sent him of the young American's notes. The fellow, he thinks, is one clever chap. Good thing Tom didn't finish him off that evening when he brained the bloke. If he had, Robin thinks, I wouldn't know now what I know now.

Estabroke calls Audley on his mobile phone. "Well done, my friend," he says, "well done indeed. Now, I think it would be best if you stay well clear of the Tremayne household for a while. Why don't we just bide our time for the next several days."

"Robin," Tom says, "I'm sorry to say that I'm stumped about how we're ever going to get our hands on that Bible. There are too many people about, the cops are on the alert, and they keep the thing under lock and key. Breaking into the house and snatching it, I think, is going to be nigh unto impossible."

"I agree, Thomas. But that's not the way we shall go."

"What other way is there?"

"Well, my friend, there's what's known as the Chicago Way."

There's a brief silence and then Tom says, "The Chicago

Way? Sir, I have no idea what you mean by the Chicago Way."

"Hard ball, Thomas?"

"Sorry, sir, you've lost me."

"Not up on your Americanisms, eh Tom?"

"Apparently not."

"Thomas, what would you say Rhys Tremayne values even more than he values that Bible?"

"Umm, probably nothing."

"Come on, Thomas, try again."

"Well, I suppose it would be his family he values the most."

"Of course he does. No man wants serious harm to come to his family. And that's how we will force him to cough up the Bible.'

"Yikes. Sir, if you seriously intend to inflict physical violence on the man and his friends, that would require you to have a cadre of strong-armed associates, associates much stronger-armed than Diana and me. The physical violence I used last time took me to the limits of my capabilities." (Although the thought of doing something like that again gives Tom a frisson of excitement.)

"No, Tom, I do not think any extreme amount of violence will be required. Not if we can make the man believe that our threat to his loved ones is genuine, that we truly mean business. We need to instill terror in the man. Fear is a very great motivator, you know."

"Well, I suppose it is. But that's beyond my experience."

"Yes, well, fortunately, Tom, it's not beyond mine."

✠ ✠

In her office at police headquarters in Plymouth, DI Eileen Corrigan looks down at the sheets she has spread out across her desk, sheets containing all of Mark Fetherston's financial transactions of recent years. She sees little here of immediate interest, no obvious red flags, though one of her team members has placed yellow tics beside several of the entries.

"Valery," Eileen says to her colleague who is sitting just a few feet away, "could you run your eyes over these sheets, tell me what I'm missing?"

Ten minutes later DS Wilson looks up and says, "They must have flagged these items because there's no obvious explanation for them. They look suspicious, coming at regular intervals from a Swiss bank."

"Hmm, seem innocuous enough to me. They aren't huge amounts, £2,500 every second month. Maybe some sort of annuity or trust fund payouts?"

"Yes, I suppose. But why would they begin when Fetherston was thirty-six? That seems a bit random. And their coming anonymously from a Swiss bank account seems a little suspicious. His financial records don't show any other dealings with Swiss banks. It would be worth knowing where that money actually originated and why it started arriving just over a year ago. The amount of the individual deposits isn't all that large, but in the aggregate it's nothing to sneeze at."

"All right, then. I'll ask the fellows to keep on digging. I grant you it is a curious anomaly, given the clear explanations for everything else in the man's financial records."

"We'll probably discover some totally innocuous explanation," Valery admits. "From all we know about Mark Fetherston, it's hard to see this upstanding antiquarian bookdealer as someone who would be engaged in small-scale money laundering or the like. But I guess you never know."

✠ ✠

"Charles, my lad," Rhys says, "your discoveries are the best medicine my poor old heart could hope for."

"Daddy," Allie says, "that's wonderful, but please don't get over excited. You have to stick to the doctor's regimen."

"Don't worry your lovely head, Pet. I shall obey the old sawbones' dictums as if they were holy writ. But one more major mystery about our Bible still remains to be solved. And Charles Bascombe, I believe, is the man to do it."

"I'm not at all sure we'll be able to reach quite so definite a conclusion about this one, sir. But we may be able to make an intelligent guess or two."

"Ah, William, there you are," says Rhys, as the professor comes into the sitting room.

"Yes, fresh from listening to the music Charlie so kindly bought for me from that slippery fellow in St. Ives."

"So, William, you also have had dealings with good old Sullen Syd?"

"I have indeed. Almost a year ago exactly. Fellow tried to palm off some inferior goods on me at an exorbitant price, and I had to call him on it. We had words, Rhys, words. In the end, though, the man saw reason and the transaction worked out to my satisfaction."

"What did Charles bring you this time? Jazz, Blues, American pop music of the '60s?"

"Otis Redding's Greatest Hits, actually."

"Nice," says Allie.

"Never heard of the chap," Rhys says.

"Even *you* might like it, my friend. If not, then there's no hope for you."

"Well, why don't we give it a listen later when we have our chess match?"

"Oh, no. It's not music to play chess by, it's music to *listen* to."

"So you haven't yet mastered the art of multi-tasking, Professor?" Rhys asks.

"No, not just yet," the professor replies. "Thank goodness for small mercies."

✢ ✢

Diana Southgate has been merging her client list with the one in Mark Fetherston's files. There is a certain amount of overlap, but not as much as she expected. The newly constructed list, she thinks, is impressive by anyone's standards. When she sends out her electronic catalogue, which she hopes to do tomorrow, she'll be surprised if she doesn't get quite a few positive responses right away.

She's nearly finished preparing it. The items it contains come primarily from her own stock accumulated in the year since she left her previous job at a London publishing house. But after looking over what Fetherston had on hand, she decided to include a few of his titles as well. All in all, it amounts to quite an impressive initial offering. As a fresh face bursting upon this field, she feels confident that "Southgate Antiquarian Books" will generate more than a ripple of excitement amongst these sedate and serious-minded folks.

Diana brews herself a cup of tea and carries it into Fetherston's sitting room. Maybe she'll thumb through his spy novels, she thinks, and see if anything jumps out at her. Fetherston's encoded file continues to nag at her, and she knows it will until she figures the bloody thing out. Where should she start? Her eyes meander along the spines of the books, all familiar authors and titles. Then they stop.

What's *that* doing there? She knows that Vladimir Nabokov had an interest in codes, but she doesn't think *Lolita* logically belongs among Fetherston's group of spy novels. And the copy she sees is a tattered paperback copy, not a respectable hardback edition like all the books surrounding it. Strange. Maybe the man had been reading it and then temporarily re-shelved it near at hand, intending to return to it soon; or maybe his cleaning woman found it lying on the chair and just shoved it in somewhere. In any case, the book has seized her attention.

Diana reaches for the copy of *Lolita* and pulls it from the bookshelf. Then, for a long moment, she holds it closed over her lap with both hands. Slowly she lessens the pressure her hands exert on the front and back of the book. It's something she often does with a book in the off chance that the book will open to a place of particular interest. This old paperback novel does precisely that. It looks to Diana's practiced eye that at some time someone must have left the book lying face down at this spot.

Diana recognizes the celebrated passage. It's Humbert Humbert's monologue, which he forces Quilty to read, a monologue that berates and excoriates Quilty: *"Because you took advantage of my disadvantage . . . because you took advantage of my inner essential innocence . . . ,"* etc.

A sudden thought strikes her and now Diana lays the book down open-faced on her chair and dashes to Fetherston's little office to retrieve the page of coded numbers she's printed out from his secret file.

In a minute she's back. All she needs to do is look at the first number on the sheet and compare it to the page number in the book. Huzzah! They are the same!

Diana decides not to spend the time right now to decode the whole message. Now that she has the key to it, she can take her time unravelling this mystery.

Then another idea strikes her. Among Mark Fetherston's stock of books, she remembers, is quite a nice first edition of *Lolita*. It's a far cry from this cheap mass-produced paperback edition. Diana thinks she just might include that first edition in the list of items in her initial electronic catalogue. The idea amuses her. And there's a chance that it might serve to more than amuse one of the recipients of her catalogue, if *Lolita* holds the key to some deep, dark secret. Diana Southgate, she says to herself, you are one sly twenty-first century fox. But just maybe Diana Southgate is being too sly by half.

29

Tom Audley arrives in Totnes at eight on Sunday evening. Diana has agreed to let him stay there for a few days, since Robin Estabroke has instructed them to lie low. Following his directions, the two of them will map out a plan of attack designed to terrify Rhys Tremayne. Both of them have perverse senses of humor and doing that amuses them, Diana more so than Tom.

"You'll be staying in the guest bedroom," she tells him.

"That's a rotten deal," he replies.

"You do a good job of earning your way around here, and then we shall see."

"I'm an excellent worker," he says. "I can provide references."

"I'm sure you can."

On Monday morning Tom and Diana sit together at the kitchen table concocting a first draft of the email message they intend to send in a day or two to Rhys Tremayne. They want this first one to be terse and to the point. They plan to follow it up a couple of days later with a specific proposal about how he can turn the Bible over to them. But they plan to let him stew for a few days first.

Their draft message says:

WE WANT THE BIBLE. WE GET IT, NO HARM WILL COME TO ANYONE. YOU MUST <u>TELL NO ONE</u> YOU'VE RECEIVED THIS MESSAGE — NOT YOUR FRIENDS OR FAMILY OR THE COPS. AWAIT FURTHER INSTRUCTIONS

"Looks good to me," Diana says, "but why don't we sleep on it for now. If we're happy with it by Wednesday, then we can send it."

"So, I have to sleep on it in the guest room?"

"In the guest room," she says firmly, "until further notice."

✢ ✢

On Monday morning Allie, with a chance to return to her painting, tells Charles to stay away until lunchtime. So alone and carrying his second cup of coffee, he walks down through the terraced back gardens to where the coastal path overlooks the sea and a bench where he and Allie often sit together. He wishes she were here now, but he understands her need to paint. The sea mist blows in from the southeast, parting now and then to allow the morning sun to peek through. Waves crash in the rocky cove beneath him. Sea birds swirl and squawk above him.

A pair of walkers, an older man and a woman, nod to him as they pass by on the coastal path. This is a popular stretch of the path, and rarely do many minutes go by without at least a few hikers appearing. Charles loves the fact that public footpaths are available to all and sundry in so many lovely spots throughout the U.K. His coffee is no longer warm, but not minding at all, he sips from the cup.

A solitary walker suddenly appears coming from the right, from the westward direction, in contrast to most hikers, who start around Lizard Point and walk toward the villages and towns on their way to Marazion. When the man spots Charles sitting on the bench, he seems to hesitate for a moment, then approaches a bit hesitantly.

"Good morning," he says.

"It is," Charles says. "Perfect day for a hike. Heading for Looe Pool or Kynance Cove?"

"Oh, umm, yes, I am," the man says, a little uncertainly. "How much farther are they from here?"

"At least a twenty-minute stroll to Looe Bar and Pool, more like forty-five minutes or an hour to Kynance. Have you been there before?"

"No, but I've seen pictures."

"Photos don't do Kynance justice. It's a perfect place to pause for a while, if it isn't too crowded. Popular spot. Pretty steep up and down getting there, but definitely worth it if you have the time."

"Well, thank you. I'll leave you to enjoy your coffee, shall I?" They exchange nods.

Charles watches as the man moves slowly along the path. The fellow is hatless, Charles notices, not a good idea; and the shoes he's wearing aren't really suitable for trekking on a rugged rocky and muddy trail. The man doesn't appear to be an experienced outdoorsman, and Charles hopes he hasn't bitten off more than he can chew. It's quite a hefty hike from here to Lizard Point, even if he does stop off and take a long rest break at Kynance Cove.

Charles takes a final sip of coffee and then tosses the rest out over the edge of the cliff. He would like to stay here longer, but he knows Rhys and the professor will be itching to ponder the matter of a possible second annotator of the Geneva Bible. So, he starts back up through the sloping gardens. As he reaches the upper terrace, he turns to enjoy one final look out over the sea. There by the bench he spots a hiker. It's the same hatless fellow he chatted with just a few minutes ago. Now the man is headed back in the direction from which he'd originally come. Must've changed his mind, Charles thinks. Probably a good idea, given the fellow's obvious inexperience.

"Christopher Marlowe was how old when he died?" Rhys asks.

"I think twenty-nine," the professor says."

"Stabbed in a brawl in a pub?" Rhys asks.

"Apparently," Charles says. "Lots of questions and uncertainties surround his death."

"As there are about everything connected to the man," the professor says.

"He and Shakespeare were the same age?" Rhys asks, continuing his questioning.

"A couple of months apart. But their lives up to the early 1590s, it appears, could hardly have been more different—though both of their lives are filled with mysteries. Shakespeare was a modestly educated fellow who took a while to find himself. Marlowe grew up in Canterbury, was educated at a private school there, before going on to Cambridge, where he was something of a phenom. By his mid-twenties he'd established himself as a major dramatist, well before Shakespeare had written a play or even arrived in London.

"Do you think they might have known each other?'

"It's certainly possible," the professor says. "They must have had mutual acquaintances and they probably moved in similar circles during the early '90s. Of course, Marlowe was dead by the end of 1592, and the first recorded reference to Shakespeare—a derogatory one at that—comes in 1593. Marlowe's theatrical company put on their plays at the Rose Theater. Whereas Shakespeare seems to have acted and written for various companies throughout the '90s before becoming attached to the famous and ill-fated Globe Theater."

"Built in 1599, destroyed by fire in 1612," Charles says.

"Lots of irresponsible speculations about Kit Marlowe," Rhys says. "But two things serious scholars can agree on. Marlowe didn't write Shakespeare's plays; and the ones he did write are truly superb."

✤ ✤

Tom Audley arises early on Wednesday morning. There are no signs of life in the small house and he assumes Diana is still in her bedroom. He slips on a sweater and sets off to have a stroll about the town. He walks down to the River Dart and looks at the boats and the wharf area, then finds his way to the main street, which he slowly walks up. Painted low on a wall is a sign that says "Brutus Stone," with an arrow pointing downward. There is indeed a stone set in the pavement. He makes a mental note to ask Diana what that's all about.

He continues his exploring and finds himself in the green space surrounding the small castle. A set of steep steps lead up to the entryway into the castle and he thinks that later on he might return and check it out more thoroughly. Then he spots a teashop called "Anne of Cleves." It's open, so he decides to pop in for a coffee and a croissant.

"Good morning," sings out a cheerful voice when he steps inside, "sit wherever you like." Tom seats himself at a small table for two near a window. The cheerful woman approaches and takes the menu already on the table and opens it for him. "We don't do a full breakfast," she says, "but we have a wide variety of muffins and scones and the like."

"Croissants?" he asks.

"Oh, yes." She points to a section of the menu toward the bottom.

"Brilliant," he says. "How about two croissants, a pot of strawberry jam, and coffee with cream." The woman smiles and nods.

She is back in a minute and places a tray down on the table. "Oh, splendid," Tom says. "This looks grand."

Tom tears the croissants into smaller pieces, butters each of them, and slathers them generously with jam. The coffee is strong and flavorful, just the way he likes it. As he is eating, a few other customers come in, a couple, and a solitary man. The man glances in Tom's direction, then takes a seat at the only other two-person table. The couple sits at a larger table in the far corner.

The man, Tom decides, is probably late middle-aged

and he has just a hint of a military bearing. Probably completed his service and then retired to this pleasant part of Devon, Tom decides. Perhaps he was originally from this area and has returned home. The man glances about him with interest and when he sees Tom looking at him, he smiles and nods a silent hello. Tom nods back. The man has a smile on his thin lips, but his cold, deep-set eyes convey a different message. Tom suppresses a shiver. The man looks familiar. Has he seen him before? Hmm, he isn't sure.

When the woman comes to ask Tom if he wants anything else, he says to her, "Did you happen to know a local man named Mark Fetherston?"

"Oh, yes, Mr. Fetherston was our dear friend, the nicest man in the world. What a terrible shock to us his death was."

"Oh, goodness, I'm sure it was. Some sort of ghastly accident, I imagine."

"It must have been. Some folks have suggested he took his own life, but we—my friend Mavis and I—we don't credit that for a moment. He would never have done that. Mr. Fetherston was a happy and contented man. We loved having him visit us, which he did several times a week."

Tom notices that the man at the other table has been attending to this conversation. His face gives no hint of an emotional response to this talk of another man's death. Tom finds that surprising. Maybe it's old news to him, or maybe he doesn't care about the tragedies that occur in other people's lives. Still, Tom wonders how he could be so completely stoical and disinterested.

"There's talk that a young woman has come to take over Mark's business," the woman says, "but we haven't met her."

Five minutes later Tom walks to the counter, pays his bill, and thanks the woman. "Maybe I'll see you again in the coming days," he says.

"We would like that," she replies.

As Tom departs from the teashop, the man with the cold eyes seated at the other table watches him leave, his face bearing a small, knowing smirk. Then it comes to Tom when he'd seen the fellow before. He is the very man who had come to the estate sale that Saturday morning a month or so ago and was infuriated to learn that the books had already been sold to Mark Fetherston.

30

It's nearly mid-morning when Tom Audley reenters the small house that had belonged to Mark Fetherston and is now owned by Diana Southgate. Diana is up and drinking coffee in the sitting room. She looks up as Tom comes in. "Seeing the sights?" she asks.

"Indeed," he replies. "Quaint little town. I think it suits you, Diana."

"I'm easy to please," she says.

Tom gives her a dubious look. "If you say so," he says, and she laughs.

"Unless you think differently, I'm ready to fire off our email message to Rhys Tremayne."

Tom reflects on her words for a moment, then nods. "Yes, let's go ahead. We can make the threats more explicit in the next one. I have to admit that what we are doing gives me some pause. I'm not normally a cruel person, you know."

"No, Tom, you are an absolute pussy cat." She grins at him, Cheshire Cat style.

"At least we know that our threats are empty ones."

"Do we know that, Tom?"

"As far as *I'm* concerned, they are."

"But what do we really know about Robin Estabroke? Aside from the fact that he's good for a paycheck. We've never even met the man, just talked with him a few times."

"No, you're wrong. I have met him, the time he came to the estate sale and reviled me for having sold the books to Fetherston. In fact, I think I saw him just a few minutes ago in a teashop. The fellow's a nasty piece of work, you ask me."

"Terrorizing Rhys Tremayne rather proves that, doesn't it?"

"Diana, are we making a mistake? Should we sever our ties with the fellow, even if it means having to give him some of his money back? Oh, and you are certain we can send this message without it being traced back to us?"

"Yes, I'm sure we can. I've created a fictitious Gmail account, and although it probably isn't necessary, I plan to create an account at a cyber-café in Exeter and then send it from there. Gmail also offers a feature called Confidential mode which allows you to have your message disappear. Do you remember how in those old "Mission Impossible" TV shows the message would self-destruct? We can actually do that. We can decide how long we want the message to be good for, and I think on this first one we'll make it good for five minutes before it disappears. Then on the next one, maybe a lot less. Also, since I have some errands to run in Exeter, I'll send it from a cyber-café there, as I said before."

"Diana, you're a whiz." Then Tom, repeating his apprehension, says, "Diana, are we sure we should be doing this?"

"A bit late for getting cold feet, Tom—and for growing a conscience. We're well in on this thing. We need to see it through to the end."

Tom Audley doesn't dispute Diana's statement. But he doesn't look at all happy about it.

✣ ✣

Rhys Tremayne isn't fanatical about checking his email, but he normally has a look each morning and again late each afternoon. Most of his messages come from book dealers or other antiquarians. On Wednesday morning when he opens his email, he finds a message in his in-box from a sender whose address he doesn't recognize. His first instinct is to delete it, but the subject line grabs his attention: "Geneva Bible Hoax." So, Rhys opens the message. "This is no hoax!" he reads. And then in all caps,

**WE WANT THE BIBLE. WE GET IT, NO HARM WILL COME TO ANYONE,
ESPECIALLY YOUR FAMILY.
TELL NO ONE YOU'VE RECEIVED THIS MESSAGE
NOT FRIENDS OR FAMILY OR COPS — OR YOU WILL
<u>REGRET IT</u> —
YOU WILL RECEIVE FURTHER INSTRUCTIONS SOON**

Rhys Tremayne is stunned. He stares at the screen. Some sort of sick joke? He reads the message several times, then studies the sender's name—"Mikie Magpie." Sounds like a character from a children's book, though magpies, Rhys knows, are said to be notoriously thieving birds.

For several minutes he just sits there and does nothing. Then, to his startlement, he sees that the message on the computer screen has disappeared. Must've been somebody's idea of a joke, he decides, a very sick one at that. But he can't help feeling distraught.

Finally Rhys makes up his mind. The message had warned him against telling anyone about it, but he decides to anyway. He can't help it. He has to—not the professor and certainly no one in his family. The one he must tell is Charles. So when Maria brings him his morning cup of tea, Rhys asks her to see if Charles can come to his room.

Five minutes later Charles taps at the door.

"Come in, come in," Rhys calls out.

When Charles enters the room, he sees the man still in his robe, sipping his cup of tea.

"What can I do for you, sir?" he asks.

"Charles, something very strange happened this morning. I need to tell you about it, then I'd like your advice." Rhys describes the message, its content and the none-too-subtle threat, and then the message's sudden disappearance. "So, what do you think? Someone's idea of a pernicious joke?"

"Gosh, yes, perhaps so. Anyway, for now, I suppose you probably shouldn't do anything. Wait and see if a follow-up message does come with 'further instructions'."

"I must say, Charles, that joke or no joke, it's a bit frightening."

"I can understand that, sir."

"Don't say a word to any of the others, eh?"

"I certainly won't. Uh, sir, if another message does arrive, do you think you could take a screenshot of it before it disappears? And let me know immediately if that happens."

"Charles, do you think someone really would harm my family if they don't get the Bible?"

"Sir, we will not let that happen."

"But I can't keep Eilish and Allie under lock and key like the book. And I can't even tell them to be extra careful. They would want to know why I was warning them."

"For now, let's just sit tight. I know this is terrible for you. It is for me, too."

Charles Bascombe walks out alone along the path that leads to the small stone circle. Rhys' predicament, which to a degree is his predicament also, completely occupies his mind. He hadn't consciously intended to walk to the stones, but after a few minutes he looks up and realizes he's there. It's a cool, gray morning, the weather matching his mood. He perches himself atop one of the three-foot high stones and stares off blankly into space. Charles is unsure what he should do. Nothing drastic or dramatic, nothing that might complicate the situation or endanger anyone; but, he finally decides, he cannot do *nothing*. He has to act.

Charles pulls out his wallet and extracts a card from it. It's the card the policewoman from Plymouth had given him last week. He hesitates a moment, then takes out his cell phone and makes a call to DS Valery Wilson in Plymouth. Charles had liked the woman and been impressed by her knowledge and intelligence. He knows that trusting her is a risk, but he decides to take it.

"DI Wilson," comes the woman's voice over the phone.

"Hello," Charles says, "this is Charles Bascombe. You came down to Cornwall last week and showed me some photos."

"Yes, of course. Hello again, Mr. Bascombe."

"Detective Wilson, I would like to say some things to you in strictest confidence, if I may," he says. "There are things I think it's best I make you aware of. Then, perhaps, you can offer me your advice."

There's silence on her end of the phone while Charles' words sink in. "Yes," she says, "you can speak to me in strict confidence."

Charles isn't sure about that, but he proceeds to tell her about the email message Rhys received that morning, its contents and the implied threat, the fact that it disappeared, and the suggestion that he await a subsequent message.

"Clearly," he says, "the sender warns Mr. Tremayne to fear for the safety of his family unless he willingly gives up the Geneva Bible. He also warns him not to inform anyone else—including the police—about the message."

"Apparently someone's decided the best way to obtain the Bible is through intimidation," Valery says.

"Yes, if it's not just someone having a lark."

"I think we must assume it's a genuine threat," Valery says. "Did he happen to notice the sender's email address?"

"Yes. It was from someone called 'Mikie Magpie' at a Gmail address. Detective, what do you suggest we do?" Charles asks.

Again there's a short silence on Valery's end of the call. "I would suggest just biding your time for now. It would be best if you didn't tell anyone else about Mr. Tremayne's email message and that you continue your normal daily routine. But if a second message does arrive, you must let me know immediately. And if possible, do try to take a screen shot of it before it disappears. If Mr. Tremayne doesn't know how to do that, you must show him."

"Okay," Charles said. "His health is pretty precarious, and this threat doesn't help matters. He's a courageous man, but I don't know how well he can hold up under this pressure."

"We may be able to put a security team on alert in your area. If you notice a strange vehicle or two wandering about, don't be too concerned, it's probably us. If he does get a second message, that's the time to be extra vigilant."

"Well, thanks a lot for your advice, Detective Wilson. You will hear from me right off if there's second message. And if we hear nothing further in the next few days, I'll let you know that, too."

"Perfect. I'm terribly sorry someone is putting Mr. Tremayne and you through this."

"Boy, me, too."

After ending the call, Charles feels a great sense of relief. The woman hadn't really offered a whole lot of constructive advice, but at least the police have been alerted, and now he knows what to do should a second message arrive. The big thing is to stay calm and carry on as if everything is normal. Which it certainly isn't.

Charles lingers at the stone circle for a few more minutes. Today if feels like a lonely place. The stones look cold, inert, unfeeling. Rhys Tremayne had called them his girls, but Charles disagrees. There is nothing human about them at all. They are nothing like Allie Tremayne. *She* is Rhys Tremayne's girl. And she is Charles' girl, too.

"Daddy's not feeling well," Allie says to Charles as he comes back in from his walk. "He just wants to rest in bed today, though he hopes you might come and keep him company for a while and maybe read to him before he naps."

"Of course I will," Charles says. "What's the professor's plan?"

"He's already gone. Packed a lunch and headed off to explore the area around Loe Pool. Said he'd be back in time for his late afternoon chess match. But I doubt that Daddy will feel like playing today. You may have to substitute for him."

"Oh, my. Maybe I had better brush up on the Sicilian Defense."

"You don't know the first thing about the Sicilian Defense," Allie scoffs.

"You're right. That's why I'd better brush up on it."

31

On Thursday morning Thomas Audley settles into the chair before the desk in the guest bedroom. He has some routine paperwork to take care of pertaining to the new job in admissions he will soon be starting at Rugby School. It won't be a hugely challenging job but it will be a welcome change from the chores he's been doing for the last five years at the ancient stately home in Derbyshire. He's looking forward to a fresh start, surrounded by fresh faces. Unlike a lot of the "Old Boys," Tom had actually enjoyed his years as a student at the school and he's always enjoyed going back there. And now he likes the fact that being on an academic schedule, with its various breaks and vacations, will give him a good bit of time to use as he chooses.

Robin Estabroke's surprise evening visit two days ago had been unsettling, and Tom was glad when the fellow had bid them adieu. Sitting in the same room with the man gave Tom a feeling of being in the presence of evil. Estabroke didn't indicate where he was off to, but Tom had a feeling he might be heading down to Cornwall to do who-knew-what. Anyway, he said he would stay in close touch in order to know how events were proceeding.

Their association with the man doesn't seem as unnerving to Diana as it was to him. Tom knows that Diana isn't a wicked woman. Venial and amoral for sure, but not truly immoral. Tom himself is no choirboy, but what they've gotten themselves into is becoming something more than he had bargained for. He's always prided himself on his ability to negotiate the boundary between licit and illicit activities. And he has to admit that when he'd delivered that blow to the head of the young man down in Cornwall, it had given him a thrill like never before. But thinking about it later had made him nauseous.

Now Tom Audley is experiencing pangs of conscience. Even if they have no real intention of inflicting harm on the book collector's family, Tom finds the idea of threatening to do that repugnant. Then he remembers looking into Robin Estabroke's cold, reptilian eyes, and being suddenly struck by a thought. Could Robin Estabroke have done for Mark Fetherston? The man seems totally capable of it. Fun and games is one thing, killing people is quite another.

Tom Audley wants out.

Diana Southgate is in a cheerful mood when Tom comes down for lunch. She's actually been baking, and the smell of bread fills the small house.

"I don't know you had such domestic skills, Diana," he says.

"There's a lot you don't know about me," she replies.

"Yes, but I am willing to learn."

"I bet you are."

"Teach me tonight?"

"Ha. Don't you wish."

"You seem very upbeat today, Diana. Any reason for that—besides my scintillating company?"

"There is, actually," she says. "The first batch of replies to my book list have begun to come in. Tom, you are looking at a businesswoman with superlative skills."

"Sold a book or two, have you?"

"More than just one or two."

"That's grand, Diana. I've never doubted you for a moment."

"I did get one rather odd reply, though."

"What was that?"

"As a kind of afterthought I'd slipped into my book list a first edition of Nabokov's *Lolita*. It didn't fit in at all with the others, but I went ahead and added it on a whim. I haven't had any offers for it yet, but someone did write back about it. All the message said was, 'Are you sure you want to do that?'"

Tom knitted his brow. "I don't get it," he says.

"Yes, it's a rather enigmatic message."

"Maybe just saying what you already knew, that it didn't fit in well with the other books on your list."

"Probably. But I couldn't help reading sinister overtones into it."

"Maybe you, like me, are feeling a little uneasy about what we've got ourselves involved in."

"No, I'm good with things. Just so long as no great amount of violence is involved."

"Just a modicum of violence is all right?" Tom asks.

"Yes. Just as long as it's you doing it and not me."

"They say it gets easier the second time," he says.

"Well, maybe you will have a chance to find out if that's true."

※ ※

Professor William Wentworth encounters quite a few walkers on the coastal footpath as he makes his way toward Loe Pool. Usually they exchange greetings and maybe a word or two in passing. At one point he asks a man about the tide, and the man says it's low tide at the moment and that he can walk safely on the bar separating the pool from the sea. "It's perfectly safe for the next hour or so. After that the tide will turn, and you don't want to be caught on the bar when that happens."

The professor safely crosses the bar before the tide turns. He walks a bit farther, then finds a scenic spot to sit and enjoy his lunch. After he's finished eating, he leaves his knapsack where he's been sitting and goes down to explore a small cove he's noticed below him where the waves have carved out a natural cave. He takes several photographs, then makes his way back up. His knapsack is right where he's left it. And as he looks down at it, he sees that someone using chalk has drawn a skull and crossbones on the flap. He stares at the drawing for a moment, slightly taken aback. "Goodness," he thinks, "I've been beset by pirates. Captain Billy Bones, or someone."

※ ※

Today Robin Estabroke has dressed more appropriately for hiking along the coastal path. He has traversed the entire route from Porthleven to the parking lot above Kynance Cove, and in the process he's learned what he needs to know in order to formulate his plan. Early in his walk, when he'd just about reached the bench perched on the cliff top below the terraced gardens of the home of Rhys Tremayne, he'd seen a man come down from the gardens and join the path heading off to the east. He didn't know the man but he knew he was neither Rhys Tremayne nor the younger man he'd seen a few days earlier. Nevertheless, Robin trails along keeping about a hundred yards behind the man. When the man sets off across the soft sands of Loe Bar, Robin does, too. When the man stops to take his lunch break, Robin walks on past him on the trail without either of them acknowledging the other. Then he finds a secluded spot of his own and waits.

When the fellow goes down to the cove, leaving his knapsack behind, Robin can't resist having a bit of fun. Using a small piece of chalk he has in one pocket, he scrawls a skull and cross bones on the flap of the man's knapsack. Then Robin Estabroke continues on his way making the long walk to Kynance Cove.

Robin Estabroke believes it has been a profitable morning. He has sussed out the entire route, and now he believes he has a handle on all the details that will be so vital to the plan he's been hatching in his active brain.

32

Also on Thursday morning, retired rare books librarian Nigel Cummings makes the short drive back to the Exeter University and parks near the library. He plans to make an effort to establish the identities of Margaret and Kit, the names from the photos Valery had shown him. He knows he could probably do just as well staying at home and doing the work on-line, but he wants to feel surrounded by scholars and be in a learned environment. He's decided to assume at the outset that Kit is Kit Marlowe, and then go from there, trying to identify the man's extended family members and then, if possible, their family friends. He knows it's a virtual impossibility to do that, but he'd promised Valery he would try.

Nigel spends the whole day on the matter, trying every avenue of attack he can think of. Finally he discovers a potential lead. In several records he's encountered a woman named Margaret Woodbury. She had served as the tutor to the daughters of some well-to-do families who lived in Canterbury in the 1580s, the celebrated city in Kent where Christopher Marlowe had grown up. In her younger days, this same Margaret Woodbury had briefly served at the court of Queen Elizabeth. Indeed, it was possible that for a short time she had even been young

Elizabeth's Latin tutor. There was speculation that she was the one who had introduced the Queen to Boethius's *The Consolation of Philosophy*, the great medieval classic that Elizabeth actually translated from Latin into English.

Nigel didn't have absolute proof that this woman was the same Margaret who'd signed the flyleaf. But the pieces seemed to fit together. It must be true, he thought. In any case, he couldn't wait to call Valery and let her know the theory he'd been formulating.

✣ ✣

"How was your walk, William?" Rhys asks the professor, after the four of them—Rhys, William, Charles, and Eilish—are seated around the little kitchen table for their evening meal, Allie having gone to St. Ives for her three-day weekend duties at the art gallery.

"My walk was splendid, splendid. But I hope I didn't overdo it. I rather pushed these old bones to the limit."

"Could be a song by The Eagles," Charles says.

"But one curious thing occurred," the professor goes on, ignoring Charles' remark.

"What was that?" Eilish asks.

"I'd gone down into a picturesque little cove to have a look at a cave I'd spotted down there, a bit beyond Loe Pool."

"I believe I know the very spot," Rhys says.

"And when I got back to where I'd left my knapsack—"

"It was gone?" Rhys interjects.

"No, it was there. But here's the odd thing. In the few minutes I'd been away, someone had decorated it in chalk with a skull and cross bones."

"Oh, my," Eilish says with lifted eyebrows.

Charles and Rhys exchange nervous glances.

"Did you see anyone?" Eilish asks.

"Saw no one in either direction. Quite odd, really, right out of *Treasure Island*. At least whoever did it didn't give me the Black Spot."

Again Charles and Rhys glance at each other.

"Well, I can top that," Eilish says. "What do you think of this? When I went out to my car after work all four tires were completely flat."

"My word," Rhys says, a stricken look on his face, "all four of them?"

"Umm. So I called the RAC. They had a team there in just a few minutes, and when the men checked the tires, they said they all looked fine, that someone had just let the air out of them. Probably local hooligans having a laugh. They inflated them again and I was on my way, no problems. But like the drawing on your knapsack, one wonders why."

For the rest of the meal, Charles and Rhys keep their own counsel. But Rhys, to Charles' eyes anyway, looked especially unsettled, his demeanor uncharacteristically subdued.

"What was your odd event today, Charles?" Eilish asks him.

"Didn't really have one. Spent a while on the phone with Mrs. Hawkins, my landlady in Oxford, discussing my plans for vacating the flat next month. She says her dog is missing me and she hopes I'll be able to spend a week or two there before I leave for the States."

"Nice to know that someone, somewhere, cares about you, Charles," the professor says with a smile in his eyes, "even if it's just a dog."

"There's someone right here at this table who cares about Charles," Rhys says, "someone who isn't a dog."

"Three someones right here," Eilish says, "and another one who's gone to St. Ives."

After the meal, Rhys returns to his room for the evening. With trepidation, he fires up his computer to make a last check of his email. As he fears, there's a message from Mikie Magpie:

> **Cutting the fuel lines or the break lines in an automobile is easily done and a bit more dangerous than just deflating the tyres, wouldn't you think?**
>
> **Such things could happen—in Truro, in St. Ives, or even in one's own garage. More explicit instructions to arrive soon.**
>
> **PAY CLOSE ATTENTION.**

Before Rhys has the presence of mind to save a screenshot of the message, it disappears.

✣ ✣

"Well," Diana Southgate says to Tom Audley late on Friday evening, a serious look on her face, "the play is moving toward its climax."

"Is it a tragedy or a comedy, Diana? And what roles are the two of us playing?"

"It's at least a tragi-comedy," she replies. "Our roles?

In your case, you hardly have one at all. You're more the 'second murderer' figure than a real player. No speaking lines at all.

"Not even an understudy?"

"As for me, looks like I will be assisting the play's villain in procuring the Bible."

"How familiar are you with the overall plot, Diana?"

"Only somewhat. But it looks like you've gotten your wish. Robin really does hope to avoid any serious violence, though he says he's prepared for it, should it come to that. Your job, Thomas, will simply be to wait in his parked Land Rover at a handy car park until he turns up with the goods. Then your job will be to whisk him safely away with his prize."

"So I get to be the get-away driver?"

"Yes, though I don't believe Elizabethan dramas had them."

"More a Chicago thing, I imagine," Tom says.

The truth is, Tom Audley is not at all disappointed in being given such a minor role. In fact, it's a huge relief. Now that he has a better sense of what is afoot, he wonders whether he should call the policewoman in Plymouth and alert her. He decides to reflect on the matter a bit more before acting upon that inclination. He wishes he knew more.

33

On Saturday morning, a cold gray rain is falling all over the southwest of Britain. It's a perfect morning for curling up with a good book and a warm cup of cocoa. That's precisely what Eilish and Professor Wentworth have chosen to do. They sit quietly and companionably on the sofas in the sitting room each with a book in their lap. Rhys Tremayne has not appeared as yet, and Charles has wandered off to the screened porch that Allie uses as her temporary painting studio. He notices a protective cover over an unfinished painting on the easel. He knows Allie wouldn't want him taking a peek at her unfinished work, but he lifts the cover anyway.

Goodness, it's a colorful semi-representational work in a style he's never seen her use. After he's studied it for a few moments it registers on him that it's a highly imaginative rendition of the St. Christopher legend. Charles makes out the figure—a looming figure of St. Christopher, whom Allie has rendered as a huge African. There on his shoulder is the tiny, luminous figure of the Christ-child. Down in the far left-hand corner is another small figure. Is it meant to be a mermaid?

Charles can't help laughing. The painting strikes

Charles as being slightly in the style of works in Picasso's Blue Period, though he is admittedly clueless about such things. He carefully replaces the protective cover knowing he must never breathe a word about having taken an unauthorized peek. Allie would be riled.

Stealing a look at her painting, however, was not his ordinal purpose in coming here. Charles was seeking privacy so he could make a phone call away from others' ears. Now he takes out his mobile phone and punches in the number of a policewoman in Devon.

"Hello, this is Valery," the woman answers. "Is this Charles?"

"It is," he says. "Listen, there's been some recent events I thought you should know about, things that happened yesterday." He proceeds to tell her about the skull-and-cross-bone image that was chalked on the professor's knapsack and about the deflated tires on Mrs. Tremayne's car.

"Sounds like both of those things were meant as warnings or clear reminders of what could happen if Mr. Tremayne doesn't cooperate," DS Wilson says.

"Yes, to me as well," Charles replies. "Anyway, I wanted you to know about them."

"And it sounds like the second shoe may be about to drop. Please stay in close contact with Mr. Tremayne and keep me informed about any additional messages. We have a team in the area already, but I believe I shall wander down that way myself just to be nearer at hand, should the need arise."

"I really appreciate that," Charles says. "I also have a

feeling that something major is about to happen."

"Let me know of any additional developments just as soon as you can."

"I shall. It's a relief to know that people who can help will be nearby."

"Talk again soon," Valery says. She rings off.

Charles leaves the screened porch and goes quietly up to Rhys's room without disturbing Eilish or the professor in the sitting room. He finds the man still curled up in his bed snug beneath the counterpane. Charles sits down in a comfortable chair, intending to remain until Rhys awakes. Then he hears a ping from Rhys's computer. A message has just come in.

Charles creeps over to the machine, strikes a random key, and the computer screen flashes up. Charles opens the mail folder and clicks on the most recent message:

TOMORROW MORNING—10 O'CLOCK.

Put the Geneva Bible, in its protective box and place the box inside a plastic shopping bag. Take it down and leave it on the coastal path bench, the one nearest to the bottom of your garden overlooking the sea. Leave the Bible there <u>at precisely 10 a.m</u>. Then turn around and walk away. Do not look back. <u>Do not contact or inform anyone</u> about these instructions. If you follow these instructions precisely, no harm will come to anyone. If you don't, you can expect grievous consequences—to you and to your loved ones.

Charles is able to save a screenshot just in the nick of time, for only seconds later the message vanishes. Charles glances toward the bed. Rhys Tremayne is now awake, his anxious eyes peering out from above the edge of the counterpane.

"Good morning, sir," Charles says. "Well, we've just received our instructions. The message is gone now, but I've saved it and will show it to you."

"Do I really want to see it?"

"Probably not. I guess now we have a couple of tough decisions to make, ones that aren't at all easy."

Rhys gives an audible sigh. "Charles," he says, "I shall screw my courage to the sticking place."

Using Rhys' computer, Charles immediately sends an email message to Detective Wilson containing the screenshot he's saved of the message with the instructions. Then, after returning to the screened porch, he phones her.

"Hello," she says, "I'm currently en route, so we probably shouldn't be chatting."

"I just sent you a crucial email message. After you've had a chance to see it and think about it, please get back to me. Looks like we are now on the verge of the main events. Looks like tomorrow is going to be the big day."

"Okay. Thanks. And you will certainly hear back from me within a couple of hours."

"Great," Charles says. "I won't do anything further until I do."

Rhys Tremayne isn't alone in having to make a tough decision. Tom Audley has a tough decision to make, too. Should he simply go along with things as Robin Estabroke has laid them out or should he, acting upon his conscience, make an effort to undermine this project in which he is so deeply implicated? As usual, Tom decides to split the difference. He *will* do what Robin Estabroke wants him to do; being the getaway driver isn't such a big deal, he tells himself. But, he decides, he will also call the policewoman in Plymouth and tell her the limited amount he knows. By having it both ways, he hopes to protect himself against the wrath of Robin Estabroke by following his orders, and at the same time creating a measure of legal cover if Robin's plan goes completely awry and they are all nabbed by the police.

Tom places his call to Detective Sergeant Valery Wilson, but it goes directly to an answering machine, Tom leaves the message that he needs to speak with her urgently and that he will try her again soon. At least, he thinks, there will be a record of his attempt to contact her.

34

On Saturday afternoon, following the instructions Robin Estabroke has laid down for them, Diana Southgate and Tom Audley check into a small hotel in Marazion. At this point they both understand how Robin Estabroke hopes events will transpire the following morning; and now they each want to go to the actual locations today to familiarize themselves with the lay of the land.

Diana is the one who has the key task of retrieving the Bible—assuming that the old bibliophile acquiesces. All Tom has to do is drop Diana off and then go to the car park where he will wait until Estabroke appears. Then he will drive himself and Robin, along with the purloined Bible, back to Totnes. Assuming that Diana avoids being apprehended, she will drive herself back from Marazion.

That's if all goes well. If all doesn't go well, they could be arrested. If that happens, Tom is prepared to argue that he was an unwilling participant and that he tried his best to blow the gaff.

Diana, wanting to familiarize herself with this entire stretch of coastal path, sets off on foot from the hotel in Marazion. It should take her about an hour's hike to reach the spot where she needs to be in the morning. After forty-five minutes she passes the bench where the bibliophile is supposed to leave the Bible, then she walks on to where Robin wants her to be at 9:30 in the morning. Diana finds the spot, takes a short breather, and then begins the walk back to Marazion. When she passes the bench again, she pictures herself snatching up the bag containing the Bible and stashing it in her backpack. A couple hundred yards farther along will be where she and Robin exchange backpacks, him taking the one with the Bible and her an identical one containing a few random paperback novels. If the police stop her and search her pack, they won't find her carrying the Bible.

Tom Audley drives along the main road that runs lengthwise down the Lizard. He sees the sign for the turnoff to Poldhu Cove. Only a minute later he pulls Robin's Land Rover into the parking area where he is to wait for Robin. For Tom, it all seems quite easy. It's his compatriots who will face tougher challenges. Tom likes it that way. And he also likes it that the plan seems to obviate the need for violence.

On Saturday evening, Rhys Tremayne is a wreck, his face pale, his nostrils pinched, dark circles under his eyes. He does his best to appear normal, but Eilish and the professor can see that something is very wrong.

"My dear," Eilish says when they've all gathered in the sitting room after their evening meal on Saturday, "is there anything I can do for you? You do look knackered."

"Maybe you could spare just a nip of your Glenfiddich?" he asks. "The doctor said a tiny bit would be all right."

"Perhaps we could all do with a little nip," she replies, "so long as Charles has left us enough to go around. Just kidding, Charles," she quickly adds with a smile.

"Whew," says Charles. "Good thing I just bought a replacement bottle."

Their attempts at light-heartedness are partially successful and the whiskey helps a little bit, too. Still, it's obvious from Rhys and Charles' demeanors that they are both under considerable strain. Eilish knows it's best to leave it alone. Poking and prodding at her husband would only exacerbate the situation.

After a few minutes, Charles excuses himself to make a phone call, and Rhys says he needs to spend a few minutes attending to something back in his private study.

Eilish says to the professor, "It warms my heart to see how much Charles dotes on Alwyn. Those two have meshed perfectly, despite all their superficial differences."

"She's been very good for him, and him for her. I'm optimistic about their future together. Domestic bliss is not easily achieved, you know."

Eilish decides not to comment on the professor's observation.

Belying their assumptions, Charles has sought privacy not to phone Ally. The person he calls is Dectective Sergeant Valery Wilson.

In his study, Rhys goes into his private closet where he keeps his most revered treasures and retrieves the protective case that contains the Geneva Bible. He is completing his preparations for the morning when he will carry it down through the terraced gardens and place it on the bench by the coastal path. 10 a.m. is the time specified in the latest email message. Rhys is having second thoughts about following those directions, but he knows what he must do. Still . . . .

35

At 9:45 on Sunday morning, Charles walks beside Rhys down through the terraced gardens toward the sea. When they reach the last pergola, they stop. Charles places his hand on the older man's shoulder and gives it a small squeeze.

"I'll remain here just out of sight until you are back," Charles says. Rhys gives him a tight-lipped nod. Then, walking stick in one hand and carrier bag in the other, he begins to make his way slowly down the last 150 yards to the bench beside the coastal path overlooking the sea.

When Rhys reaches the bench, he pauses for a moment standing behind it. Charles wonders if the man is having second thoughts. Finally Rhys extends his arm out over the bench and lowers the carrier bag down onto it. He settles the bag containing the book box into one corner of the bench so that it leans against the bench arm. He continues to stand there, then glances down the coastal path in one direction and then the other. As far as Charles can tell, there's no one to be seen.

Finally, Rhys Tremayne turns around and moves slowly up the gradual incline. By the time he reaches Charles, it's obvious that this walk has taken a physical toll. Rhys is breathing hard, but he's managed it.

"You must rest here for a moment before heading back to the house," Charles says, "and then you must take it very slowly. I'm going to remain here out of sight. I'll be keeping an eye on you and also on the bench and the bag you left there. I'm going to remain here until something happens to the book. I'll come back to the house after a bit and fill you in on whatever I see."

"Thanks, lad," the older man says, his words punctuated by his shortness of breath. "You be careful, eh? No heroics from you, lad."

Charles grins. "Heroics from me? There'll be no heroics from me, you can be sure of that."

Rhys smiles, then leaning heavily on his walking stick, he begins tottering on up through the gardens to the house.

It's five minutes later that someone appears on the coastal path, a slender figure in a navy-blue anorak. This individual—who has come from the left, from the direction of Lizard Point—carries a dark backpack strapped over both shoulders. The hood of the anorak is pulled up, and the bill of a ball cap extends just below the hood. Charles can't tell if it's a man or a woman.

Careful to remain out of sight behind the wisteria-enshrouded pergola, Charles watches as the person pauses beside the bench, takes off the backpack, unzips it, and then thrusts the carrier bag Rhys left on the bench into the backpack and re-zips it. After shouldering the backpack again, the person sets off along the path, moving quickly toward to the right, the direction of Marazion.

Once this person has passed from his view, Charles takes out his mobile phone and calls DS Valery Wilson.

"The book has been retrieved," he says. "I couldn't tell if it was a man or a woman, but the person is wearing a dark blue rain jacket and has put the book into a black or dark blue backpack."

"Yes, we've seen her. It's a woman. My colleague, Constable Barnes, is following her at a safe distance. You should catch sight of him soon."

"There he comes now," Charles says, as he sees a tall fellow appear striding along the path, also from the left, a couple of hundred yards behind the woman in the anorak.

"His job," Valerie says, "is to be sure she doesn't double back or leave the coastal path at some point. Basically, he's herding her toward the team we've posted half a mile further on along the coastal path. They will stop her and search her. Assuming they find the Bible on her, they will take her into custody and retrieve the Bible."

"Very neatly done, Detective. Sounds like it all could be concluded within the next few minutes."

"We shall see. Talk to you soon," she says, then disconnects.

Although there's no longer any particular need for Charles to remain at his post, he decides to wait a little longer. And it's a good thing he does.

Five minutes later he sees someone approaching along the coastal path, this time coming from the right. As he watches, he thinks it might possibly be the same person he'd seen before. Then he realizes it can't be. This person looks to be about the same height but is definitely stouter, and Charles realizes that this person's anorak is a lighter shade of blue. The hood of the rain jacket isn't pulled over this person's head and he wears no cap. It's definitely a man, not a woman. The backpack the man wears, Charles thinks, looks identical to the one the woman had been carrying. But that means nothing since it's one of those currently popular brands. Anyway, this person must not have aroused the suspicions of the policeman tailing the first woman or he surely would have been stopped.

As Charles watches the man hurrying along the coastal path, he suddenly realizes that he's seen him before. He looks to be the same fellow Charles watched a couple of days earlier, the fellow who said he was going to Kynance Cove—and then a few minutes later turned around and returned.

His curiosity aroused, Charles strides down toward the coastal path. There he turns to the left and begins pursuing the fellow.

A quarter of a mile along the coastal path to the west, the direction opposite to the one Charles is going, a pair of policemen have stopped the woman Charles had seen take the carrier bag from the bench.

"Excuse us, miss," one of them says to her, showing his warrant card. "I hope you won't mind if we quickly inspect the contents of your backpack. Just a routine matter is all. That be okay?"

She glares at the men. "No, that is not okay," she replies with some heat. "I would find it a clear violation of my privacy. Let me assure you, sir, I am not in possession of any illegal substances. And I don't think you have any right to search me without proper cause."

"It's not drugs we're looking for, miss," the constable tells her, "and I can assure you we do have the right to search your pack. Frankly, your reluctance to let us do that suggests you may have something to hide."

"Well, if you must, then go ahead. But I protest your actions. And I certainly have nothing to hide." Diana removes the backpack and places it on the ground.

The other constable rummages through the pack, finally extracting a carrier bag from a Waitross grocery store.

"Let's just take a peek inside this bag," the man says.

He reaches in and pulls three paperback books from inside the bag. The policemen glance at the titles: Rachel Carson's *The Silent Spring*, Elizabeth Kolbert's *The Sixth Extinction*, and Jackie Collins's *Lethal Seduction*. The incongruity of the third title, in company with the previous two, is lost on the policemen, but Diana blushes anyway—Robin Estabroke has played a little joke on her. The important thing to both Diana and the policemen, of course, is the absence of the Geneva Bible.

The two policemen are momentarily dumfounded at not finding it.

"Do you mind, sirs, if I continue on my way now?" Diana says, rather disdainfully.

"Um, yes, miss, you may, though first we need to take your name and your contact information. A driver's license will suffice."

Still looking huffy, Diana cooperates and hands over

her license, and the information is duly recorded.

"Sorry if we've inconvenienced you, miss," the man says. "Just doing our job."

With the books now replaced inside her backpack, Diana shoulders it again and sets off on her way. As soon as she is out earshot, one of the policemen is on his mobile phone, calling DS Valery Wilson.

"We stopped her. No Bible in her backpack, just a few odd paperbacks. Maybe she stashed it somewhere along the way."

"Yes, walk back along the trail and make a very thorough search. It's possible, I guess, that the old fellow decided *not* to put the Bible in the carrier bag. But I rather doubt that. How you seen Constable Barnes yet? He was trailing her."

"Here he comes now. We'll find out if he saw anything helpful."

Diana Southgate moves quickly along the coastal footpath, her goal, Marazion still an hour's walk ahead of her. She's relieved that her confrontation with the police has gone so smoothly. She and Robin had prepared for the possibility of police intervention, and their quick exchange of backpacks behind the little copse that Estabroke had sussed out a few days earlier had proved a crucial expedient. Now she can be amused that the man had put in a lurid Jackie Collins romance along with the two serious titles. At the moment of discovery, she wasn't. If Robin had been in her shoes and she was the one choosing the paperbacks, she might have put in a copy of *Lolita*. But that probably would have been a little over the top.

A few miles to the east, in the car park for Poldhu Cove, Tom Audley sits inside Robin Estabroke's Land Rover. Knowing it could be a long morning, he's brought a coffee flask and a couple of sausage rolls to tide him over. He guesses that if all goes well, Robin should be turning up between eleven and half past. It's a pretty hefty hike and Tom is glad he's not the one doing the hiking. Robin and Diana have given themselves the more demanding but also more exciting parts in this drama. Tom's is the truly boring part—and he doesn't mind that one single bit.

Having reached a bench on the cliff top a quarter of a mile beyond Loe Bar, Robin Estabroke pauses to catch his breath. He quickly unzips the backpack, reaches in and pulls open the plastic wrap surrounding the book box. He lifts the lid and peeks in at the Bible. It's there, all right. He knew it would be, but actually seeing it is reassuring. It's better to be certain than to harbor any lingering doubts.

Ahead of him on the path he sees a few scattered walkers. He's met only a few so far, mostly older couples engaged in hiking from one scenic location to another, no one who poses any kind of a threat to him. When Robin glances at the stretch of path behind him, he spots a solitary walker who has just about finished crossing Loe Bar. Robin hops up to his feet and strides forth. He decides it might be advisable to keep a good distance ahead of the figure behind him—just to be on the safe side.

36

Dectective Sergeant Valery Wilson had arrived at her post near Poldhu Cove at nine a.m. It was about nine-thirty when she and the young policeman with her, Constable Barnes, saw the figure clad in a dark-blue anorak move along the coastal path near where they were concealed. She'd sent the constable on his way to keep tabs on the suspicious figure, while she remained where she was to monitor activity nearby. Valery had checked out a few additional hikers in the intervening hour and a half, but none of them seemed in any way involved. She was hugely disappointed when she learned from the phone call that the woman the constable had trailed hadn't had the Bible in her possession when they searched her. Valery had felt certain the woman was a key part of things—and she still does. Had they been outfoxed in some way? It began to look like it.

When Charles Bascombe called her to tell her about the man he was following, her spirits rebounded. The man coming her way is almost certainly the one they want. It's unfortunate that now she has no backup, in the event of a physical confrontation, but she has confidence in her abilities to cope with whatever might arise. She is fit and well-trained, and on a couple of previous occasions she's taken down men considerably larger than herself.

Charles, realizing that the man ahead of him has stepped up his pace, does too. He doesn't want to catch up to the guy, but he doesn't want to risk the possibility of losing sight of him, should the fellow veer off the path for some reason. Charles now feels certain that this man is the one he'd seen before. On that day the fellow must have been reconnoitering, familiarizing himself with the lay of the land.

Is the man actually carrying the Bible in his backpack right now? And is the backpack he's wearing the same one into which the woman deposited the carrier bag Rhys left on the bench? Charles thinks that's likely to be the case. It's imperative, then, that he not lose visual contact with this fellow.

Now, not far ahead of them, is Poldhu Cove, a scenic spot Charles and Ally have walked to on their late afternoon walks. Here, Charles knows, there are numerous places where the man could wander away from the main coastal path. So, with a sense of urgency, he breaks into a jogtrot.

Detective Valery Wilson sees the man on the trail as he draws nearer to where she's stationed herself. He's now maybe 200 yards distant. Well beyond him, she sees someone moving quickly along the trail. She suspects it is Charles Bascombe. She glances in the other direction but sees no one. It's a beautiful spot but a lonely one where she prepares to confront the man she feels certain is at the center of all these nefarious events.

Robin Estabroke regrets that he's not in better shape. It wasn't so long ago that this trek would have been child's play, but now, in his semi-retirement, he's allowed himself to go to seed. Being in the military had kept him on his toes. Well, henceforth, he resolves, he take better care of himself.

Suddenly a woman appears on the path ahead of him. She's holding up some sort of official-looking credentials.

"Sir, I'd like you to stop," she says. And he does, "Where are you off to today, sir?"

"Just making my way toward Kynance Cove, which I've heard is quite a special place."

"It is," she says, "though on a Sunday it's likely to be jam-packed with picnickers. Sir, these are just routine inquiries, but I need to take a look at the contents of your backpack. We're doing our best to keep the public safe, as you can understand."

"Hmm. Yes, I suppose I can." He unzips one of the front pockets on the pack and holds it open for her inspection. When she bends forward to look inside, he suddenly whirls the entire backpack, cracking it against her head. The weight and solidity of the book container in the pack's main pocket has turned the backpack into a vicious weapon.

The unexpected blow staggers Valery. As she tries to right herself, the man shoves her. He pushes her toward the cliff's edge. Still stunned by the blow, she feels helpless against the unexpected strength of the man's arms.

He gives her a final powerful shove, and Valery finds herself sliding down the wet, grassy incline toward the lip above the cove. She has no way to slow her momentum. Before she can react, she slides over the edge of the cliff and falls toward the rocky inlet thirty feet below her. For a split second she feels her body collide with the cold water and the sharp rocks that rim the edge of the cove. Then she feels nothing more.

From fifty yards away Charles observes the confrontation. Seeing DS Wilson's body slip over the edge of the cliff sends a bolt of terror through his body.

He breaks into a sprint. He's too late to prevent Valery's body from plunging into the cove, but he's determined to exact swift vengeance on the bastard who has perpetrated this horrific deed.

Hearing Charles' footsteps, Robin Estabroke whirls about to face him. He still grasps the straps of the backpack, and as Charles rushes toward him he swings the backpack in a vicious half-circle. Charles swerves. The backpack brushes his shoulder. Charles is filled with a rage like he's never before experienced. Lowering his head he smashes straight into the man's chest. The impact staggers the man. He tries to place one foot behind him to brace himself, but his feet slip out from under him.

Robin Estabroke's body gathers speed as it slithers down the wet incline. Like Valery, he has no way to break his downward motion. Like Valery, Robin plunges downward onto the sharp rocks of Poldhu cove.

37

Charles Bascombe stands alone atop the cliff overlooking the cove. His body is trembling, his mind whirling. He knows he has to collect himself and act. From where he stands, he can't see down into the area below the cliff above the cove, but he knows he has to climb down and find DS Wilson.

Charles casts a glance in each direction along the coastal pathway. Off to the east maybe a quarter mile away he sees what looks like a pair of hikers. Charles waves and yells—"*Help!* We need *help!*" He thinks one of the hikers returns his wave.

There is a small trail that leads down to the cove, a trail made over the years by hikers wanting a closer look at the cove. It's one he and Allie have used before also. Now Charles locates it and begins a careful descent. The footing is treacherous and he moves with caution. It takes him a minute to reach the end of the little path. Now he can see the entire inner portion of the cove. The waves come crashing in, and then they recede with a rush.

For one short moment water covers the rocks, and then in the next moment the rocks reappear.

Charles sees no sign of Robin Estabroke or the backpack. The rushing water must have taken them when it receded. Valery's body is still there. Charles has no idea whether she has survived the fall, and if so, how badly she may have been injured. But he knows he must retrieve her body immediately—or she will either drown or be washed out to sea. Charles steps thigh-deep into the cold water and splashes his way toward Valery. He is soon soaked to the chest. Valery is wedged between two of the larger rocks. Charles figures that's why she hasn't been pulled out to sea. Had she landed a foot in either direction, the rocks would surely have inflicted irreparable damage. Now, maybe, she has a chance.

Charles knows that moving her risks hurting her even more, but he can't leave her where she is or she will die for certain. He carefully extracts her body from between the rocks. He cradles her with both arms, lifts her to his waist, turns and struggles to reach the bottom of the little path. He knows that he will never be able to carry her up the steep hill by himself. He lays her gently on the grass beside the little path and pauses to catch his breath.

"Hello," calls a voice from above. "Can we help?"

"Call for the EMTs. There's a policewoman here who is seriously injured. She needs help immediately."

"What number do I call? I'm from America."

"Call 9-9-9. It's like 9-1-1 in America."

"You got it."

✣ ✣

Tom Audley is worried. It's nearly half-past eleven and Robin Estabroke still hasn't turned up. Tom has used the public Gents in the car park twice already, his nerves speeding up his bodily functions. Maybe he should try calling Diana? He hopes nothing untoward has happened to her. If the plan has gone as expected, Diana should be in the clear—she would have had the Bible in her possession if only briefly—but she's probably not back at the hotel in Marazion quite yet, he realizes, so he'd better wait a bit longer.

Suddenly Tom sees flashing lights. Are the police arriving on the scene? Is he in trouble? He breathes a sigh of relief when he sees it's not the police but an emergency vehicle. Tom watches it pass through the car park and begin to make its way cautiously along the coastal path. It's headed in the direction from which Estabroke should be coming. Some hiker must have had an accident, he thinks.

Tom remains there in the Land Rover. Less than half an hour later the emergency vehicle returns, lights still flashing. Still no sign of Robin Estabroke.

At 12:15 Tom calls Diana. She's arrived safely back to the hotel. She tells him about the brief encounter she had with the police and their surprise when they discovered she didn't have the Bible. He tells her that Robin has not turned up but that an emergency vehicle has come and gone. Could the hiker who had an accident have been Robin Estabroke? Diana says that if Robin doesn't turn up by one o'clock, or if they haven't heard from him by then, the two of them should simply return to Totnes. She will drive to the car park and pick him up; they will leave Robin's Land Rover in the car park as if they had nothing to do with it. The crucial thing is for the two of them to try to distance themselves from whole endeavor.

Tom Audley sits tight for another hour. By day's end, he and Diana are back in Totnes. They haven't heard a word from Robin Estabroke—and they never will.

38

Charles Bascombe sits slumped low in a chair in the Helston Community Hospital waiting room. In chairs nearby are the American college students, Jason and Jennifer, who came to his aid at the cove. They chose to ride along with him in the rescue vehicle that carried DS Wilson to the hospital.

Charles' spirits have never been so low, his brain so numb. The day's events have drained him physically and emotionally. His deepest concern is for the well being of DS Valery Wilson. He knows that her injuries have to be life threatening. He knows it's possible she is no longer alive. When he last saw her she was breathing and had a faint pulse; but that was all she had.

And what about the Bible? It must have been in the backpack the man still held when he plummeted down into the waters of the cove—now man and book are both gone.

And what will the impact of losing his most cherished possession be on Rhys Tremayne? Charles fears the worst.

And Charles also can't help thinking about the man who went over the cliff. His body, like the backpack, was apparently washed out to sea. Could he have survived? Not likely. As vile a human being as he must have been, did he deserve to die? Does anyone ever deserve to die? And if he is dead, does that make Charles responsible for his death?

A soft voice intrudes on Charles' bleak reflections. "Is she a close friend of yours?" Charles realizes the young woman named Jennifer is speaking to him. Her question draws him from his oppressive thoughts.

"A close friend of mine?" Charles says, repeating her words. He pauses only for a second before saying, "Oh yes, she is." Valery is hardly a close friend—Charles has only met her a couple of times—but given the present circumstances, he has no reservations about claiming her as such. He does like the policewoman very much. And he's been impressed by her intelligence and courage. There's nothing he wants more than for her to survive this terrible ordeal.

Before he can continue his remarks to Jennifer, his mobile phone rings. It's DI Eileen Corrigan. She tells him she's on her way and should be there by late afternoon. She wants to know all that Charles knows—which will certainly include, he believes, a full account of his actions on the cliff top that morning, especially as it pertains to the man's assault on Valery and then his own actions toward the man with the backpack.

✣ ✣

"Where am I?" DS Valery Wilson whispers. She thinks she's alone in the darkened room.

"My dear," says an elderly woman, who's sitting in a corner knitting, "you're in Helston Community Hospital. I am so glad, dear, that you are awake. You have had quite a time of it. But we know you are made of stern stuff."

"I feel ghastly," Valery says.

"You've a perfect right to feel that way, dear. But I can tell you you are going to make the doctor a happy man. And quite a few others, too. What you need now is lots and lots of rest."

"What's happened to my head?" Valery asks. She runs the hand of her free arm, the one not attached to a welter of tubes, over the top half of her head. All she feels are bandages.

"You got yourself bashed about a good bit down in one o' those wicked coves, dear. But your head held together just fine. They've shaved off some of your lovely locks, they have. Shame, but it'll grow back afore ya know it. Now, you just shut those pretty eyes and rest for a bit. The doctor will be in to see you again soon."

✣ ✣

The sound of footsteps rouses Charles from his lethargy. DI Eileen Corrigan of the Devon Constabulary is striding toward him, accompanied by a young constable. When she spots Charles and the two young Americans seated close by, she approaches them.

Charles gets to his feet. "Hello, Detective," he says.

She stands still for a moment and looks him over good. Finally she asks, "How are you doing, Mr. Bascombe? All right, I hope."

"Umm, not so great, actually, but I'm surviving."

"You are a hero, sir," she declares. "You're the man who saved Valery's life."

"Umm, maybe. But it's these two who saved the day," Charles says, gesturing toward his companions. "If they hadn't arrived when they did, we would have had no chance. Now maybe Valery still has a chance?" he asks.

"From what the doctors tell me, yes, she does. Could you spare me a few minutes to provide a more detailed account of what exactly happened this morning?"

"I'll give it my best shot, though there's quite a lot about these events I don't fully understand myself."

"Let's find a private place where we can talk, shall we?"

Charles nods. Then he turns to Jason and Jennifer. "Keep an eye out for my friend Allie. She should be arriving fairly soon. Then we can run you back to your hostel in Penzance. Maybe the four of us can have a meal there in a local pub?"

"That sounds great," Jason says. Jennifer nods her agreement.

"Allie knows all the best ones," Charles says.

For the next half an hour, Charles does his best to recount the mornings' untoward events to DI Corrigan. He relates how his instincts told him to follow the man with the backpack, whom he suspected of having the Bible; and how he'd nearly caught up to him when the fellow assaulted DS Wilson. "I got there as fast as I could but I was too late. He'd whacked her in the head with the heavy backpack and shoved her over the brink. When I reached the spot, he went for me, too. I dodged his blows and pushed him back. His feet slipped out from beneath him and he slid down the wet grass to the cliff's edge. A second later he'd gone over. I heard his scream, then nothing more, not even a splash.

"After a moment I gathered my wits and worked my way down to the cove. When I got there I could see DS Wilson's body wedged between two large rocks. There was no sign of the man. I freed her from the rocks and carried her to where I could lay her down on a grassy place.

"She was breathing, but I didn't know what to do. There was no way I could carry her up the steep incline by myself and I knew that in view of her injuries it would be dangerous to even try. That's when I heard the college students calling from up above. They phoned the EMTs, who arrived in maybe twenty minutes. They did a superb job of getting her up to the ambulance. It was probably no more than an hour from the time of the accident until we arrived here at the hospital. I only wish I'd reached her on the path thirty seconds sooner."

DI Corrigan listens to Charles' account intently, the constable with her taking notes. When he finishes, she reaches out and pats his arm. "You have absolutely nothing to blame yourself for. You did all you could. It's likely you saved Valery's life. As for the man who attacked you and Valery, if his body was washed out to sea, there's a good chance it will be found. There's little likelihood, of course, that he survived. I will call you in the morning and give you an update on Valery and if there's any news about the Bible. It's even possible you can come and see Valery, but I can't promise that."

"I do hope so. That would be wonderful."

When Charles returns to the main waiting room, Allie is there chatting with the two college students. All three get to their feet to greet him.

"You've all met, then," Charles says, then feels stupid. "I guess that's kind of obvious."

"Let's go to Penzance," Allie says, "the Admiral Benbow pub serves excellent pub grub. And you, Charlie, look like a man who could use a drink."

"Or two or three," Jason adds with a grin.

Their meal at the pub is peasant but subdued. Charles is drained by the day's events, and the students are exhausted too. Jennifer and Jason attend different universities in the U.S. and met for the first time at the beginning of the summer in a study-abroad program in Bath. It's obvious they are fond of one another. They remind Charles of his own students—who he will be back with in less than a month. Justin is in a pre-law program at his school, and Jennifer has a double major in English and Business.

When the meal wraps up, they exchange contact information, and Charles promises to let the students know how everything turns out with DS Wilson. When he and Allie drop them at the door of the hostel, the four of them exchange final hugs.

"It was really nice to meet you," Jennifer says, "despite the circumstances."

"Safe travels," Charles says.

Once they are back on the road and finally headed for home, Allie asks about the Bible. "Is it lost for good?"

"Barring a miracle, it is."

"Bloody hell. I hope that news doesn't crush my father."

"Me too. What do you suggest? Should I hold off telling

him until we know for sure?"

Allie scrunches up her face in thought, then says, "No, I think you should tell him straight away exactly what you know, no dilly-dallying. It will be a terrible blow. But Daddy can be surprisingly strong. It will be quite a shock but it won't destroy him."

"Okay, I'll tell him right off. But I want you, Eilish, and the professor to be there when I do."

"Yes, that would be best."

39

Eilish, Rhys, and the professor are in the sitting room when Allie and Charles come in.

"Charlie, you look knackered," the professor says. "I'm guessing you've had quite a day."

"You aren't wrong, sir. I've never had one like it, and I hope I never will again."

"Dare I inquire, Charles?" Rhys says, his upturned face reflecting his anxiety. "Dare I inquire about the Bible?"

"Sir, it's been lost. There's very little chance that we'll ever see it again."

Rhys chews on his lips. No one else speaks. Charles walks over to him, then drops down beside him on the sofa.

"Tell us the whole thing, Charles," Rhys says softly.

Charles offers an abbreviated account of his adventure leading up to the crucial part: "After the man whacked the policewoman and shoved her over the cliff, then he came at me. He swung at me but lost his balance and then he went over too, still clutching the backpack with the book inside.

"By the time I got down to the cove, the man and the backpack were gone. Washed out to sea. I was able to retrieve the detective's body. Then two college students turned up and they called the EMTs. Those fellows got there quickly, bless them, and we took her to the hospital in Helston. She's alive but in a very precarious condition. Fortunately, the doctors think she will survive."

"That's good, Charles. Thank heavens you were there. But . . . the Bible . . . it's truly . . . *gone?*"

"Sorry to say, sir, but it is."

"Vanity of vanities," intones the professor, "all is vanity."

Eilish gives the professor the bent eye, and Allie frowns at him.

But Rhys says, "William is right. I would be willing to sacrifice the rarest book in the world if it would guarantee the safety of those I love. It was, after all, just a book."

Charles and the professor exchange surprised glances, startled by the man's unexpected equanimity. Allie was right, Charles thinks. The man, frail as he seems, can be surprisingly strong.

Half an hour later, Allie and Charles ascend the stairs to their rooms.

When they pause on the landing just outside Allie's room she asks, "Charlie, would it be all right if I come up to your room in a bit to tell you goodnight?"

"I would like that more than I can say."

Charles drags his weary self on up to his room. After taking a steamy shower, he stands by his window looking out toward the sea. He wants to imprint this ever-changing view on his brain, a view he knows he will miss once he's back in America.

Charles is already in bed when Allie creeps into his room. She climbs into the bed and snuggles up against his back. She wraps her arms about his torso.

"If that's a mermaid trying to seduce me," he mumbles, "tonight she's going to be out of luck. Tonight I am impervious to her charms."

"If I were a betting woman," Allie replies, "I would bet against that statement. But tonight this Cornish mermaid will settle for just holding you tight."

"Yes, Allie, please do hold me tight. And don't you ever let go."

Charles falls asleep in Allie's arms and sleeps the sleep of the just. But when he wakes up in the morning, he is all alone.

At mid-morning on Monday, Charles takes a call on his mobile phone from DI Eileen Corrigan. "I'm at the hospital," she says, "and there are various bits of news, mostly good. First of all, Valery is now awake and the doctors say she's in a stable condition."

"Wonderful," Charles says.

"They say that beginning tomorrow it should be fine for her to have visitors. You and an old mentor of hers from Exeter University are at the top of her list."

"Perfect," Charles says. "Just let me know the best time, and I'll be there."

"Here's the second bit of news. The backpack containing the antiquarian book has turned up."

"Fantastic," Charles says.

"I'm no expert on these things, but I'm sorry to say that

the book appears to be a total ruin."

"No surprise there, I guess," Charles says.

"We can turn it over to you at the hospital tomorrow, unless you really want it sooner."

"Tomorrow should be fine."

"And lastly—the man who attacked Valery and who fell down into the cove—his body has been recovered as well."

"He's dead?"

"Oh, yes indeed." Charles had expected as much, but having it confirmed gives him a sinking feeling.

"Do you know who he is?"

"I see no harm in telling you that. He was a man named Robin Estabroke, a book dealer from the London area."

"The name means nothing to me," Charles admits. "Maybe it will to Mr. Tremayne. So he was the one who was behind the threats to Mr. Tremayne's family?"

"As far as we know, yes."

"With that man dead and the book ruined, I hope that means that now there's no further danger to the Tremaynes. Is that right?"

"That's what we think, but we will remain vigilant until we are absolutely sure."

"Well, thank you for that. And I will plan to be at the hospital tomorrow once you've told me the best time."

⁜ ⁜

Diana Southgate has yet to decode the secret file she had found on Mark Fetherston's computer. But she's reached several tentative conclusions about it. It must contain damning information on Robin Estabroke, perhaps information concerning underage women, given Estabroke's history and the *Lolita* quotation. That compromising information may have been a major factor in Mark's death. She feels quite certain that Robin Estabroke killed him. Maybe Mark's selling the Bible to the Cornish bibliophile was a factor as well; indeed, it may have been the straw that broke the camel's back. Anyway, since Robin Estabroke is now dead, there seems little point in wasting any more time or energy on the secret file.

Diana sits before her computer contemplating the matter. Finally, she clicks on the file to highlight it, then hits the delete key. Presto—no more secret file. Let the dead take their secrets to the grave.

Thomas Audley taps at her office door, then pokes his head in. Diana looks up.

"Tom," she says, "I just had an inquiry from a Bible-collector in Chepstow, a fellow named James Addison. He wondered if we'd acquired any interesting Bibles lately we might like to sell?"

Tom suppresses a giggle as he thinks about how close they came to nabbing the Geneva Bible. "And what did you tell him?"

"I said we'd just missed out on a gem, but we would surely let him know if anything in that line should happen to come our way."

"So, there's still no news about Estabroke?" Tom asks.

"No. And maybe there never will be."

"Diana, do you think we are in the clear?"

"I do, Thomas. There is nothing that connects us with

any certainty to the theft of the Bible. When the police stopped me on the coastal path, they found nothing incriminating on me. So I don't think they have any evidence that implicates us."

"What about our break-in at the Tremaynes'?"

"Again, I don't think we left any traces, and aside from the man you knocked on the head, no one even saw us. So there are no witnesses. If the police had anything on us about that, we surely would have heard from them by now. So, you can relax."

"In that case, if you don't mind, I think I shall be shoving off in a day or two."

"To head for Rugby School?"

"Yes, eventually, but I thought I might treat myself to a brief holiday in between."

"Not down on the Lizard, I hope!" she says, grinning.

"Uh, no, I've had enough of Cornwall to last me a few years."

"You've been a big help in getting me settled here, Tom. Thank you for that. And you will always be welcome here. Come whenever you can."

"You mind your p's and q's, Diana."

"And when have I ever not done that?" The two incorrigible friends laugh.

40

A nurse leads Charles, who holds a vase of flowers, to DS Wilson's hospital room. The policewoman is hooked up to an array of serious-looking machines on which a panoply of lights and numbers flash.

"Wow, look at you," he says. "They're pulling out all the stops."

Valery smiles wanly at him. "There's only one of these things I really care about," she says. "It's the morphine drip. That I can control by myself, and believe me, I do. And please, whatever you do, don't tell me how well I'm looking. I know better."

Charles grins. "Then I probably shouldn't say that compared to the last time I saw you, you look magnificent."

"At some future time, sir, I may have the fortitude to listen to you tell me just what happened on that ill-fated day. But this isn't the time for it."

"No, today I shall stay away from anything to do with that. Besides, I'm sick of telling people about it."

A young nurse, her hair arranged up beneath her nurse's cap comes in, takes the flowers and puts them on the windowsill. "You're a popular woman, Ms. Wilson, you have another visitor," the nurse says, "an older gentleman. Shall I tell him to wait?"

"Have him wait five minutes, then bring him in. I'd like him to meet Mr. Bascombe."

"I'd prefer you to call me Charles rather than Mr. Bascombe. After what we've been through together, I think we deserve to be on a first name basis. Is it all right if I call you Valery?"

"I would nod, but it hurts to move my head."

"So you have a very sore neck and a few cracked ribs as well?"

"Yes, several. No serious damage to my four limbs, thank heavens, and they say no major damage to internal organs. My head and neck injuries are the really painful ones, but the doctors think they will come around, given enough time. Probably a few weeks."

"I suspect that your excellent health before the accident has been a crucial factor."

"*Accident?*"

"Umm, not really sure what's the best word to use."

"Nor am I, actually. And to tell you the truth, I'm sorry the man has died. He was a rotter, but . . . "

"He tried to do to me what he did to you. I got lucky and it really cost him."

"I thought we weren't going to talk about it today?"

"Sorry. I'll shut up."

The young nurse looks in through the open door. "All set?"

"Oh, yes."

Nigel Cummings, who is standing behind the nurse, steps into the room. He nods toward Charles.

"Hello, sir," Valery calls out, sounding almost cheerful.

"Sir, this is Charles Bascombe, an American academic. He's been assisting Rhys Tremayne in his study of the Geneva Bible. In addition, he happens to be the man who saved my life three days ago."

"I am eternally grateful to you, Charles. Valery is one of the finest people I have ever known."

"She's a remarkable woman, Mr. Cummings. And I believe you deserve a lot of credit for her knowledge of books?"

"Perhaps a bit. But tell me, Charles, what's happened to the Bible? From all I've heard and the two photos Valery shared with me, it appears to be quite a unique copy."

"I'm told it's been recovered but that it's a total loss."

"Water damage is one of the worst kinds. I've made a lot of attempts at book restorations in my time, Charles, and I'm willing to have a crack at it, if Rhys Tremayne is interested."

"I haven't seen the book yet myself, but the reports are that it's damaged beyond salvation."

"Where is it?" Valery asks.

"I believe your colleague still has it. She said she would bring it here today. So I think I will just wait around in the hospital until she arrives," Charles says.

"Maybe I will too, if you don't mind," Nigel says. "I can't help wanting to see this Bible for myself, even if it is a total loss."

"Good," Charles says. "That will give us a chance to get to know each other while we wait together."

Valery is fading, her eyes drooping.

"You must get more sleep, Valery," Nigel says. He steps

over to the bed and touches her tubeless arm. She smiles and her eyes close.

It's early afternoon when DI Corrigan finally arrives. She apologizes for not getting there sooner and hands a wrapped parcel to Charles. Charles introduces her to Nigel.

"So, Mr. Bascombe, you'll take this woe-be-gone item to Rhys Tremayne for me?"

"Yes, I shall. Thank you."

"We've had a brief look at it and it's not a pretty sight. Sorry to deliver it to you in such a terrible condition. Will you both wait around until I've seen Valery? I have a little more information to share with you."

"Sure, no problem," Charles says. Nigel nods his agreement.

When she's gone off again, Charles says, "Well, shall we take a look?"

"Let's see if it's as bad as she thinks," Nigel says.

When Charles pulls away the layer of plastic wrap, there lies the solid book container, obviously wet through with seawater. "Oh, my," says Nigel.

Charles slowly lifts the soggy lid. The book inside does indeed look like a total disaster.

"Don't try to open the cover," Nigel says. "What we need to do is allow the book to have an extremely slow drying process. Eventually, we may be able to peel back the pages one by one. Right now they will be stuck together in a gluey mass. It's very unlikely the first pages and the last pages will ever be salvageable. But it's possible that some of the interior pages have escaped the worst of it. That's the optimistic view."

"And the pessimistic view?"

"You don't need to be told the pessimistic view."

"This is the second saddest thing I've seen this week," Charles said.

"The first being?"

"Valery's unconscious body jammed between rocks down in Poldhu Cove."

Nigel grimaces. "You've had yourself quite a week," he says.

When DI Corrigan returns, she reads the men's body language. "Not good news, I take it."

"No, not so good," Charles says. "Mr. Cummings has offered to see what he can do to restore portions of the book. But first I need to show it to Mr. Tremayne."

"There are a few things I can try," Nigel says, "but I don't think there's any chance of truly restoring the precious thing. That's a terrible shame. This was an extremely rare treasure. Now, it's essentially ruined."

'Could you come by the house in an hour and meet Mr. Tremayne before you head back to Devon? Then I could turn this pitiful thing over to you."

"Yes, I can do that. I look forward to meeting the famous book collector I've heard so much about."

"How do you find Valery?" Charles asks DI Corrigan.

"She's coming right along. By week's end we may move her up to a facility in Plymouth. The doctors say they are okay with that."

"That will be much handier for me," Nigel says.

"Mr. Bascombe, how much longer do you plan to be in the U.K.?"

"I'm leaving on August 15th. So, less than three weeks."

"We'll need to get a formal written statement from you describing the events of that day. We can send someone down here to take it."

"How about if I were to bring it to Plymouth in a week or so? That would give me a chance to say goodbye to Valery, too."

"And," Nigel says," that might give me sufficient time to complete my efforts at salvaging some portions of the book and have it ready to be returned to Mr. Tremayne."

"Waiting a week for the statement is not a problem," she says. "Well, I'm about to head back up now, if you have no questions for me."

"If Valery is awake, I'd like to see her again," Nigel says.

"I won't join you," Charles says. "It's back to the Tremaynes' for me, with my little, umm, bundle of treasure."

41

Ten days later, Charles Bascombe pulls Eilish's Jaguar out from the gravel drive leading to the Tremayne home and passes between the two gray plinths topped by stone choughs. As he does, it strikes him that his may be one of the last times he will do that for a good long while.

His visit with DS Valery Wilson in the convalescent home in Plymouth is quite affecting. The woman is in good spirits and looks a lot more like her old self. Her gratitude to Charles is palpable: "I owe you *everything*," she whispers at one point. And like DI Corrigan, she tries to assuage Charles' nagging conscience about the death of Robin Estabroke. "I'm not a vindictive woman, Charles, but I've no sympathy for the villain. *He* was responsible for his unfortunate demise, not you."

An hour into Charles' visit, Nigel Cummings also arrives at the convalescent home, and Charles can't help noticing how fond the elderly gentleman is of the much younger woman. Careful, old chap, Charles thinks to himself, that way madness lies. Nigel has brought the sad remains of the Bible in a carrier bag, and after the three of them have visited amiably for a bit, he opens the bag and brings out the book box, which looks a lot drier than the last time Charles saw it.

"I had more success with it than I expected," he says. "It's still an unmitigated disaster, but now at least some portions of it are readable." Nigel places the Bible on the coffee table and opens it up somewhere in the middle. "I didn't expect to have any success with the initial pages or the final pages, and I didn't. This is in the middle of Isaiah. The verses of scripture are readable, but just barely."

"How about the Gospels?" Charles asks.

"Not too bad," Nigel says. He closes and then reopens the Bible to Matthew. Charles turns a few pages and finds the "Judge not lest ye be judged" verses in Matthew 7.

Charles stares at the words, then says, "But where's the underscoring?"

"Should there be underscoring?" Valery asks.

"Yes, there should. And there was a squiggle in the margin that I couldn't make out. It's not there now. The marginalia couldn't have dissolved or been washed away by the salt water, could they?"

Valery and Nigel's faces bear puzzled looks.

"You kept a full register of all the annotations?" Nigel asks.

"I did. But these I don't even need to look up. I *know* they were there. How could they disappear?" Neither Valery nor Nigel offers any explanation.

"Or maybe," Charles says after a long pause, "maybe they didn't disappear."

Nigel's eyebrows shoot up. "You aren't suggesting, are you," he says, "that this might be the wrong book?"

Charles, with compressed lips, nods slowly. Earlier he'd been somewhat taken aback by Rhys Tremayne's unexpectedly calm reaction to the news about the Bible. Now he realizes there may be a good reason for that.

"My word," Valery says.

At half past five, Charles, in Eilish's Jaguar, passes up the gravel drive to the house where his mentor, William Wentworth, and the famous Cornish bibliophile, Rhys Tremayne, are probably locking horns in a contentious chess game.

"Have a good outing?" Rhys asks Charles as Charles comes into the sitting room.

"Yes, thank you. And I have something to show you." Charles sets the book box on the coffee table. "The man worked some miracles, but the Bible is still an unholy mess, as one might say."

"Well, let's have a look, shall we," the professor says. "I hope at least some of the annotations have survived, especially those in Ecclesiastes."

The professor slowly opens the damaged Bible, hoping to find the book of Ecclesiastes. "Rats! These pages still aren't separable."

"The Gospels aren't quite so bad," Charles says. "Try Matthew 7."

The professor finally manages to find the right page. "This one is one of the ones with underscoring, right? One of the ones by your hypothetical *second* annotator?"

"That's correct."

"Well, hmm, . . . where's the underscoring? What's happened to the underscoring?"

"I couldn't find it either. In fact, I haven't been able to

find any annotations of either kind anywhere in any of the readable pages."

"The sea water dissolved them?"

"Either that, or . . . "

Suddenly the professor turns his eyes upon Rhys Tremayne.

Rhys tries to maintain a poker face, but he can't. "So you've caught me out, have you?"

"What did you do, my friend? Or rather, what didn't you do?"

"I *couldn't*, William, I just *couldn't*. Not with the rarest book in the world."

William Wentworth shrugs his shoulders, then grins at his dear old friend.

"Besides," Rhys goes on, "the email said to give them the Geneva Bible. I did do that, I *did* give them the Geneva Bible."

"Just not the one they wanted."

"They didn't indicate that they wanted a *specific* Geneva Bible. They just said the Geneva Bible. So it seemed to me that the 1620 edition should work as well as the 1572."

"Uh, huh," the professor scoffs dubiously.

"Besides, I knew they weren't going to get away with it. Not with Charles on the job."

"Uh, huh," the professor scoffs again. "My friend, you and your rationalizations are so transparent even Stevie Wonder could see through them."

"William, I *couldn't*. I just *couldn't*. You can understand that, can't you?"

"I can, Rhys, of course I can," he replies, rolling his eyes.

Allie, standing in the doorway, has caught the last part of this exchange. "What couldn't you do, Daddy?" She asks.

"Allie," Charles says, "do you remember what happens on Mount Doom when Frodo is supposed to toss the One Ring into the Cracks of Doom?" Three blank faces turn toward him.

"*Now* what are you on about, Charlie?" the professor asks.

"Frodo can't bring himself to do it. It isn't until Gollum bites his finger off that the ring and Gollum fall into the Cracks and are destroyed."

"A rather strained analogy, Charles," Rhys says.

"Daddy," Allie says, "when it came to losing the book, you couldn't do it? The Bible was just too *precious* to you?"

"Well, Pet, you are right. But that Bible is no evil talisman like the Ring in Tolkien. It's a holy object in more ways than one. The last thing I would ever want is to destroy it."

"Where is it, Daddy?"

"Ah. It's in my *sanctum sanctorum* where it belongs."

Professor Wentworth is laughing. "Rhys," he says, "you are truly a classic. They don't make them like you anymore."

"Thank you, William. You're a bit of an old relic yourself."

Allie gives her father a hug.

"Eilish and I are safe, Daddy, and you didn't even have to sacrifice your precious Bible."

"That's all that matters."

"All's well that ends well," the Professor says, "never mind the blurry morality of the thing."

"Oh, William, you surely know that the police and Charles, working in tandem, wouldn't have allowed any harm to come to Alwyn and Eilish. They wouldn't, would they?"

"Of course not, Rhys, of course not," he replies, rolling his eyes. "Not Charlie and the police wirking in tandem."

At mid-morning the next day the three men are looking at the Geneva Bible, the 1572 edition, not the 1620 edition that Rhys had substituted for it. They've opened it to the verses in Chapter 7 of Matthew. "Now, there's the underscoring that was missing in the other Bible," the professor says. "And there's that mysterious little squiggle in the margin."

"I was never sure about it," Charles says, "so I noted its presence but didn't attempt to interpret it."

"Let's enlarge it," Rhys says. He holds the magnifier over it. "It looks like there are two words. The first one looks like the word 'two.' Yes?"

"Maybe so," the professor says.

"And the second word?" Charles asks. "Looks like it starts with the letter 'J'. Could it be 'Judges'?"

"Two Judges would fit the 'Judge not lest ye be judged' context, William says.

"Hmm," Rhys says. "Two judges. Isn't that what Shakespeare's *Measure for Measure* is about? One honest judge and one corrupt judge who learns the error of his ways?"

"Yes, at least sort of," Charles says. "And it's this passage from Matthew that underlies the moral lesson of the play. Oh, my goodness. Who do you think might have written the two words in the margin?"

"Must have been the Bard himself!" Rhys declares. "We've suspected all along that it was Shakespeare who did the underscoring. Now we have a pair of words that were written in his own hand."

"Well, maybe," Charles says.

"No maybe about it, Charles," Rhys declares, "it must be

so. If it is so, then there can be no doubt that this truly is the rarest book in the world."

"Annotations by the two greatest Elizabethan dramatists," the professor says. "That certainly makes it a very special book."

"It makes it the rarest book in the world," Rhys avers once more.

"Well, maybe," Charles says again.

"Maybe me no maybes," Rhys says. "This book was owned by Christopher Marlowe. Then later it came into the hands of William Shakespeare. Each of them left their mark upon it. There's no other book in the world that comes close to that."

42

Allie, Eilish, Rhys, William, and Charles are seated at the breakfast table on the day that Charles plans to bid adieu to Cornwall. Allie will be running him and the professor up to Oxford in the middle of the day. Charles has just a week before his flight back to the U.S., and he needs to pack up everything in his flat and collect all his research materials from the Bodleian. He will be going alone. That's not what he or Allie had wanted, but they are both reconciled to it—at least somewhat. They both realize how important it is for Allie to remain behind until Rhys Tremayne's health has stabilized.

"So, Rhys?" the professor asks, "what are your plans for the Bible, now that Charlie has done all the hard work for you?"

"Charles and I will co-author an article describing our discoveries and laying out our hypotheses about the Bible. Our article will shake the scholarly world, that's for sure."

"Yes, of course you'll do that, and of course it will cause a big fuss. But what I mean is, what do you actually plan to do with the 'rarest book in the world,' as you love calling it? You realize that it will have to be made available to the true experts in the field. You, me, and Charles, smart as we are, we don't qualify. Charlie and I are medievalists, not Renaissance scholars, let alone Marlowe or Shakespeare scholars. And you are an antiquarian, a book-man, not a Shakespearian. I suspect, Rhys, that you won't be eager to have droves of scholars turning up on your doorstep, announced or unannounced."

"No, I certainly don't want that. What do you suggest,

William?"

"You should give Bible to the Bodleian on 'permanent loan'."

"The Bodleian! Never in life! No, William, my Bible will never set foot in Oxford!"

"Then maybe you could lend it to the British Library or the John Rylands in Manchester."

Rhys makes a rude noise with his lips.

"You could lend it to the Folger Shakespeare Library in the U.S., if you want to avoid it ending up in England," Charles suggests.

"How about none of the above. No, Charles, I know the Folger is a wonderful library, but I wouldn't want such a treasure to leave the country. There's too much of that sort of thing already in the world, and especially here in Britain. Perhaps I could lend it to the National Library of Wales or maybe my graduate school, the University of Edinburgh. That might be worth considering."

"What about Exeter University?" the professor suggests. "They have a fine rare book collection."

"And their former rare book librarian gave us some indispensable assistance," Charles adds. "He not only spent a lot of time restoring your 'substitute' Bible, but he came up with the identity of the woman who gave the book to Kit Marlowe."

"True, true. Yes, that's a good suggestion."

"Well," Eilish says, shifting the subject, "we shall miss you, Charles. It's been wonderful having you here. You will come back for the Christmas holidays, won't you?"

"If I'm invited." He glances at Allie. She's grinning ear to ear.

"Oh," Rhys says, "I think you might be able to inveigle an invite."

"Of course you are invited, Charles," Eilish says. "You must come. The professor is welcome, too."

"I might be able to get a free pass for a couple of days after New

Years," the professor says. "I wouldn't want to miss all the fun of hanging out with this lovable bunch of loonies."

"Then we shall look forward to having you both."

"What Daddy needs most is some quiet months this autumn without you two hanging about causing him aggravation," Allie says. "That's what his heart needs most of all. He doesn't need any chess games with the professor getting him all riled, and he doesn't need any wild adventures with Charlie down on the coastal footpath."

"Speaking of the footpath . . . ," Charles says.

"Yes," Allie says. "Charlie and I are going to take one last walk before our drive to Oxford. Professor, we'll be back in an hour or so."

"I'm packed and ready," the professor replies.

It's a beautiful August day on the Lizard—a cloudless sky, a gentle breeze wafting in from the southwest, sunlight glinting off the waves. Even the seabirds are less raucous than usual. Hand in hand, Allie and Charles stroll down through the terraced gardens to the coastal footpath. They pause and stand, shoulders touching, together just behind the bench where Rhys had left the book container two weeks earlier. This is the first time Charles has been here since he followed the man who nearly killed DS Valery Wilson.

"Which way?" Allie asks.

"Let's go the right," he says, which is the direction the woman in the anorak went on that fateful morning. Somewhere ahead of them in this direction, she must have handed off her backpack to Robin Estabroke, the fellow who assaulted Valery. It was a neat plan, Charles thinks, and it would have worked, had not some instinct told him to follow Estabroke. Of course, unbeknownst to all of them (except Rhys), Estabroke didn't actually have the Bible he thought he had.

Allie and Charles walk for a quarter of a mile, then stop at a spot overlooking a small scenic cove. "Come here," Allie says. She takes Charles in her arms and holds him tight. "Oh, how I am going to miss you," she says.

"I will miss you every day," Charles replies.

"Tell me all the things you will miss about not being in the U.K.," Allie says.

"That's a long list."

"Tell me."

"Of course I will miss the people the most, beginning with you. I will miss the beauties of Cornwall and I, unlike your father, will really miss Oxford. To me, Oxford will always be a special and remarkable place. I shall miss Cornish pasties and fish & chips, and I will miss our various wanderings about the countryside in Devon, Dorset and Somerset. And I will miss all the scholarly stimulation and the research opportunities that are available to me here in he UK.

"It was only a little over a year ago," Charles goes on, "that I first heard of the Lizard—when the professor told me about his friend who had come into possession of a mysterious medieval manuscript he wanted us to look at."

"Which was when you first stumbled upon me."

"What a fateful event that turned out to be!"

"I immediately recognized you, Charlie, as someone who needed to have his boring old scholarly world spiced up a bit."

"Well, you certainly succeeded. Allie, you were and are just the spice I need."

"Charlie, I hope I will never stop spicing up your world."

"I don't think that's possible." Charles bends his head down toward Allie who raises her lips up to meet his. Neither one is in a hurry to break off their kiss.

"Yum," Charles says, "sugar and spice and everything nice. Might I have another of those?"

"I think you might," she says. Their second kiss lasts longer than the first.

When they return to the house, the other three are gathered in the sitting room. The professor's bag stands next to Charles' by the entryway, ready to be carried out and put into the boot of Allie's car.

"Well, William, I give you fair warning," Rhys says. "This fall I shall be studying up on the Ruy-Lopez chess opening. Once I've mastered it, that will fix your wagon."

"Ha, my friend. I'll believe that when I see it."

"Charlie," Allie says with a grin, "it's time for you to pack the professor off home to Oxford. He's just about worn out his welcome with me." The professor nods his head sadly in agreement.

"C'mon, sir," Charles says. "Let's grab our bags and go."

Ten minutes later, Eilish and Rhys stand in the portico. They watch as Allie starts up her car, then lift their arms and wave farewell to Charles Bascombe and Professor William Wentworth. Charles and William wave back.

When Allie's car reaches the end of the gravel drive, Charles gazes up at the pair of stone birds—choughs—perched on their plinths. He gives them a final nod. *You brave birds of Cornwall,* he thinks, *I'm counting on you to watch over my dear friends until I get back.*

✧ ✧

Acknowledgments

I wish to express deep gratitude to my writing compatriots in Williamsburg: Kathleen Jabs, Sally Stiles, Len Shartzer, and Jim Tobin. Their suggestions and criticisms were invaluable. I am also grateful to Cory Ragsdale and to my brother, Roger Conlee, for their careful reading of the manuscript. The errors that still remain are solely my responsibility.

-- John Conlee

✣ ✣

Printed in the USA
CPSIA information can be obtained
at www.ICGtesting.com
CBHW030247130324
5262CB00001B/7

9 781939 917287